Mary Somerville

On Molecular and Microscopic Science

Vol. II

SALZWASSER
VERLAG

Mary Somerville

On Molecular and Microscopic Science
Vol. II

Reprint of the original, first published in 1869.

1st Edition 2022 | ISBN: 978-3-37504-794-8

Verlag (Publisher): Salzwasser Verlag GmbH, Zeilweg 44, 60439 Frankfurt, Deutschland
Vertretungsberechtigt (Authorized to represent): E. Roepke, Zeilweg 44, 60439 Frankfurt, Deutschland
Druck (Print): Books on Demand GmbH, In de Tarpen 42, 22848 Norderstedt, Deutschland

ON

MOLECULAR and MICROSCOPIC SCIENCE

SCIENCE

VOLUME THE SECOND

ON

MOLECULAR

AND

MICROSCOPIC SCIENCE

BY MARY SOMERVILLE

AUTHOR OF 'THE MECHANISM OF THE HEAVENS' 'PHYSICAL GEOGRAPHY'
'CONNECTION OF THE PHYSICAL SCIENCES' ETC.

Deus magnus in magnis, maximus in minimis — St. Augustine

IN TWO VOLUMES—VOL. II.

WITH ILLUSTRATIONS

LONDON
JOHN MURRAY, ALBEMARLE STREET
1869

CONTENTS

OF

THE SECOND VOLUME.

—◦◦—

PART III.

ANIMAL ORGANISMS.

ILLUSTRATIONS

TO

THE SECOND VOLUME.

———◦◦———

* From Dr. Ernst Haeckel's ' Radiolarien.'

* From Voght's 'Syphonophores de la Mer de Nice.'

MOLECULAR AND MICROSCOPIC SCIENCE.

PART III.

ANIMAL ORGANISMS.

SECTION I.

FUNCTIONS OF THE ANIMAL FRAME.

ALTHOUGH animal life is only known to us as a manifestation of divine power not to be explained, yet the various phases of life, growth, and structure in animals, from the microscopic Monad to Man, are legitimate subjects of physical inquiry, being totally independent of those high moral and religious sentiments which are peculiar to Man alone.

The same simple elements chemically combined in definite but different proportions form the base of animal as well as of vegetable life. But besides the elementary gases and carbon, many substances, simple and compound, are found in the animal frame; the phosphate and carbonate of lime, iron which colours the blood, and common salt which, with the exception of water, is the only article of food we use in a mineral state. Animals derive their nourishment, both directly and indirectly, from vegetables. Their incapacity to change inert into living matter is one of the most characteristic distinctions between the animal and vegetable kingdoms.

Protoplasm was shown to be rudimentary formative vegetable matter: so Sarcode, or rudimentary flesh, forms the whole or part of every animal structure. It is a semi-fluid substance, consisting of an albuminous base, mixed with particles of oil in a state of very fine division. It is tenacious, extensile, contractile, and diaphanous, reflecting light more than water, but less than oil. It is rendered perfectly transparent by citric acid, and is dyed brown by iodine. This substance, in a homogeneous state, constitutes the whole frame of the lowest grade of animal life; but when gradually differentiated into cell-wall and cell-contents, it becomes the origin of animal structure from that which has little more than mere existence to man himself; in fact, cellular origin and cellular structure prevail throughout every class of animal life. Unicellular plants and animals live for themselves independently and alone; but the cells which form part of the higher and compound individuals of both kingdoms, may be said to have two lives, one peculiarly their own, and another depending on that of the organized beings of which they form a part.

Flesh or muscle, which is organized sarcode, consists of two parts, namely, bundles of muscular fibre imbedded in areolar tissue. Nervous matter also consists of two parts, differing much in appearance and structure, the one being cellular, the other fibrous. The vital activity of the nerves far surpasses that of every other tissue; but there is an inherent irritability in muscular fibre altogether independent of nervous action: both the nervous and muscular tissues are subject to decay and waste.

The blood, which is the ultimate result of the assimilation of the food and respiration, conveys nourishment to all the tissues during its circulation; for with every breath, with every effort, muscular or mental, with every motion, voluntary or involuntary, at every instant of life, asleep or awake, part of the muscular and nervous substances becomes dead, separates from the living part, is returned to the circulation, combines with the oxygen of the blood, and is removed from the system, the waste being ordinarily in exact proportion to the exertion, mental and physical. Hence food, assimilated into blood, is necessary to supply nourishment to the muscles, and to restore strength to the nervous system, on which all our vital motions depend; for, by the nerves, volition acts upon living matter. Waste and repair is a law of nature, but when nature begins to decay, the waste exceeds the supply.

However, something more than food is necessary, for the oxygen in the blood would soon be exhausted were it not constantly restored by inspiration of atmospheric air. The perpetual combination of the oxygen of the air with the carbon of the blood derived from the food is a real combustion, and the cause of animal heat; but if the carbonic acid gas produced by that chemical union were not continually given out by the respiratory organs, it would become injurious to the animal system. Thus respiration and the circulation of the blood are mutually dependent; the activity of the one is exactly proportional to that of the other: both are increased by exercise and nervous excitement.

External heat is no less essential to animals than to vegetables; the development of a germ or egg is as dependent on heat as that of a seed. The amount of heat generated by respiration and that carried off by the air is a more or less constant quantity; hence, in hot countries, rice and other vegetable diet is sufficient, but as the cold increases with the latitude, more and more animal food or hydrocarbon is requisite for the production of heat.

The waste of the tissues, and the aëration of the vital juices, that is, the exchange of the respiratory gases, are common to all animals. The heart, upon whose expansions and contractions the circulation of the blood depends, is represented in the lower animals by propelling organs of a variety of forms; and the organs of respiration differ exceedingly, according to the medium in which the animals live. Water, both fresh and salt, though a suffocating element to land animals, contains a great deal of air, not only in the state of gas, but also in solution, the quantity in solution being directly as the pressure; so that animals living in the deepest recesses of the ocean breathe as freely as those that live on land, but with respiratory organs of a very different structure. In the lowest classes, which have no respiratory organs at all, the gases are exchanged through their thin delicate skins.

The mechanical forces act within the living being according to the same laws as they do in the external world: the chemical powers too, which are the cause of digestion, heat, and respiration, follow the same laws of definite and quantitative proportion as they do in inert matter; but neither the mechanical forces, nor the physical powers, could create a germ; nor could they even awaken its dormant state to living energy, unless a vital power existed in it, the origin of which is beyond the reach of man.

Animals are endowed with nerve-force, in addition to mechanical force and the physical powers which are common to them and vegetables; a force which constitutes their prime distinction, which is superior to all the other powers from its immediate connection with mind, and which becomes more evident, and more evidently under the control of the animal, in proportion as the animal approaches the higher grades of life, and only attains its perfect development in the human race.

The bones of man and the higher animals are clothed with a system of muscles, so attached that the head, eyes, limbs, &c., can be moved in various directions. In each of these muscles the fibres of two sets of nerves ramify, namely, the sensory and the motor nerves.

The sensory nerves convey external impressions to the brain, and by them alone the mind is rendered conscious of external objects. The impressions made by light and sound upon the eye and the ear, or by mechanical touch on the body, are conveyed by the sensory nerves to the brain, where they are perceived, though the impressions take place at a distance from it. Conversely, the mind or will acts through the brain on the motor nerves, which by alternately contracting, relaxing, and directing the muscles, produces muscular motion. Thus the motor nerves convey the emotions of the mind to the external world, and the sensory nerves convey the impressions made by the external world to the mind. By these admirable discoveries, Sir Charles Bell has proved that 'we are placed between two worlds, the invisible and the material;' our nervous system is the bond of connection. The connection, however, between the mind and the brain is unknown: it has never been explained, and is probably inexplicable; yet it is evident that the mind or will, though immaterial, manifests itself by acting on matter; that is, as a power which stimulates the nerves, the nerve-force acting on the muscles. Mental excitement calls forth the most powerful muscular strength, and an iron will can resist the greatest nervous excitement. The nervous and muscular forces are perpetually called into action, because, for distinct perception, the muscles require to be adjusted. Mind is passive as well as active: we may see an object without perceiving it, and we may hear a sound without attending to it. We must look in order to see, listen in order to hear, and handle in order to feel; that is, we must adjust the muscular apparatus of all our senses, of our eyes, ears, &c., if we would have a distinct perception of external exciting objects: and that is accomplished by the power of mind acting upon matter.

Dr. Carpenter has shown that it is by a series of forces acting upon matter that man conveys his ideas to man, the sonorous undulations of the atmosphere being the medium between the two. On one side the will, or power of mind, acts upon the nerves, nerve-force acts upon the muscles of speech, and these muscles, while in the act of speaking, produce sonorous undulations in the atmosphere. On the other side, these undulations are communicated by the mechanism of the ear to the auditory nerves, exciting nerve-force, and nerve-force acts upon the mind of the hearer. ' Thus the consciousness of the speaker acts upon the consciousness of the hearer by a well-connected series of powers.'

Nerve-force generates, directly or indirectly, light, heat, chemical power, and electricity. When the optic nerve is pressed in the dark, a luminous ring is seen round the eye, and a blow on the face excites a flash of light. Nervous excitement, by accelerating respiration, increases the chemical combination of the oxygen of the air with the carbon of the blood, and thus produces animal heat. But the development of electricity by nervous and muscular force, is one of the most unexpected and singular results of physiological research.

MM. Matteucci and Du Bois Reymond have proved that the intensity of the nervous and muscular forces is at a maximum when the muscles are contracted; and that if each arm of a man be put in contact with a wire of a galvanometer so as to form an electric circuit, an instantaneous deviation of the needle will take place, now in one direction and now in the other, according as he contracts his right arm or his left. The electricity thus evolved, when conveyed to the needle through several miles' length of coiled insulated wire, will cause a deflection amounting to sixty or seventy degrees, according to the strength of the man—that is, according to his muscular and nervous force; the amount of the electricity being exactly in proportion to the amount of muscular force.

It appears that the electric currents in the nerves are eight or ten times stronger than those in the muscles. M. Helmholtz found that the time required to contract a muscle, together with the time required to relax it again, is not more than the third of a second, and is a constant quantity, for the compensation of energy prevails also in organic nature. He also found that the motion or velocity of the electric current in a man is at the rate of 200 feet in a second. The electric equivalent, as determined by M. Helmholtz, is equal to the electricity produced in a voltaic battery by the seven millionth part of a milligramme of zinc consumed in the ten-thousandth part of a second, a milligramme being the 0·015432 part of a grain.

The contraction and muscular action or mechanical labour produced by the passage of an electric current through a nerve is 27,000 times greater than the mechanical labour which results from the heat disengaged by the oxidation of that small quantity of zinc requisite to generate the electricity; that is to say, the mechanical labour really produced by the contraction of the muscles is enormously greater than the labour corresponding to the zinc oxidized. In fact, the electric excitement of a nerve is analogous to an incandescent particle or electric spark that sets fire to a great mass of gunpowder. This result, and the association between the greatest activity of respiration and the intensity of the muscular energy, led M. Matteucci to suspect that a chemical action must take place in the interior of a muscle during its contraction; and he found by experiment that there actually is what he calls a muscular respiration, namely, that the muscles themselves absorb oxygen, and give out carbonic acid gas and nitrogen when contracted. This kind of respiration is more or less common to all animals; if impeded, the blood is imperfectly oxygenized, and loss of animal heat is the consequence. The heat that is perpetually escaping from animals is replaced, by the combustion of the carbon of the tissues or of the food with the oxygen inhaled by the lungs and the skin.

In the highest class of animal life the brain is at once the seat of intelligence and sensibility, and the origin of the nervous system. In the lower animals intelligence and sensibility decrease exactly in proportion to the deviation of their nervous system from this high standard. The forms of the nervous system are more and more degraded as the animals sink in the scale of being, till at last creatures are found in which nerves have only been discovered with the microscope; others apparently have none, consequently they have little or no sensibility.

The brain and the spinal cord enclosed in the vertebræ of the backbone form a nervous system, which in the vertebrated creation is equal to all the contingencies and powers of these animated beings, but is beyond all comparison most perfect in the human race. The brain alone is the seat of consciousness, for the spinal cord, though intimately connected with it, and of a similar 'mysterious albuminous electric pulp,' appears to have no relation to the faculties of perception and thought, yet it is essential to the continuance of life. It is a distinct nervous centre which generates muscular energy in man and animals corresponding to external impressions, but without sensation, and is entirely independent of the will; the vegetative functions of respiration, the contractions of the heart, circulation of the blood, and digestion, are carried on under every circumstance, even during sleep. The reason of their being independent of sensation and the will is, that the nerves in the organs performing these functions never reach the brain, which is the seat of intelligence and sensation, but they form what is called the reflex system; for any impressions made upon them are carried to the upper part of the spinal cord alone, and are reflected back again to the muscles of the heart, lungs, &c., which, by their contractions, produce these involuntary motions. For instance, the flow of blood into the cavities of the heart while dilating, acts upon the nerves, and these excite a rhythmical movement in the muscular fibres of the heart. For there is a vital contractility in muscular tissue which is one of the most universal attributes of living beings, and is probably the sole cause of motion in the lowest grades of life, and the movements produced by it in the higher grades are in all cases the most directly connected with the vegetative functions. The involuntary reflex system of nerves constitutes the chief locomotive power in a number of the lower animals; but it forms a continually decreasing portion of the whole nervous system in proportion as animals rise in the scale of life, till in man its very existence has been overlooked. If the spinal cord were destroyed, instant death would be the consequence; whereas infants born without brain have sucked and lived for a day or two.

There are numerous actions, especially among the lower animals, as little under the influence of the will or intelligence as the reflex nerves, which nevertheless depend upon sensation for their excitement. The sensation may call the muscular apparatus into action without any exertion of reason or will, in such a manner as to produce actions as directly and obviously adapted to the well-being of the individual as the reflex system. For example, a grain of dust irritates the nostrils, and involuntarily excites the complicated muscular movements concerned in the act of sneezing. This class of actions, which is called sensori-motor, or consensual, includes most of the purely instinctive motions of the lower animals, which, being prompted by sensations, cannot be assigned to the reflex group.

Purely emotional movements are nearly allied to the preceding. Sensation excites a mental feeling, or impulse, which reacts upon the muscular system without calling either the will or the instinct into exercise. These emotional movements are often performed in opposition to the strongest efforts of the will, as when a sense of something ridiculous may excite irresistible laughter at an improper time. It is probable that the strong emotions exhibited by many of the lower animals, which have been ascribed to instinct, are referable to this group.[1]

The movements of such animals as have no nerves are merely owing to the vital contractility of muscular fibre.

In the highest province of animal life, which includes the mammalia, birds, reptiles, and fishes, the general structure of the nervous system consists of a double lobed brain, from whence a spinal cord proceeds, protected by articulated bones, which extend along the back of the animals, and from thence nerve-fibres extend to every part of the body. But in order to suit a great variety of forms, this system undergoes many modifications. In all the lower grades of life that have nerves, the system chiefly consists of small globular masses, or

[1] The nervous system is ably explained in Dr. Carpenter's ' Manual of Physiology.'

nuclei, of nervous matter, technically called ganglia, which are centres of nervous energy, each of which is endowed with its own peculiar properties; the nervous cords and filaments proceeding from them are merely organs of transmission. The arrangement of these centres of nerve-force is symmetrical, or unsymmetrical, according to the form of the animal.

In the lower portion of Articulated animals, such as insects, crustacea, annelids, worms, &c. &c., there is a double cord extending along the ventral side of the animal, united at equal intervals by double nerve-centres, or ganglia. These two cords diverge towards the upper end, surround the gullet, and unite again above that tube to form a distinct bilobed principal nerve-centre or brain. A third form of the nervous system is only a ring round the gullet; the points in it from whence the nerves radiate are swollen nerve-centres, or ganglia. Those on the sides and upper parts of the ring represent the brain, and supply the eyes, mouth, &c., with nerves: other centres, connected with the lower side of the ring, send nerves to the locomotive organs, viscera, and respiratory organs. In animals of a still lower grade there are single nuclei irregularly scattered, but in every case they are centres of energy from whence filaments are sent to the different parts of the creature. The last and lowest system consists of filamentous nerves, chiefly microscopic.

Intelligence, or the mental principle, in animals differs in degree, though not in kind, from that in the human race. It is higher in proportion as the nervous system, especially the brain, approximates in structure to that of man; but even in many of the lower orders may be traced the dawn of that intelligence which has made man supreme on earth. Every atom in the human frame, as well as in that of other animals, undergoes a periodical change by continual waste and renovation; but the same frame remains: the abode is changed, not the inhabitant.   Yet it is generally assumed that the living principle of animals is extinguished when the abode finally crumbles into dust, a tacit acknowledgment of the doctrine of materialism; for it is assuming that the high intelligence, memory, affection, fidelity, and conscience of a dog, or elephant, depend upon a combination of the atoms of matter.   To suppose that the vital spark is evanescent, while there is every reason to believe that the atoms of matter are imperishable, is admitting the superiority of matter over mind: an assumption altogether at variance with the result of geological sequence; for Sir Charles Lyell observes, that 'sensation, instinct, the intelligence of the higher mammalia bordering on reason, and lastly the improvable reason of man himself, presents us with a picture of the ever-increasing dominion of mind over matter.'

The physical structure of a vast number of animals has been investigated from such as are a mere microscopic speck to the highest grade of animal life; but very little is comparatively known of their intelligence and means of communication.   We know not by what means a pointer and greyhound make an agreement to hunt together; nor how each dog is not only aware that his companion possesses a property which he has not, but that by their united talents they might accomplish their purpose, which is merely sport, for they never eat the game.[2]   The undulations of the air and water are no doubt the means by which most animals communicate; but there is reason to believe that many inhabitants of the earth, air, and water are endowed with senses which we do not possess, and which we are consequently incapable of comprehending.

[2] A pointer and greyhound, belonging to a friend of the author's, repeatedly brought home hares. Upon watching the dogs, the pointer was seen to find the hare, which was coursed and killed by the greyhound. Singular as this may seem, it is by no means unprecedented.

SECTION II.

PROTOZOA.

THE Protozoa are the very lowest forms of animal existence, the beginning and dawn of living things. They first appear as minute shapeless particles of semi-fluid sarcode moving on the surface of the waters. The pseudopodia, or false feet, with which they move, are merely lobes of their own substance which they project and retract. In creatures of a somewhat higher grade the form is definite, the pseudopodia, numerous and filamental, serving for locomotion and catching prey; and from the resemblance they bear to the slender roots of plants are called Rhizopods.[3] The microscopic organisms possessing these means of locomotion and supply, are of incalculable multitudes, and of innumerable forms. Thus the waters, as of old, still 'bring forth abundantly the moving creature that hath life;' in them the lowest types of the two great kingdoms have their origin, yet they are diverse in the manifestation of the living principle, that slender but decided line which separates the vegetable from the animal Amœba.

CLASS I.—RHIZOPODA.

The Amœba, which is the simplest of the group, is merely a mass of semi-fluid jelly, 'changing itself into a greater variety of forms than the fabled Proteus, laying hold of its food without members, swallowing

[3] From *rhizon*, a root, and *pous, podos*, a foot.

it without a mouth, digesting it without a stomach,
appropriating its nutritious material without absorbent
vessels or a circulating system, moving from place to
place without muscles, feeling (if it has any power to do
so) without nerves, multiplying itself without eggs, and
not only this, but in many instances forming shelly
coverings of a symmetry and complexity not surpassed
by those of any testaceous animal.'

Such is the description given by Dr. Carpenter of the
Amœba and its allies. The Amœba princeps, which

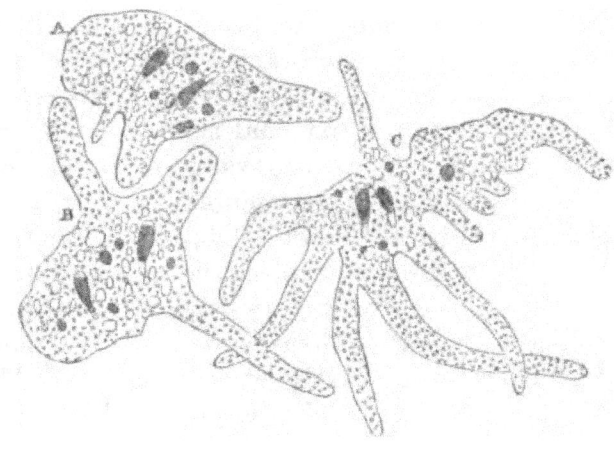

Fig. 86. Amœba princeps.

is the type of the naked group, fig. 86, is merely a
shapeless mass of semi-fluid sarcode, coated by a soft,
pellucid and highly contractile film, called diaphane by
Mr. W. J. Carter, and in many forms of Amœba the
whole is inclosed in a transparent covering. It is in
the interior semi-fluid sarcode alone, that the coloured
and granular particles are diffused, on which the hue
and opacity of the body depend, for the ectosarc or
external coat is transparent as glass. These creatures,
which vary in size from the $\frac{1}{2800}$ to the $\frac{1}{70}$ of an inch in
diameter, are found in the sea, but chiefly in ponds

inhabited by fresh-water plants. They move irregularly over the surface of the water, slowly and continually changing their form by stretching out portions of their gelatinous mass in blunt finger-like extensions, and then drawing the rest of it into them; thus causing the whole mass to change its place. Before it protrudes these pseudopodia or false feet, there is a rush of the internal semi-fluid matter to the spot, due to the highly contractile power of the diaphane, which is often so thin and transparent as to be scarcely perceptible.

When the creature in its progress meets with a particle of food, it spreads itself over it, draws it into its mass, within which a temporary hollow or vacuole is made for its reception; there it is digested, the refuse is squeezed out through the external surface; the nutritious liquid that is left in the vacuole seems to be dispersed in the sarcode, for the vacuole disappears. An Amœba often spreads itself over a Diatom, draws it into a vacuole newly made to receive and digest it; the siliceous shells of the diatom are pushed towards the exterior, and are ultimately thrust out; then the vacuole disappears, either immediately or soon after. These improvised stomachs are the earliest form of a digestive system.

Besides the vacuoles of which there may be several at a time, the slow and nearly rhythmical pulsations of a vesicle containing a subtle fluid may be seen, which changes its position in the interior of the sarcode with every motion of the Amœba. It gradually increases in size, then diminishes to a point, and as some of the digestive vacuoles nearest the surface of the animal are observed to undergo distension when the vesicle contracts, and to empty themselves gradually as it fills, Dr. Carpenter thinks it can hardly be doubted that the function of the vesicle is to maintain a continual movement of nutritious matter, among a system of channels and vacuoles excavated in the substance of the body. It is the first obscure rudiment of a circulating system.

In all the Amœbæ the semi-fluid sarcode, with the numerous bodies suspended in it, rotates at a varied rate within the pellucid coat; a motion presumed to be for respiration, that is to exchange carbonic acid gas for oxygen, so indispensable for animal life.[4]

Although like other animals, the Amœba cannot change inorganic into organic matter, as the vegetable Amœba can do, these two Protozoa are similar in one mode of reproduction; for portions of the animal Amœba or even one of the pseudopodia separate from the gelatinous mass, move to a little distance on the surface of the water, and become independent Amœbæ.

With a high microscopic power, many bodies besides the digesting vacuoles and pulsating vesicles may be seen imbedded in the sarcode of the Amœba princeps; namely, coloured molecules, granules, fat-globules, and nuclei. All these bodies were seen by Mr. Carter, in certain Amœbina he found at Bombay, together with what he believed to be female reproductive cells, and motile particles similar to spermatozoids, or male fertilizing particles.

The Actinophrys, a genus of the order Radiolaria, differs from the Amœba princeps in having a definite nearly spherical form with slender root-like filamental pseudopodia radiating from its surface in all directions as from a centre. They taper from the base to the apex, and sometimes end in knobs like a pin's head, but vary much in length and number, and can be extended and retracted till they are out of sight. They are externally of a firmer substance than the sarcode of the body, which is merely a viscid fluid inclosed in a pellucid film. The Actinophrys sol, which is the type of

---

[4] ' On the Amœba princeps and its reproductive cells,' by Mr J. H. Carter: *Annals of Natural History,* July 1863.

the genus, is a sphere of from $\frac{1}{1300}$ to $\frac{1}{650}$ of an inch in diameter, with slender contractile filaments the length of its diameter extending from its surface as rays from the sun. It can draw them in and flatten its body so as to be easily mistaken for an Amœba. This creature, which is common in fresh-water pools where aquatic plants are growing and even in the sea, has little power of moving about like the Amœba; it depends almost entirely on its pseudopodia for food. They have an adhesive property, for when any animalcule or diatom

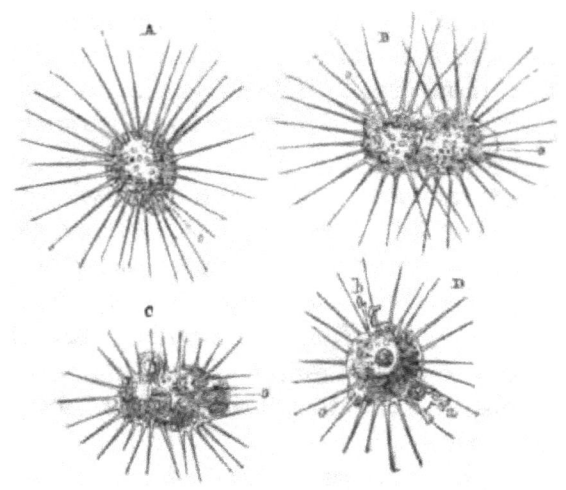

Fig. 87. Actinophrys sol.—A, ordinary form; B, act of division or conjugation; C, process of feeding; D, discharge of fæcal matter, a and b; o o, contractile vesicles.

comes in contact with one of them, they adhere to it; the filament then begins to retract, and as it shortens the adjacent filaments apply their points to the captive, enclose it, coalesce round it, the whole is drawn within the surface of the Actinophrys, the captive is imbedded in the sarcode mass, and passes into a vacuole where it is digested, and then the pseudopodia thrust out the undigested matter by a process exactly the reverse of that by which the food was taken in (D fig. 87). The pseudopodia are believed by Professor Rupert Jones to have the power of stunning their prey, for if an animalcule be touched by one of them, it instantly becomes motionless, and does not resume its activity for some time. The pulsations of the contractile vesicle are very regular, and its duty is the same as in the Amœba princeps.

The Actinophryna are propagated like the lowest vegetables by gemmation and conjugation, shown in B fig. 87; moreover Mr. Carter saw the production of germ-cells and motile particles in the Actinophrys exactly after the mode already described in the Amœba.

Mr. Carter mentions an instance in which the Actinophrys sol showed what may possibly be a certain degree of instinct. An individual was in the same vessel with vegetable cells charged with particles of starch; one of the cells had been ruptured and a little of the internal matter was protruded through the crevice. The Actinophrys came, extracted one of the starch-grains, and crept to a distance; it returned, and although there were no more starch-grains in sight, the creature managed to take them out from the interior of the cell one by one, always retiring to a distance and returning again, showing that it knew its way back, and where the starch-grains were to be found. On another occasion Mr. Carter saw an Actinophrys station itself close to the ripe spore cell of a plant, and as the young zoospores came out one after another, the Actinophrys caught every one of them even to the last and then retired to a distance as if instinctively conscious that no more remained. Like Amœbæ these animals select their food, but notwithstanding the superior facility and unfailing energy with which they capture prey larger and more active than themselves, they are invariably overcome even by a very small Amœba which they avoid if possible. When they come into contact the Amœba shows unwonted activity, tries to envelope the Actinophrys with its pseudopodia, but failing to capture the whole animal

ACANTHOMETRA BULBOSA.

it tears out portions and conveys them to improvised vacuoles to be digested. Dr. Wallich mentions that he had seen nearly the half of a large Actinophrys transferred piecemeal to the interior of its enemy, where it was quickly digested.

As every part of the body of the Actinophrys is equally capable of performing the part of nutrition, respiration, and circulation; and as in the absence of muscles and nerves they may be presumed to have no consciousness, the marks of apparent intelligence can only be attributed to a kind of instinct, and their motions to the vast inherent contractility of the sarcode and its enclosing film, which is also the case with the Amœbæ.

The Acanthometræ (see fig. 88, Acanthometra bulbosa) are all marine animals; their skeleton consists of a number of long spicules which radiate from a common centre, tapering to their extremities. These spicules are traversed by a canal with a furrow at the base through which groups of pseudopodia enter, emerging at the apex. Besides, there are a vast number of pseudopodia not thus enclosed, resembling those of the Actinophrys in appearance and action. The body is spherical, and occupies the spaces left between the bases of the spicules. The exterior film covering the body seems to be more decidedly membranaceous than that of the Actinophrys, but it is pierced by the pseudopodia which radiate through it. This exterior film itself is enclosed in a layer of a less tenacious substance, resembling that of which the pseudopodia are formed. There is a species of Acanthometra (echinoides) extremely common in some parts of the coast of Norway, which, to the naked eye, resembles merely a crimson point.

The Polycystina are an exceedingly numerous and widely dispersed group of siliceous rhizopods. They are inhabitants of the deep waters, having been brought up from vast depths in the Atlantic and Pacific oceans.

Their bodies are inclosed in siliceous shells, which have either the form of a thin hollow sphere perforated by large openings like windows, or of a perforated sphere produced here and there into tubes, spines, and a variety of singular projections: so they have many varied but beautiful microscopic forms. The animal which inhabits these shells is a mouthless mass of sarcode, divided into four lobes with a nucleus in each and covered with a thick gelatinous coat. It is crimson in the Eucyrtidium and Dictyopodium trilobum of Haeckel (figs. 89 and 90): in others, as the Podocyrtis Schomburgi, it is olive brown with yellow globules (fig. 91). These creatures extend themselves in radiating filaments through the perforations of their shells in search of food, like their type the Actinophrys sol, to

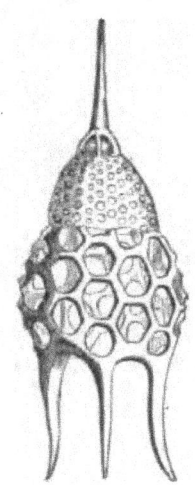

whose pseudopodia the filaments are perfectly similar in form, isolation, and in the slow movements of granules along their borders. The Polycystine does not always fill its shell, occasionally retreating into the vault or upper part of it, as in the Eucyrtidium (fig. 89, frontispiece to vol. i.). Sometimes the shell is furnished with radiating elongations, as in the Dictyopodium trilobum (fig. 90). In both of these shells the animal consists of four crimson lobes. These beautiful microscopic organisms are found at present in the Mediterranean, in the Arctic and

Fig. 91. Podocyrtis Schomburgi.

Antarctic seas, and on the bed of the North Atlantic. They had been exceedingly abundant during the later geological periods; multitudes are discovered in the chalk and marls in Sicily, Greece, at Bermuda, at Richmond in Virginia and elsewhere; in all 282 different fossil forms have been described, grouped in 44 genera.

DICTYOPODIUM TRILOBUM.

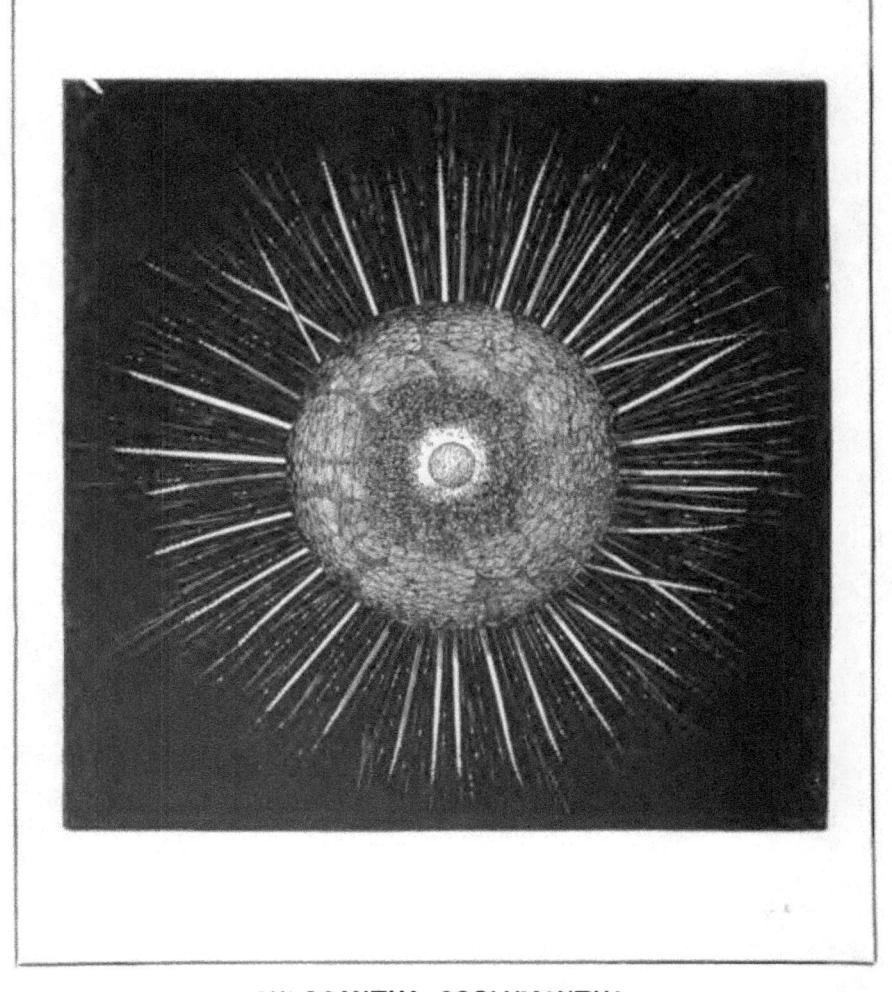

AULOCANTHA SCOLYMANTHA.

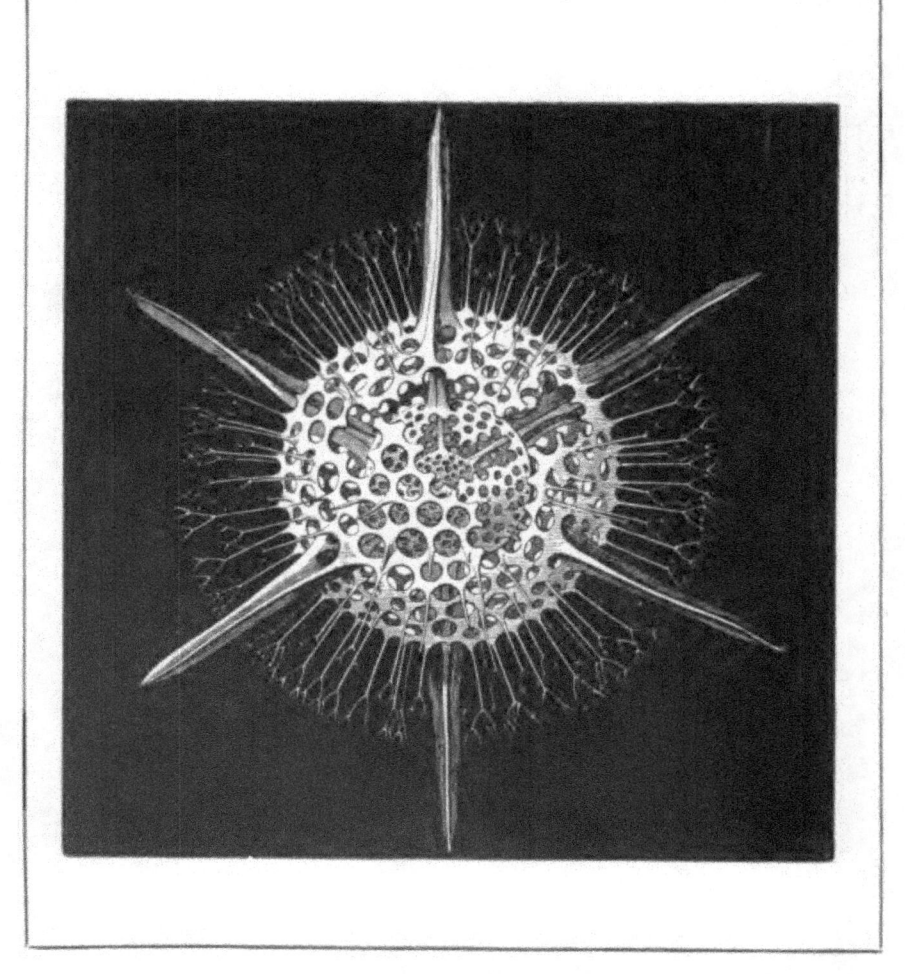

ACTINOMMA DRYMODES.

HALIOMMA ECHINASTER.

In certain Polycystina, the perforations of the shell are so large and so close together, that the sarcode body of the animal appears to be covered by a siliceous net. This connects them with the Thalassicollæ, minute creatures found passively floating on the surface of the sea. Th. morum, which is one of the most simple of the few forms known, has a spherical body of sarcode covered with a siliceous net, through which the pseudopodia radiate in all directions, as in the Actinophrys, but it is studded at regular distances with groups of apparently radiating siliceous spicules.

The Aulocantha scolymantha (fig. 92), found by M. Haeckel in the Mediterranean, may be taken as an example of the most general form of the Thalassicolla. The siliceous skeleton of some of the Radiolaria resembles the Chinese ivory toy of ball within ball. That of the Actinomma drymodes (fig. 93) consists of three perforated concentric spheres, with six strong spicules attached to the outer surface, perpendicular to one another and prolonged in the interior to the central sphere. Hundreds of finer bristle-like spicules radiate from the surface. The animal is chiefly contained in the central sphere, and from it a perfect forest of fine, long pseudopodia radiate in thick tufts through the apertures of the exterior sphere.

The skeleton of the Haliomma (fig. 94) consists of only two concentric spheres. In many species of Haliomma and Actinomma the animals are of the most vivid vermilion or purple colour. Little or nothing is known of the reproduction of these microscopic organisms.

The Actinomma drymodes and the Haliomma are two of the most beautiful microscopic rhizopods discovered by M. Haeckel.

There is a family of fresh-water testaceous rhizopods of which one group secretes its shell and the other builds it. The horny shell secreted by the group of the Arcella presents various degrees of plano-convexity, the convexity in some cases amounting to a hemisphere. They rarely, if ever, have mineral matter on their surface, which is studded with regular but very minute hexagonal reticulations. The aperture or mouth of the shell is small, and invariably occupies the centre of the plane surface, its margins being more or less inverted. The form of the shell is exceedingly varied, sometimes it even has horns indefinite in number, sometimes symmetrical, sometimes not; when its test or covering becomes too small for its increasing size, it quits it, and secretes a new one. The filamental pseudopodia proceed from the mouth of the shell only, and by means of these it creeps about on its mouth in search of food.

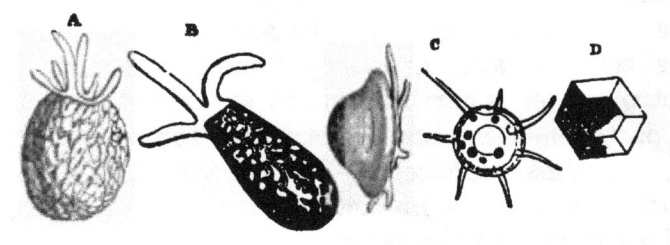

Fig. 95.   Simple Rhizopods.—A, B, Difflugiæ ; C, D, Arcellæ.

The Difflugia build their own shells, which are usually truncated spheres, ovate, or sometimes elongated into the form of a pitcher or flask. The most minute recognisable of these shells is about the $\frac{1}{1000}$ of an inch in diameter, but they are constructed with the most perfect regularity. The Difflugia pyriformis or symmetrica has the form of an egg with an aperture at the small end. It is entirely made up of rectangular hyaline plates, arranged with the greatest regularity in consecutive transverse and longitudinal rows, the smaller ones being at the extremities, while the larger ones occupy the central and widest portion of the structure. The inhabitant of this abode is an Amœba with a sarcode body covered with a thin film, from whence it sends off pseudopodia through the mouth of its shell. The Difflugia is propagated by conjugation, but before that takes place it becomes densely charged with chlorophyll-cells and starch-grains. The former disappear during the subsequent changes, and are replaced by a mass of colourless cells full of granules which are supposed to be the elements of a new generation. The embryo or earliest form is a minute truncated sphere, but the animal builds up its habitation very much according to local circumstances.

The greater number of the Difflugiæ secrete a substance which forms a smooth layer in the interior, which the animal covers with sarcode from its mouth, and then it drags itself with its pseudopodia to the particles which it selects, and they adhere to it. The particles selected are invariably mineral matter. 'The selective power is carried to such an extent that colourless particles—sometimes quartzose, sometimes felspathic, sometimes micaceous—are always chosen.' 'The particles seem to be impacted into the soft matter, laid on the exterior in the same way that a brick is pressed into the yielding mortar, and that too, in so skilful a manner as to leave the smallest possible amount of vacant area; whilst in the specimens of Difflugia in which tabular or micaceous particles are used, they are sometimes disposed with such nicety that there is no overlapping, but the small fragments are placed so as to occupy the space left between the larger ones. These excellent architects seem to know that in the valves of the Diatoms are combined the properties best suited to their wants, that is, transparency and form, capable of being easily arranged.'

Both the Difflugia and Arcella are Amœbæ in the strictest sense of the word; their bodies consist of sarcode, which sends out finger-like lobes from the mouth of the shell at one end, while the other end has an adhesive property, which fixes it to the bottom. The nucleus and contractile vesicles are identical in character with those of the Amœbæ, and exhibit the same tendency to subdivision at certain periods of the creature's history that is witnessed on a large scale in the Amœba proper; and the reproductive process is the same.[5]

The Difflugiæ are found in rivulets and pools containing aquatic plants; the condition of the water and the nature of the soil have a great influence on the form of their shell.

The Euglyphæ is the third group of fresh-water rhizopods. They are extremely minute, and there are no mineral particles whatever on their shells, the axes of which do not coincide with the aperture. The interior of the animal is like that of the Arcella and Difflugia, but it differs from them in as much as the pseudopodia and ectosarc, or external coat, are finely granular, and the whole mass of the body possesses a decided degree of adhesive viscidity. The pseudopodia are filiform, tapering, radiating, and readily coalesce; and 'as if to compensate for the restricted power of locomotion, compared with that of the Amœba proper, the pseudopodia of the Euglyphæ are much more active. The rapidity with which they admit of being projected outwards, and withdrawn into the shell, is unequalled in any other form, presenting the most wonderful example of inherent contractility in an amorphous animal substance, that is to be met with in either of the great organic kingdoms.'[6]

The order Reticularia, with a very few exceptions, are animals dwelling in calcareous microscopic shells, and differing essentially in constitution from all the

[5] 'On Difflugian Rhizopods,' by 'G. C. Wallich 'M.D. *Annals of Natural History*, March, 1864.   [6] Dr. Wallich.

preceding Rhizopods. The ectosarc or surface-layer of the sarcode in the Amœba and Actinophrys has so much consistence, that their pseudopodia, which are derived from it, have a decidedly firm outline and never coalesce; whereas in the order Reticularia, the sarcode is merely a semi-fluid protoplasm or colourless viscid fluid, without the smallest surface-layer or film, so that their pseudopodia possess no definiteness either in shape, size or number. Sometimes they are cylindrical, and sometimes form broad flat bands, whilst they are often drawn into threads of such extreme tenuity, as to require a high magnifying power to discern them. They coalesce and fuse into each other so freely and so completely when they meet, that no part of their substance can be regarded as having more than a viscous consistence. Their margins are not defined by continuous lines, but are broken by granules irregularly disposed among them, so that they appear as if torn; and these granules, when the animal is in a state of activity, are in constant motion, passing along the pseudopodia from one end to the other, or passing through the connecting threads of this animated network from one pseudopodium to another, with considerable rapidity, analogous to the movement of the particles in the cells of the hairs of the Tradescantia and other plants.[7]

The sarcode body of the Gromiæ is inclosed in a yellowish brown horny envelope or test of an oval shape, with a single round orifice of moderate size, through which the pseudopodia extend into the surrounding water, some forms of the animal being marine, others inhabitants of fresh water. When the animal is at rest all is drawn within the test, and when its activity recommences, single fine threads are put out which move about in a groping manner until they find some

[7] 'Introduction to the Study of the Foraminifera,' by W. B. Carpenter.

surface to which they may attach themselves. When
fixed, sarcode flows into them so that they rapidly
increase in size, and then they put forth finer ramifications, which diverging come in contact with those from
other stems, and by
mutual fusion form
bridges of connec-
tion between the
different branching
systems; for the pro-
toplasm spreads over
the exterior of the
test, and from it
pseudopodia extend
and coalesce, wher-
ever they meet, so
that the whole forms
a living network,
extending to a dis-
tance of six or eight
times the length of
the body. Fig. 96
represents the Gro-
mia oviformis with
its pseudopodia ex-
tended.

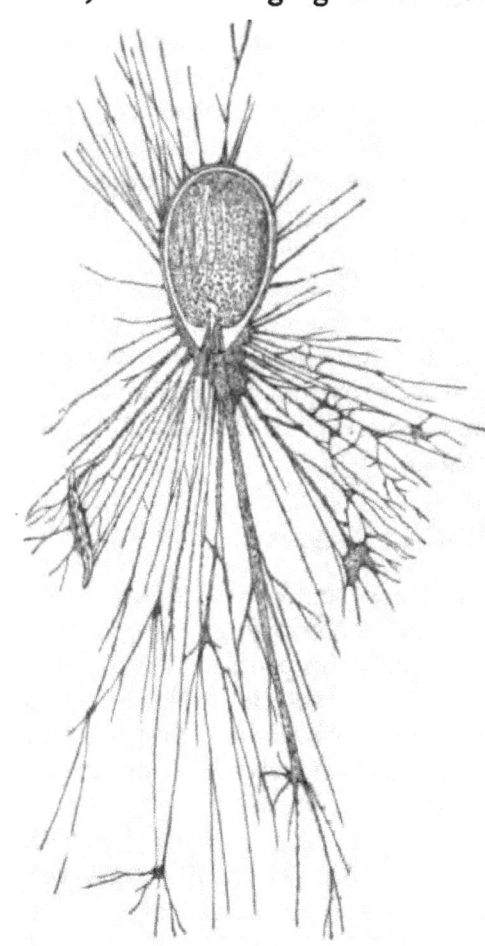

Fig. 96. Gromia oviformis.

In the Gromiæ the
granular particles in
the semi-fluid proto-
plasm are in con-
stant motion. In
the finer filaments
there is but one current, and a particle may be seen to
be carried to the extremity, and return again bringing
back with it any granules that may be advancing; and
should particles of food adhere to the filament they

take part in the general movement. In the broader filaments two currents carrying particles pass backwards and forwards in opposite directions at the same time, and the network in which these motions are going on is undergoing continual changes in its arrangements. New filaments are put forth sometimes from the midst of the ramifications, while others are retracted; and occasionally a new centre of radiation is formed at a point where several threads meet. The food consists of diatoms and morsels of vegetable matter; but the Gromiæ have no vent, so that the indigestible matter collects in a heap within them. However, as the form of the test is such that the animal cannot increase its size, it leaves it when it becomes too small for its comfort and forms another, and it is supposed to get rid of the effete matter at the same time. The Gromiæ have no nucleus or contractile vesicle.

CLASS II.—FORAMINIFERA.

The geological importance of the Foraminifera, their intrinsic beauty, the prodigious variety of their forms, their incredible multitude, and the peculiarity of their structure, have given these microscopic organisms the highest place in the class of Rhizopods. The body of these animals consists of a perfectly homogeneous sarcode or semi-fluid protoplasm, showing no tendency whatever to any film or surface-layer. It is inclosed in a shell; and the only evidence of vitality that the creature gives, is a protrusion and retraction of slender threads of its sarcode, through the mouth or pores of the shell, or through both according to its structure. Fig. 97 shows some of their forms.

By far the greater number of the Foraminifera are compound or many-chambered shells. When young, the shell has but one chamber, generally of a globular form; but as the animal grows, others are successively added by a kind of budding in a definite but different arrangement for each order and genus of the class. When the creature increases in size, a portion of its semi-fluid sarcode projects like a bud from the mouth of its shell. If it be of the one-chambered kind, the bud separates from its parent before the shelly matter which it secretes from its surface consolidates, and a new individual is thus produced. But if the primary

Fig. 97. Various forms of Foraminifera:—A, Oolina claxata; B, Nodosaria rugosa C, Nodosaria spinicosta; Cristellaria compressa; K, Polystomella crispa; F, Dendritina elegans; G, Globigerina bulloïdes; H, Textularia Mayeriana; I, Quinqueloculina Bronniana.

shell be of the many-chambered kind, the shelly secretion consolidates over the sarcode projection which thus remains fixed, and the shell has then two chambers, the aperture in the last being the mouth, from which, by a protrusion of sarcode, a third chamber may be added, the new chamber being always placed upon the mouth of its predecessor, a process which may be continued indefinitely, the mouth of the last segment being the mouth of the whole shell.

By this process an ovate shell with a mouth at one extremity may have a succession of ovate chambers added to it, each chamber being in continuity with its predecessor, so that the whole shell will be straight and rod-like, the last opening being the mouth. If the original shell be globular, and if all the successive gemmæ given out be equal and globular, the shell covering and uniting them will be like a number of beads strung upon a straight wire. Sometimes the successive gemmæ increase in size so that each chamber is larger than the one which precedes it; in this case the compound shell will have a conical form, the primary shell being the apex, and the base the last formed, the aperture of which is the mouth of the whole shell; a great many Foraminifera have this structure. The spiral form is very common and much varied. A series of chambers increasing in size may coil round a longitudinal axis, like the shell of the snail; but if each of the successive chambers, instead of being developed exactly in the axis of its predecessor, should be directed a little to one side, a curved instead of a straight axis would be the result; there is a regular gradation of forms of Foraminifera between these two types. The convolutions are frequently flat and in one plane, but the character of the spiral depends upon the successive enlargement or not of the consecutive chambers; for when they open very wide and increase in breadth, every whorl is larger than that which it surrounds; but more commonly there is so little difference between the segments after the spiral has made two or three turns, that the breadth of each whorl scarcely exceeds that which precedes it.

However varied the forms may be, the mouth of the last shell is the mouth of the whole, either for the time being or finally. For all the chambers are connected by narrow apertures in the partitions between them. Each chamber is occupied by a segment of the gelatinous sarcode body of the animal, and all the segments are connected by sarcode filaments passing through the minute apertures in the partitions between the chambers, so that the whole constitutes one compound creature.

Although the character and structure assumed by the semi-fluid bodies of the known Foraminifera have been determined in most cases with admirable precision, it is still thought advisable to arrange them according to the substance of the shell : consequently they form three natural orders ; namely, the Porcellanous or imperforate, which have calcareous shells often so polished and shining that they resemble porcelain; secondly, the Arenaceous Foraminifera, consisting of animals which secrete a kind of cement from their surfaces, and cover themselves with calcareous or siliceous sand-grains ; and lastly, the Vitreous and Perforated order, which is the most numerous and highly organized of the whole class, has siliceous shells transparent as glass, but acquires more or less of an opaque aspect in consequence of minute straight tubes which perforate the substance of the shell perpendicularly to its surface, and consequently interfere with the transmission of light.

Order of Porcellanous Foraminifera.

The Miliolidæ constitute the porcellanous order, which consists of twelve genera and many species, varying from a mere scale to such as have chambered shells of complicated structure.

The genus Miliola has minute white shells resembling millet seeds, often so brilliantly polished that they are perfectly characteristic of the porcelain family to which they belong. No Foraminifera are better suited to give an idea of the intimate connection between the shell and its inhabitant than the Miliola, the fundamental type of this genus. The shell is a spiral (1, fig. 97), which is made up of a series of half turns arranged symmetrically on its two sides. Each half turn is longer and of greater area than that on the opposite side, so that each turn of the spire has a tendency to extend itself in some degree over the preceding one, which gives a concave instead of a convex border to the inner wall of the chamber. The sarcode body of the Miliola consists of long segments which fill the chambers, connected by threads of sarcode passing through the tubular constrictions of the shell. As the animal grows, its pseudopodia extend alternately now from one end, and now from the other extremity of the spiral, and by them it fixes itself to seaweeds, zoophytes, and other bodies, for these Foraminifera never float or swim freely in the water. The genus Miliola is more extensively diffused than almost any other group of Foraminifera; they are most abundant between the shore and a depth of 150 fathoms, and are occasionally brought up from great depths. Beds of miliolite limestone show to what an extent the Miliola abounded in the seas of the Eocene period; but the type is traced back to the Lias.

The genus Peneroplis is distinguished by a highly polished opaque white shell; its typical form is an extremely flat spire of two turns and a half opening rapidly and widely in the last half whorl. It is strongly marked by depressed bands which indicate the septa or shelly partitions between the chambers in the interior. The polished surface of the shell is striated between and transversely to the bands by parallel platted-looking folds $\frac{1}{1400}$ of an inch apart. But the peculiarity of this shell and its congeners is, that the partitions between the chambers in its interior are perforated by numerous isolated and generally circular pores which in this compressed type are in a single linear row. Their number depends upon the length of the partition between the chambers, which increases with the age of the animal and size of the shell. There is but one pore in each of the consecutive partitions from the globular centre to the fourth chamber. From the fourth to the seventh chamber the communication is by two pores; after this the number is gradually increased to three, four, six, &c., up to forty-eight, so that the last segment may send out forty-eight pseudopodia from the mouth of the shell. In its early youth one pseudopodium appears to have been sufficient to find food for the animal, but as the shell increased in size and the segments in number, a greater supply of food was requisite and a greater number of pseudopodia were necessary to fish for it. Moreover when an addition to the shell is required the pseudopodia coalesce at their base and form a continuous segment upon which the new portion of the shell is moulded.

In varieties of the Peneroplis where the spire is less compressed there are sometimes two rows of pores in the partitions between the chambers. The Dendritine variety deviates most from that described. It is characterised by a single large aperture in each partition which sends out ramifications from its edges. The form of these openings depends upon that of the spire; when compressed the aperture is linear and less branched at its edges; but in shells which have a very turgid spire it is sometimes broader than it is long, and much branched; but these extremes are connected by a variety of forms. The shells of this variety of the Peneroplis are strongly marked by the depressed bands and striæ, as in the Dendritina elegans (F, fig. 97). The segments of the animal inhabiting these shells must be more intimately connected than in most of the other Foraminifera; and the pseudopodia sent through these large apertures out of the mouth of the shell must be comparatively quite a mass of sarcode. The Dendritinæ are inhabitants of shallow water and tropical seas, while the other members of the genus Peneroplis abound in the Red Sea and the seas of other warm latitudes, especially in the zone of the great laminarian fuci. They do not appear in a fossil state prior to the beginning of the Tertiary period.

The last whorls of some of the compressed spiral Foraminifera of the Porcellanous order so nearly encompass all their predecessors, that the transition from a flat spiral to the Orbitolite with its flat disk of concentric rings is not so abrupt as might at first appear. The gradual change may be distinctly traced in the species of the genus Orbiculina. The exteriors of the shells of the genus Orbitolites have less of the opaque whiteness than many others of its family. In its simplest form it is a disk about the $\frac{1}{500}$ of an inch in diameter, consisting of a central nucleus surrounded by from ten to fifteen concentric circular rings. The surface is usually plane, though sometimes it is concave on both surfaces in consequence of the rings increasing in thickness towards the circumference. The rings or zones are distinctly marked by furrows on the exterior of the shell, and each of these zones is divided by transverse furrows into ovate elevations with their greatest diameter transverse to the radius of the disk, so that the surface presents a number of ovate elevations arranged in consecutive circles round the central nucleus. The margin of the disk exhibits a series of convexities with depressions between them; in each of these depressions there is a circular pore surrounded by a ring of shell: these pores are the only means the animal possesses of communicating with the water in which it lives.

Fig. 98 is a horizontal section of the simple Orbitolite showing the internal structure of the disk. A pear-shaped chamber with a circumambient chamber forms a nucleus which is surrounded by series of concentric rings of ovate cavities. The chambers of the nucleus

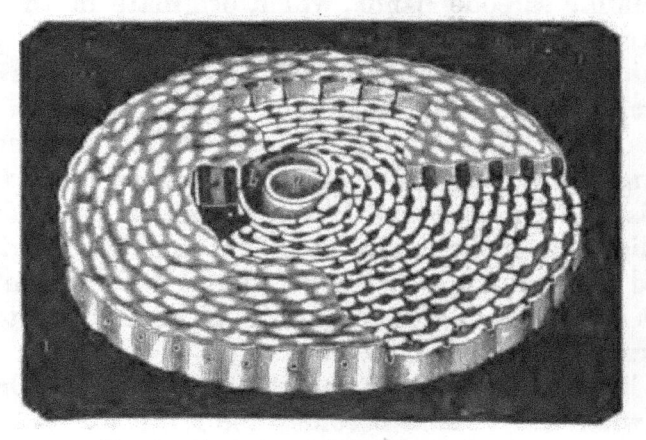

Fig. 98.   Simple disc of Orbitolites complanatus.

and all the cavities are filled with segments of homogeneous semi-fluid sarcode, which constitute the body

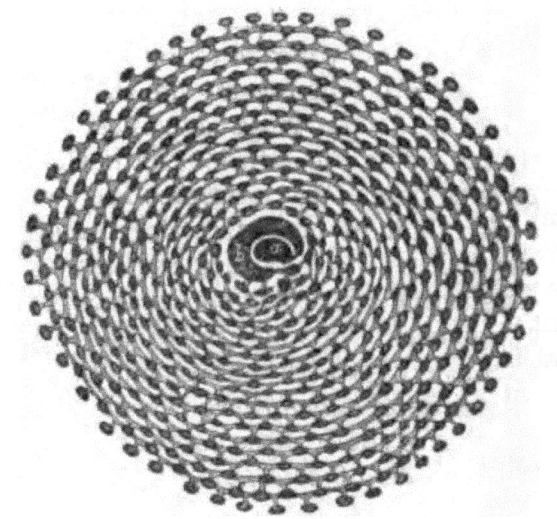

Fig. 99.   Animal of Orbitolites complanatus.

of the animal (fig. 99). The segments in the rings are connected circularly by gelatinous bands of sarcode extending through passages which connect the cavities laterally. The segments are also connected radially by similar sarcode bands, which originate in the mass of sarcode filling the nucleus, and extend to the pores in the margin of the disk. The cavities of each zone alternate in position with those of the zones on each side of it. The animal sends out its pseudopodia through the marginal pores in search of food, which consists of Diatoms and Desmidiaceæ; they are drawn in, digested without any stomach, and the nutritious liquid is conducted by the gelatinous bands from segment to segment and from zone to zone, even to the innermost recesses of the shell.

It is supposed that during the growth of the Orbitolite, when the animal becomes too large for its abode, its pseudopodia coalesce and form a gelatinous massive coat over the margin of the exterior zone, which secretes a shelly ring with all its chambers and passages, each ring being a mere vegetative repetition of those preceding it. That vegetative property enables the animal to repair its shell or add a part that is wanting. For, if a small portion of a ring be broken off and separated from the living animal, it will increase so as to form a new disk, the want of the central part or nucleus not appearing to be of the smallest consequence; indeed, the central rings are very often imperfect. The sarcode of these animals is red, and although the shell is of a brownish-yellow by transmitted light, it is so translucent that the red tint is seen through it.

The simple Orbitolite has many varieties. Sometimes it begins its life as a spiral which changes to a circular disk as it advances in age. It varies in thickness, and some of its very large varieties may be said to consist of three disks or stories of concentric chambers and many marginal pores instead of one. The upper and base stories of concentric chambers are alike, the intermediate one very different, but the sarcode segments in all the three are so connected as to form a very complex compound animal.[8] Different as this structure is from that of the simple Orbitolite, they are merely varieties of the same species; for it has been shown by Dr. Carpenter that, although many pass their lives in the simple one-storied state, they may change into the complex form at any stage of their growth; and as an equally extensive range of variation has been proved by Professor Williamson and Mr. Parker to prevail in other groups of Foraminifera, the tendency to specific variation seems to be characteristic of that type of animal life, and consequently the number of distinct species is less than they were supposed to be.

The Orbitolites are found in the dredgings of all the warmer seas, in vast multitudes at the Philippine Islands, but those from Australia are the most gigantic, being sometimes the size and thickness of a shilling.

Order of Arenaceous Foraminifera.

In the numerous family of Lituolidæ the abode of the animal consists of a cement mixed with very fine particles of sand with larger ones imbedded in the surface. The order includes a wide range of forms divided into three genera, the simplest of which consists of a cylindrical tube twisted into a spiral gradually increasing in diameter, and attached to a foreign substance by one of its surfaces. The creature which lives in it is a uniform cord of sarcode, which sends its pseudopodia out through a large aperture at the extremity of its tube in search of food. Although the tube consists of sand imbedded in an ochreous-coloured cement secreted by the animal, its surface is smooth as a plastered wall.

---

[8] A complete description of this complex type is given by Dr. Carpenter in the Phil. Trans. 1856.

The spiral tubes of this genus take various forms, and in some cases are divided into chambers.

The members of the genus Lituola exude from their surfaces a thick coat of cement with a quantity of siliceous particles roughly imbedded in it, but in some instances the particles are so uniform in size and shape, and are so methodically arranged, that the surface resembles a tesselated pavement. The usual form of the Lituola is a mere string of oval convex chambers increasing gradually in size, and fixed to shells and corals by their flat surfaces. In some instances the shells, or rather the substitutes for shells, take a nautiloid form, and become detached from the foreign bodies to which they were attached. In the highest forms of this genus the chambers are divided by secondary partitions.

The typical form of the genus Valvulina is a three-whorled, three-sided pyramidal shell, with three chambers in every turn of the spire. The aperture is large and round, with a valve of smaller size attached by a tooth of shell to its rim. The creature itself has an exceedingly thin perforated vitreous shell, covered by an incrustation of calcareous particles, which so entirely blocks up the perforations that it can only extend its pseudopodia through the mouth of its shell.

Order of Vitreous Foraminifera.

Nearly all the Foraminifera on the British coasts belong to the Vitreous or Perforated order, which consists of three natural families and many genera. Their shells are vitreous, hyaline, and generally colourless, even although the substance of the animal is deeply coloured; in some species both the animal and its shell are of a rich crimson. The glassy transparency of the shells would be perfect were they not perforated by numerous tubes running from the interior of the chambers straight through the shell, and ending in pores on its surface. According to microscopic measurement the tubes in the Rotalia, which are the largest, are on an average the $\frac{1}{1000}$ of an inch in diameter, and as they are somewhat more than that apart, the transparency of the shell appears between them and gives the surface a vitreous aspect. The pseudopodia of the animal have been seen to pass through every part of the wall of the chambers occupied by it; the apertures of the tubuli in this case are wide enough to permit particles of food to be drawn into the interior of the shell. But threads of sarcode of extreme tenuity alone could pass through the tubuli of the Operculina, which are not more than the $\frac{1}{10000}$ of an inch in diameter, and the distance between them not much greater, which gives the shell an opaque appearance. Particles of food can hardly be small enough to pass through such tubes into the interior to be digested. Dr. Carpenter, however, is almost certain, from the manner in which the animal repairs injuries done to its shell, that the semi-fluid sarcode extends itself at certain times, if not constantly, over the exterior of the shell, as in the Gromia; and therefore it is by no means impossible that the digestive process may really be performed in this external layer, so that only the products of digestion may have to pass into the portion of the sarcode occupying the body of the shell.

In such many-chambered shells as are pierced by tubuli wide enough to permit particles of food to be drawn into the interior, each segment of the animal, being fed within its own chamber, has a life of its own, at the same time that it shares with all the others in a common life maintained by food taken in through the mouth of the shell. There are many instances of this individual life combined with a common life among the lowest tribes of animals.

Although the Perforated order contains types widely

apart, they are always connected by intermediate forms; but there is no such connection between the two great natural orders, which are not only separated by the tubuli in the shell, but in many instances by the structure of the interior and the corresponding character of the animal.

In the Lagenidæ, which form the first family of the Perforated order, the vitreous shell possesses great hardness, and is pierced by numerous small tubuli. It is very thin, and of glossy transparency. The first four shells in fig. 97 represent some of its forms.

The genus Nodosaria has a very extensive range of forms, from the elongated structure to the nautiloid spiral, depending upon the relative proportions and arrangement of the segments. The segments are separated by constrictions transverse to the axis of growth, or by bands as in the Nodosaria rugosa, B, fig. 97. It frequently happens that parts of the shell are not perforated; and there are generally longitudinal ribs which sometimes have spines projecting from every part of the interior, as in Nodosaria spinicosta, c, fig. 97.

In the genus Nodosaria, the axis of growth changes from a straight line to that of a spiral, so that the septa or divisions between the segments cross the axis obliquely, and the aperture instead of being exactly central becomes excentric. Between these extremes there is a numerous series of gradations. The Cristallaria is the highest type; the form is a nautiloid spiral, more or less compressed (D, fig. 97), of which each whorl has its chambers extended by winged projections so as to reach the centre, and entirely encloses the preceding whorl. The number of chambers in each whorl is much smaller than in most of the nautiloid spirals, not being more than eight or nine. The divisions are always strongly marked externally by septal bands, varying in character according to the species. The margin of the shell runs into a keel, which is sometimes extended into a knife-edge. Nearly all the Lagena family are found in the North Atlantic and Mediterranean, especially in the Adriatic, which is rich in species. In the Nodosaria the cells which compose the shell have so little connection one with another that they may be easily detached; which gives reason to believe that the separation of the parts may be a means of reproduction and dispersion.

The Globigerinidæ are the most numerous family of the perforated series, and the most remarkable in the history of the existing Foraminifera. They are distinguished by the coarseness of the perforations in their shells, and by the crescentic form of the aperture by which the chambers communicate with each other.

The genus Globigerina consists of a spiral aggregation of globose segments, which are nearly disconnected from each other although united by mutual cohesion. The segments are always somewhat flattened against one another in their planes or junctions, and sometimes the flattening extends over a pretty large surface as in G, fig. 97. The entire series of segments shows itself on the upper side, but on the lower side only the segments forming the latest convolution are prominent; they are usually four in number, and are arranged symmetrically round a deep depression or vestibule; the bottom of which is formed by the segments of the earlier convolutions. In this vestibule each segment opens by a large crescent-shaped orifice, the several chambers having no direct communication with each other. The entire shell of the ordinary type may attain the diameter of about $\frac{1}{30}$ of an inch, but it is usually much smaller; the typical form, however, is subject to very considerable modifications. In newly formed segments of Globigerina, the hyaline shell substance is perforated by tubuli varying from $\frac{1}{10000}$ to $\frac{1}{5000}$ of an inch in

ROSALINA ORNATA.

diameter, arranged at pretty regular distances; but in deep seas the surface of the shell is raised by an external deposit into tubercles or ridges, the orifices of the pores appearing between them.

Each chamber of the shell is occupied by a reddish-yellow segment of sarcode, from which pseudopodia are seen to protrude; and it is supposed that the sarcode body also fills the vestibule, since without such connecting band it is difficult to understand how the segments which occupy the separate chambers can communicate with each other, or how new segments can be budded off. In the Globigerina the slight cohesion gives reason to believe that the separation of the parts may be a means of reproduction.

The Rosalina ornata, one of the most beautiful specimens of this group, and remarkable for the size of its pores, is represented in fig. 100 with its pseudopodia extended, and coalescing in some parts.

The shells of the genus Textularia consist of a double series of chambers disposed on each side of an axis, so that they look as if they were mutually interwoven. As the segments for the most part increase gradually in size, the shell is generally triangular, the apex being formed of the first segment, and its base of the two last (H, fig. 97).

The aperture is always placed in the inner wall of each chamber, close to its junction with the preceding segment on the opposite side. In the compressed shells it is crescent-shaped, but it is semilunar in the less compressed, and may even be gibbous. The shell is hyaline, with large pores not very closely set, though in some varieties they are minute and near to one another. Sometimes the pores open on the surface in deep hexagonal pits. The older shells are frequently incrusted with large coarse particles of sand, and some specimens from deep water are almost covered with fine sand, but with a good microscope the pores may be seen between them.

The sarcode segments of the animal perfectly correspond in shape and in alternate arrangement with the segments of the shell, and are connected by bands of sarcode passing through the crescent-shaped apertures by which each chamber communicates with that which precedes and follows it.

The Textulariæ are among the most cosmopolitan of Foraminifera; some of their forms are found in the sands and dredgings from all shores, from shallow or moderately deep water. In time they go back to the Palæozoic period.

The Rotalia Beccarii, common on the British coast, affords a good example of the supplemental skeleton, a structure peculiar to some of the higher vitreous Foraminifera. It has a rather compressed turbinoid form with a rounded margin. Its spire is composed of a considerable number of bulging segments gradually increasing in size, disposed with great regularity, and with their opposed surfaces closely fitted to each other. The whole spire is visible on the exterior, with all its convolutions, and on account of the bulging form of the segments, their lines of junction would appear as deep furrows along the whole spire, were they not partly or wholly filled up with a homogeneous semi-crystalline deposit of shell-substance, which is very different in structure and appearance from the porous shell wall of the segments.

The genus Calcarina is distinguished by a highly developed intermediate skeleton with singular outgrowths, which is traversed by a system of canals; through these the animal sends its pseudopodia into the water for food to nourish the whole.

A homogeneous crystalline deposit invests almost the whole of the minute spiral shell of a Calcarina, and sends out many cylindrical, but more generally club-shaped spines in all directions, though they usually affect more or less that of the equator, as in the typical form Calcarina calcar, which is exactly like the rowel of a spur. The spines are for the most part thick and clumsy, and give the shell a very uncouth appearance, especially when their extremities are forked. The turbinoid spire of the shell has a globose centre surrounded by about five whorls progressively increasing in size, and divided by perforated septa into chambers. Each whorl is merely applied to that preceding it, and does not invest it in the least degree. Internally the turns of the spire are separated from each other by the interposition of a solid layer of shell-substance quite distinct from the walls of the chambers. A crystalline deposit begins at the very centre of the spire in a thin layer gradually increasing in thickness as it proceeds, and sending off club-shaped spines from time to time so that the spines are of later and later production, and become thicker and longer. From this it is evident that the intermediate skeleton grows simultaneously with the turns of the spire, but strange as it may seem, their growth is independent, though both are nourished and increased by the sarcode in the interior of the chambers. For the intermediate skeleton is traversed in every part by an elongated network of canals, which begin from irregular lacunæ or openings in the walls of the chambers, and extend to the extremities of the spines. Through these canals threads of the sarcode body of the animal within the chambers have access to the exterior, and provide nourishment for the intermediate skeleton; while pseudopodia, passing into the water through pores in the last partition of the shell, provide for its growth and procure nourishment for the animal. The communication between the adjacent chambers in the whorls, is by means of a series of pores in the septa, or partitions; and it is through the pores of the last septum that the pseudopodia of the animal have access to the water to provide for the growth of the spire, for the punctures on the surface are merely the terminations of some of the branching canals. On approaching the surface the canals become crowded together in some parts, leaving columns of the shelly skeleton unoccupied which either appear as tubercles on the surface, or, if they do not rise so high, form circular spots surrounded by punctations which are the apertures of the canals.

The Rotaline series of the Globigerina family is one of the most numerous and varied of the whole class of Foraminifera; but varied as their forms are, they all bear the characteristic marks which distinguish their order, with this essential difference, that in the genus Globigerina each chamber of the spire has a communication with the central vestibule by a crescent-shaped aperture, while in the Rotalinæ each chamber only communicates by a crescentic aperture with that which precedes and follows it.

In the Rotaline group the internal organization rises successively from the simple porous partition between the chambers, to the double partition with the radiating passages, and from the latter to the double partitions, intermediate skeleton, and complicated system of canals. To these changes the structure of the compound animal necessarily corresponds, for it may be presumed that not only the chambers but all the passages and canals in the interior of the shell are either permanently or occasionally filled with its sarcode body.

However, it is in the Nummuline family that the Foraminifera attain the highest organization of which they are capable. This family surpasses all the Vitreous tribe in the density and toughness of the shell, the fineness of its tubuli, and in the high organization of its canal system. Their forms vary from that resembling a nautilus or ammonite to a flat spiral or cyclical disk, like an Orbitolite, though vastly superior to it in organization both with regard to the animal and to the structure of the shell.

All the species of the genus Nummulite are spiral; in the typical form the last turn of the spire not only completely embraces, but entirely conceals, all that precede it. In general, the form is that of a double convex lens of more or less thickness; some are flat, lenticular, and thinned away to an acute edge, while

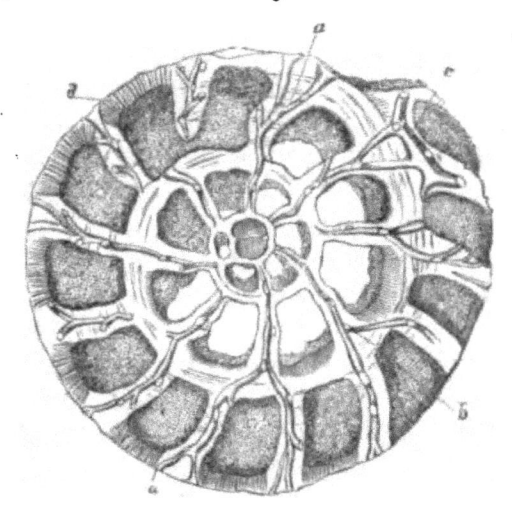

Fig. 101.   Section of Faujasina.

others may be spheroidal with a round, or obtuse edge. They owe their name to their resemblance to coins, being, in general, nearly circular. Their diameters range from $\frac{1}{16}$th of an inch to $4\frac{1}{2}$ inches, so that they are the giants of their race; but the most common species vary from $\frac{1}{4}$ an inch to 1 inch in diameter.

Fig. 101 represents a section of the Nummulite Faujasina near and parallel to the base of the shell. It shows a series of chambers arranged in a flat spiral, and increasing in size from the centre to the last turn of the spire, which embraces and conceals all that precede it. Every segment of the animal is enclosed in a shell of its own, so that they are separated from one another by a double wall and space between; however, they are connected in the spiral direction by narrow passages in the walls.

The segments of the animal in the exterior whorl have direct communication with the water by means of a shelly marginal cord, *a*, fig. 101, perforated by multitudes of minute tubes, less than the $\frac{1}{10000}$ of an inch in

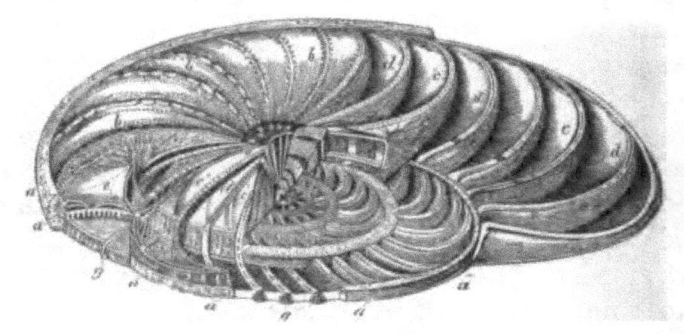

Fig. 102. Interior of the Operculina.

diameter, through which threads of sarcode finer than those of a spider's web can be protruded. These tubuli are so very fine and numerous, that they characterize the Nummuline family.

Fig. 102 represents the interior of the Operculina, which is an existing representation of the Nummuline type. Every segment of the animal is enclosed in a shell of its own, but all the segments are connected in the spiral direction by narrow passages in the walls as in the Faujasina.

Although each of the interior whorls has its perforated marginal band, the segments can have no direct access to the water; however, they are indirectly brought into contact with it by means of a system of branching shelly canals, radiating from the central chamber, ending in conspicuous pores in the external surface of the shell. During this course the canals send small tubes into the chambers on each side of them; through these the internal segments of the animal can fill the canals with cords of sarcode, and protrude them into the water, whence they are supplied with food.

The genus Polystomella is distinguished by the high development of the intermediate skeleton and the canal system that maintains it. The Polystomella crispa (fig. 97, E), a beautiful species common on the British coasts and in other temperate seas, has a lenticular form, the $\frac{1}{18}$ to the $\frac{1}{12}$ of an inch in diameter. It consists of a small number of convolutions winding round the shorter axis of the lens, increasing rather rapidly in breadth, and each one almost entirely enclosing its predecessor, so that the shell is exactly alike on both sides, and only the last convolution is to be seen. At the extremities of the axis there is a mass of solid shell-substance, perforated by orifices which are the apertures of a set of straight, parallel canals. In the figure only the last convolution is visible, upon which the convex septal bands are very conspicuous, dividing the surface into well marked segments, upon the exterior edge of each of which there are strong transverse crenulations. The only communication which the chambers have with the exterior, is by means of a variable number of minute orifices near the inner margin of the sagittate partition-plane, close to its junction with the preceding convolution; a very high microscopic power is required to see them, as well as the minute tubercles with which the surface of the shell is crowded, more especially on the septal bands and in the rows of depressions between the segmental divisions.

The sarcode animal itself corresponds exactly with the form and spiral arrangement of the chambers so strongly marked on the exterior of the shell. The segments form a spiral of crescents, smooth on the convex and crenulated on the concave side; and from the latter threads of sarcode proceed, which pass through pores in the inner margins of the partitions, and unite them into one animal.

The Polystomella lives in tropical seas; P. crispa in temperate latitudes, and P. striato-punctata inhabits the polar waters; the genus is found everywhere.

Although variety of form without specific difference is characteristic of the Foraminifera, it sometimes happens that identity of external form is accompanied by an essential difference in internal structure. Of this the Cycloclypeus is an instance; it is a rare species of nummuline, dredged up from rather deep water off the coast of Borneo. The shell is gigantic, some specimens being two and a half inches in diameter; but its mode of growth is the same with that of the most complicated Orbitolite. It consists of three superposed stages of circular discs, each circle of chambers enclosing all those previously formed. However, each segment of the animal being enclosed in its own shelly envelope, a supplemental skeleton, and a radial, vertical and annular system of canals, prove that the two animals belong to essentially different families of Foraminifera. There are many instances, especially in the Rotaline group, of isomorphism accompanied with generic difference; thus no reliance can be placed on variety of external form, unaccompanied by change of internal structure.

An attempt has been made in the preceding pages to describe a few species most characteristic of some of the genera of this multitudinous class; and of those selected a mere sketch of the most prominent features of the animal and its abode is given, that some idea may be formed of the wonderfully complicated structure of beings, which are mostly microscopic specks. Yet the most minute circumstances in the forms of the animals and their shells, with their varieties and affinities, have been determined with an accuracy that does honour to microscopic science.

They are now arranged in a natural system by William B. Carpenter, M.D. F.R.S. assisted by William K. Parker, Esq., and T. Rupert Jones, Esq., and published in the Transactions of the Ray Society in 1862. To this admirable work, the author is highly indebted.

It was known that different types of Foraminifera abound at different depths on the coasts of the ocean; but it was long believed that no living creature could exist in its dark and profound abyss. By deep-sea sounding, it has been ascertained that the basin of the Atlantic Ocean is a profound and vast hollow or trough, extending from pole to pole; in the far south, it is of unknown depth, and the deepest part in the north is supposed to be between the Bermudas and the Great Banks of Newfoundland. But by a regular series of soundings made by the officers of the navies of Great Britain and the United States, for the purpose of laying a telegraphic cable, that great plain or steppe was discovered, now so well known as the telegraphic plateau, which extends between Cape Race in Newfoundland, and Cape Clear in Ireland. From depths of more than 2,000 fathoms on this plateau, the ooze brought up by the sounding machine consisted of 97 per cent. of Globigerinæ. The high state of preservation of these delicate shells was no doubt owing to the perfect tranquillity which prevails at great depths; for the telegraphic plateau and the bed of the deep ocean everywhere is covered by a stratum of water unruffled by the commotion raised by the hurricane which may be raging on the surface. The greater number of the Globigerinæ were dead empty shells; but although in many the animal matter was quite fresh, Professor Bailly of New York could not believe that such delicate creatures could live on that dark sea bed, under the pressure of a column of water more than 2,000 fathoms high, a weight equal to rather more than that of 340 atmospheres or 5,100 lbs. on every square inch of sea-bed; wherefore he concluded that the tropical ocean and the Gulf Stream, which absolutely swarm with animal life, must have been the birth-place and home of these minute creatures, and that this mighty ‘ocean river,’ which divides at the Great Banks of Newfoundland, and spreads its warm waters like a fan over the north Atlantic, deposits their remains over its bed, which has thus been their grave-yard for unknown periods, and which, in the lapse of geological time, may be raised above the waves as dry land.

Professor Ehrenberg on the contrary concluded that residentiary life exists at the bottom of the ocean, both from the freshness of the animal matter found in the shells, and from the number of unknown forms which are discovered from time to time at various and often great depths along the coasts. This opinion has been confirmed beyond a doubt on several occasions, especially by Dr. Wallich, who accompanied an expedition sent under the command of Sir Leopold M'Clintock, to sound the North Atlantic for laying a telegraphic line.

In doing that two operations are requisite. The first is to ascertain the depth: when that is known, the nature of the sea-bed must be determined, and on that account a sample of it is then sounded for; but owing to the difficulty of ascertaining the exact time at which the ground is struck, a quantity of rope in excess of the depth is given out, which lies on the bottom of the sea while the machine is being drawn up, which occupies a considerable time when the depth is great. About midway between Greenland and the north of Ireland, when the machine was hauled up from a depth of a mile and a half, several starfish were clinging with their long spiny arms to fifty fathoms of the rope that had been lying on the surface of the sea-bed while the machine was being drawn up, and to that part of the rope alone. They continued to move their limbs energetically for more than a quarter of an hour after they were out of the water. They certainly had not been entangled in the line while swimming, because starfishes are invariably creeping animals. The deposit on which they had rested at the bottom of the ocean contained ninety-five per cent. of Globigerinæ. Abundance of these minute Foraminifera were found in the stomachs of the starfish; which seemed to prove not only that the starfish were caught on their natural feeding ground, but that their food was living organisms whose normal abode is the surface of the bed of the deep ocean.

Dr. Wallich also discovered in the ooze brought up from a depth of nearly two miles and a quarter a number of small bodies from $\frac{1}{16}$ to $\frac{1}{4}$ of an inch in length and about a line in breadth. They consisted of equal globes arranged in a straight line like the Nodosaria, or built up, each lying on part of the one below it, and increasing in size from the uppermost about $\frac{1}{1250}$ to the undermost about $\frac{1}{450}$ of an inch in diameter. Both of these forms, called coccospheres, consisted of sarcode enclosed in a calcareous deposit; and were studded at nearly regular distances by minute round or oval bodies concave below, and with an aperture on their convex surface sometimes single, sometimes double. These coccospheres were also found free in the ooze, and had been seen previously by Capt. Dayman. They have likewise been seen as free organisms living on the surface of the ocean.

The ooze in the bed of the Atlantic ocean, as well as of the Mediterranean and Adriatic contains fifty per cent. of Globigerinæ; they exist in the Red Sea, in the

vicinity of the West Indian Islands, on both sides of
South America and near the Isle of France, but not in
the Coral Sea which is occupied by different genera.
Though in utter darkness, at the bottom of a deep
ocean, these little creatures can procure food by means
of their pseudopodia, whose extreme sensibility makes up
for the want of sight; and the very excess of pressure
under which they live insures them a supply of oxygen
at depths to which free air cannot penetrate, for it is
believed that the quantity of dissolved air that water
contains is in proportion to the pressure.

Fossil Foraminifera enter so abundantly into the
sedimentary strata, that Buffon declared 'the very dust
had been alive.' 58,000 of these fossil shells have been
computed in a cubic inch of the stone of which Paris and
Lyons are built. The remains of these Rhizopods are
for the most part microscopic. M. D'Orbigny estimated
that an ounce of sand from the Antilles contained
1,800,000 shells of Foraminifera. A handful of sand
anywhere, dry sea-weeds, the dust shaken from a dry
sponge, are full of them.

When the finer portions of chalk amounting to one
half or less are washed away, the remaining sediment
consists almost entirely of the shells of Foraminifera,
some perfect, others in various stages of disintegration.
In some of the hard limestones and marbles, the relics
of Foraminifera can be detected in polished sections
and in thin slices laid on glass. It is now universally
admitted that some crystallized limestones which are
destitute of fossil remains, had been originally formed
by the agency of animal life, and subsequently altered
by metamorphic action; the opinion is gradually gain-
ing ground among geologists that such is the history of
the oldest limestones.

At certain geological periods circumstances favoured
the development of an enormous multitude of indivi-

dual animals. In the earlier part of the Tertiary period the Nummulites acquired an extraordinary size. They were like very large coins two or more inches in diameter, and were accumulated in such quantities as to constitute the chief part of the nummulitic limestone; a formation in some places 1,500 feet thick, which extends through southern Europe, Libya, Egypt, Asia Minor, and is continued through the Himalayan mountains into various parts of the Indian peninsula, where it is extensively distributed. The Great Pyramid of Egypt is built of this limestone, which gave rise to singular speculations with regard to the Nummulites in very ancient and even in more recent times. Although this is incomparably the greatest, it is by no means the only instance of an accumulation of the fossil shells of individual animals. The 'Lingula flags,' a stratum in the upper Cambrian series of North Wales, was so named from the abundance of the Brachiopod Lingula that it contains.

Professor Ehrenberg discovered that the shells of the Foraminifera sometimes undergo an infiltration of silicate of iron, which fills not only the chambers, but also their canal-system even to its minutest ramifications, so that if the shell be destroyed by dilute acid, a perfect cast of the sarcode matter remains. The greensands in the different geological strata from the Silurian formation upwards, are chiefly composed of these casts; and Professor Baily of the United States more recently discovered that a process of infiltration is even now taking place in some parts of the ocean bed, and that beautiful casts of Foraminifera may be obtained by dissolving their shells with dilute acid.

A most extensive comparison of the Foraminiferous group of Rhizopods, recent and fossil, has been made by Messrs. Parker and Rupert Jones from almost every latitude on the globe, from the arctic and tropical seas, from the temperate zones in both hemispheres, and from shallow as well as deep-sea beds. They have also reviewed the fossil Foraminifera in their manifold aspects as presented by the ancient geological faunas throughout the whole series from the Tertiary down to the Carboniferous strata inclusive; and have come to the astonishing conclusion that scarcely any of the species of the Foraminifera met with in the secondary rocks have become extinct. All that they had seen have their counterparts in the recent Mediterranean deposits. Throughout that long series of geological epochs even to the present day, the Foraminifera show no tendency to rise to a higher type; but variety of form in the same species prevailed then as it does now.

Subsequently to this investigation, a gigantic Orbitulite twelve inches in diameter, and the third of an inch thick, has been found in the Silurian strata in Canada. The largest recent species Dr. Carpenter had seen was about the size and thickness of a shilling.

The lowest stratum of the Cambrian formations has been regarded as the most ancient of the Palæozoic rocks; now, however, strata of crystallized limestone near the base of the Laurentian system, which is 50,000 feet thick in Canada, are discovered by Sir W. E. Logan to have been the work of the Eozoön Canadense, a gigantic Foraminifer, at a period so inconceivably remote that it may be regarded as the first appearance of animal life upon the earth. In a paper published by Dr. Carpenter, in May 1865, he expressed his opinion that the Eozoön would be found in the older rocks of central Europe; and in the December following he received specimens from the fundamental quartz rocks of Germany, in which he found undoubted traces of the Eozoön. Here the superincumbent strata are 90,000 feet thick; the transcendent antiquity of the Eozoön is therefore beyond all estimation.

The fossil Eozoön consists of a succession of parallel rows or tiers of chambers, in which the sarcode of the living animal had been replaced by a siliceous infiltration, so that when the calcareous shell was destroyed by dilute acid, the cast was found to be precisely like that of a Nummulite; thin slices of it taken in different directions being examined with a microscope, it was found that the siliceous matter had not only filled that portion of the chambers which had been occupied by the sarcode-body of the animal and the canal-system, but had actually taken the place of the pseudopodial threads, the softest and most transitory of living substances, which were put forth through tubuli in the shell-walls of less than the $\frac{1}{10000}$ part of an inch in diameter. 'These are the very threads themselves turned into stone by the substitution which took place, particle by particle, between the sarcode body of the animal and certain constituents of the water of the ocean, before the destruction of the sarcode by ordinary decomposition.'[9] The shell had an intermediate skeleton, but the minute tubes in the walls of the chambers are so characteristic of the Nummulites, that they were sufficient alone to determine the relationship of the Eozoön to its modern representative.

The external shape and limits to the size of the individual Eozoön have not been determined with certainty, on account of its indefinite mode of growth, and the manner in which the fossilized masses are connected with the highly crystalline matrix in which they are imbedded; there is no doubt, however, that they spread over an area of a foot or even more, and attained a thickness of several inches. As they seem to have increased laterally by buds which never fell off, they formed extensive reefs; at the same time they had a vertical growth, for in some of the reefs the older

[9] Dr. Carpenter.

portions appear to have been fossilized before the newer
were built up on them as a base, exactly like the coral
reefs in the tropical ocean of the present day,[1] with
this difference however, that shells and other crustaceans are associated with the corals, while no organic
body has been found in the Eozoön reefs; nevertheless
the Eozoön must have had food. It may therefore be
inferred that parts at least of that primeval ocean
swarmed with animal life, whose remains have been
obliterated by metamorphic action. Carbon (which in
the form of graphite both constitutes distinct beds, and
is disseminated through the siliceous and calcareous
strata of the Laurentian series, as well in Norway as in
Canada), may indicate the existence of vegetation in the
Eozoön period.

The Eozoön is by no means confined to Canada and
central Europe. The serpentine marble of Tyree which
forms part of the Laurentian system on the west of
Scotland, and a similar rock in Skye, when subjected to
minute examination, are found to present a structure
clearly identical with that of the Canadian Eozoön.
And the like structure has been discovered by Mr.
Sanford in the serpentine marble of Connemara, known
as Irish green. The age of that rock however, is
doubtful: for when it was discovered to contain Eozoön,
Sir Roderick Murchison who had previously studied its
relations was at first inclined to believe it belonged to
the Laurentian series; now however, he considers the
Connemara marble to be of the Silurian age. ' If this be
the case it proves that the Eozoön was not confined to
the Laurentian period, but that it had a vast range in
time, as well as in geographical distribution; in this
respect corresponding to many later forms of Foraminifera which have been shown by Messrs. Parker and

---

[1] Structure of the Organic Remains in the Laurentian Rocks of Canada:
by J. W. Dawson. Esq., Principal of M'Gill University, Montreal.

Rupert Jones to range from the Trias to the present epoch.' [2]

The Carpenteria found in the Indian seas forms a link between the Foraminifera and Sponges. The shell is a minute cone adhering to the surface of corals and shells, by its wide base which spreads in broad lobes. Double-walled chambers and canals form a spiral within it, and are filled with a spongy sarcode of a more consistent texture than the sarcode of the Foraminifera, which in the larger chambers is supported by siliceous spicules similar to those which form the skeletons in sponges.

CLASS III.—SPONGES.

According to the observations of Mr. Carter, sponges begin their lives as solitary Amœbæ which grow by multiplication into masses, and assume endless forms according to the species; turbinate, bell-shaped, like a vase, a crater, a fan, flat, foliaceous and lobed or branching and incrusting the surface of stones. All the Amœbæ are so connected as to form one compound animal. The whole substance of a sponge is permeated by innumerable tubes which begin in small pores on the surface, and continually unite with one another as they proceed in their devious course to form a system of canals increasing in diameter and ending in wide openings called oscula, on the opposite side of the mass. Currents of water enter through the pores on the surface, and bring minute portions of food which are seized upon by a vast multitude of Amœbæ with long cilia which form the walls of the tubes and canals; and after they have

---

[2] The discovery of Eozoön and the minute details of its structure are published in the *Intellectual Observer* for May 1865. Also the ' Laurentian Rocks of Canada,' a small work, contains articles by various authors on the occurrence, structure, and mineralogy of certain organic remains of these rocks.

extracted the nutritious part, the offal is carried into the sea through the oscula, by the current of water whose flux is maintained by the vibrations of the cilia. In the compressed and many of the tubular sponges the water passes through them in a straight line; in branched and encrusting sponges, the afferent and efferent openings are on the same surface. The water is inhaled continuously and gently like an animal breathing, but it is rapidly and forcibly ejected; and in its passage it no doubt furnishes oxygen to aërate the juices of the compound animal, whose flesh or sarcode is irritable while alive, and which has the power to open and shut the pores and oscula of the canals, for the whole sponge forms one compound creature whose mass is nourished by the myriads of Amœbæ of which it is constituted.

Within the animated sarcode mass of the sponges there is in most cases a complicated skeleton of fibrous network, either horny, calcareous, or siliceous, which supports the soft mass, and determines its form.

Besides the skeleton, the mass of sponges is for the most part strengthened and defended by siliceous, and more rarely by calcareous, spines or spicules, either imbedded among the fibres of the skeleton, or fixed to them by their bases. The fibres of the skeleton network always unite, whether they be horny, calcareous, or siliceous; the spicules never, though they often lie in confused heaps over one another. They are of innumerable forms and arrangements. Some are like long needles lying close together in bundles, pointed or with a head like a pin at one or both ends; a great number are stellate with long or short rays; there may even be several different forms in the same sponge. Many calcareous sponges have cavities full of organic matter; and when the calcareous matter is dissolved by dilute acid, the organic base is left.

The common commercial sponges have a skeleton

which consists of a network of tubular, horny, tough, and elastic fibres which cross in every direction. They have no spicules or very few; and when such do project from the horny skeleton, they are generally conical, attached by their bases, and their surface is often beset with little spines arranged at regular intervals, which gives them a jointed appearance. The common sponge which is so abundant in the Mediterranean has many forms; those from the coast of North America are no less varied, but that most used in the United States is turbinate, concave, soft, and tomentose.

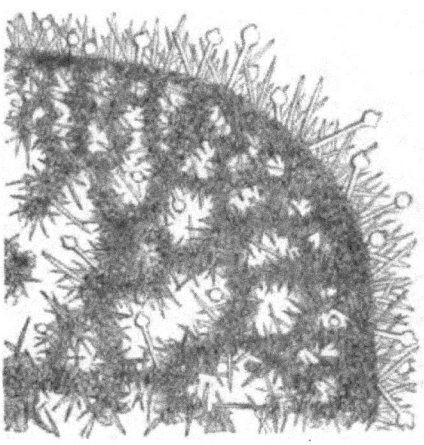

Fig. 103. Section of Sponge.

In the calcareous sponges a mass of three-rayed spicules surround the interior canals, where they are held together by a cartilaginous substance which is wanting in the horny sponges, but which remains in this order after the destruction of the more delicate matter when the sponge is dried.[3] The pores are also occasionally defended by the projecting points of half buried spines.

In nearly every species of this order the pores on the surface are protected by spicules; and they are also projected from the surface of the large cloacal cavity, and curved towards its opening, to defend it from Annelids and other enemies.[4] Some species have a long ciliary fringe at the orifice of the cavity, through which the water may pass out, but no animal can come in.

[3] 'Histoire Naturelle des Animaux sans Vertèbres,' par MM. Deshayes et H. Milne-Edwards.
[4] Memoir by Dr. Bowerbank in the Transactions of the Microscopic Society.

The spicula and skeleton of most of the marine sponges are siliceous and singularly beautiful; the skeleton of the Dactylocalyx pumiceus of Barbadoes is transparent as spun glass; and a species from Madagascar has numerous simple transparent and articulated spicules implanted in the siliceous fibres of the skeleton. The Cristata, Papillaris, Ovulata, and many more have siliceous skeletons, some garnished with spicules of various forms, and the surface occasionally covered with a layer of siliceous granules.

The variety in the size, structure, and habits of the marine sponges is very great: temperate and tropical seas have their own peculiar genera and species; some inhabit deep water, others live near the surface, while many fix themselves to rocks, sea-weeds, and shells, between high and low water mark. There are very few dead oyster, whelk, scallop, and other shells that escape from the ravages of the Cliona, an extremely minute burrowing sponge of the simplest structure, which has a coat of siliceous spicules supposed to be the tools with which it tunnels a labyrinth through the mid-layer of the shell, in a pattern that varies with the species of the sponge. A communication is formed here and there with the exterior by little round holes, through which the sponge protrudes its yellow papillæ. From the force exhibited by this little sponge, it may perhaps be inferred to possess a rudimentary muscle and nerve.[5]

Sponges are propagated twice in the year by minute ciliated globules of sarcode, detached from the interior of the aquiferous canals, which swim like zoospores to a distance, come to rest, and lay the foundation of new sponges. The little yellow eggs of Halichondria panicea are lodged in the interstices between the interior canals; when mature, they are oval and covered with cilia, and are carried out by the currents; and after

[5] Professor Huxley's Lectures.

swimming about for some days fix on a solid object, become covered with bristles, spread out into a transparent film, charged with contractile vesicles of different sizes in all degrees of dilatation and contraction, as well as with sponge ovules. Spicules are developed at the same time, and these films ultimately become young sponges, and if two happen to meet they unite and are soldered together.[6] Besides eggs, larger bodies covered with radiating spicules are produced, containing granular particles of sarcode, each of which when set free by the rupture of the envelope, becomes an Amœba-like creature, and ultimately a sponge.

Fresh-water sponges are sometimes branched, and sometimes spread over stones, wood, and other substances; and one species covers an earthy mass some inches thick formed by its own decayed matter. The skeleton of such species as have one, consists of bundles of siliceous spicules, held together and mixed with groups of needles, the rods of which project through the surface of the sponge and render it spinous. The motions in the gelatinous sarcode mass are the most remarkable feature in the fresh-water sponges, which all belong to the genus Spongilla. Mr. Carter observed that portions of the surface of some individuals of the Spongilla fluviatilis in his aquarium had long cilia by means of which they rapidly changed their places during the spring, but when winter came they emitted processes from such parts of their surfaces as were free from cilia and retracted them again just like Amœbæ. These portions often had cells, and when the Amœba-like motions ceased, a nucleus and nucleolus appeared within them, and at last the whole gelatinous sarcode mass consisted of these cells or globules. Some had no nucleus, but were filled with green or colourless granules.

At certain seasons of the year, whatever the form of

<hr />

6 M. Milne-Edwards.

the fresh-water sponges may be, a multitude of minute
hard yellow bodies are produced in their deeper parts.
They consist of a tough coat containing radiating spicules like a pair of spoked wheels united by an axle with
a pore in its surface. Within this last there is a mass of
motionless granular cells, and when put into water the
cells come out at the pore and give rise to new sponges.

Insulated groups of germs covered with cells called
swarm-cells seem to form parts of the sponges; they lie
completely within the mass of the living sponge. They
have the form of a hen's egg, are visible to the naked
eye, and when they come into the water they swim in
all directions for a day or two; become fixed; a white
spot within is enlarged; and the constituents of young
sponges appear.[7]

The generic forms of fossil sponges augment in
number and variety from the Silurian to the Cretaceous
beds, where the increase is rapid; but all the sponges
which had a stony reticulated form without spicules
passed away with the Secondary epoch, so that the
family has no representatives in the Tertiary deposits or
existing seas. The calcareous sponges which abound
in the Oolite and Cretaceous strata, and attain their
maximum in the Chalk, are now almost extinct, or are
represented by other families with calcareous spicules.
Siliceous fossil sponges are particularly plentiful. In
England extensive beds of them occur in the Upper
Greensand, and in some of the Oolitic and Carboniferous Limestones; and some beds of the Kentish Rag
are so full of their siliceous spicules, that they irritate
the hands of the men who quarry them. Since every
geological formation except the Muschelkalk is found
in England, the number and variety of fossil sponges
are very considerable. The horny sponges are more
abundant now than they were in the former seas. Ac-

[7] Professor Huxley's Lectures.

cording to M. D'Orbigny the whole number of fossil sponges known and described amount to thirty-six genera and 427 species, which is probably much below the real number.[8]

CLASS IV.—INFUSORIA.

The Infusoria, which form the second group of the Protozoa, are microscopic animals of a higher grade than any of the preceding creatures, although they go through their whole lives as isolated single cells of innumerable forms. They invariably appear in stagnant pools and infusions of animal and vegetable matter when in a state of rapid decomposition. Every drop of the green matter that mantles the surface of pools in summer teems with the most minute and varied forms of animal life. The species called Monas corpusculus by the distinguished Professor Ehrenberg, has been estimated to be $\frac{1}{2000}$ part of a line in diameter. 'Of such infusoria a single drop of water may contain 500,000,000 of individuals, a number equalling that of the whole human species now existing upon the face of the earth. But the varieties in size of these animalcules invisible to the naked eye are not less than that which prevails in almost any other natural class of animals. From the Monad to the Loxades or Amphileptus, which are the fourth and sixth part of a line in diameter, the difference in size is greater than between a mouse and an elephant; within such narrow bounds might our ideas of the range in animal life be limited if the sphere of our observation was not augmented by artificial aid.'[9]

This singular race of beings has given rise to the erroneous hypothesis of equivocal or spontaneous generation, that is to say, the production of living animalcules by a chemical or even fortuitous combination

---

[8] 'Palæontology,' by Professor Owen.   [9] Prof. Owen.

of the elements of inert matter. That question has been decided by direct experiment, for Professor Schultz kept boiled infusions of animal and vegetable matter for weeks in air which had passed through a red-hot tube, and no animalcules were formed, but they appeared in a few hours when the same infusions were freely exposed to the atmosphere, which shows clearly that the germs of the lowest grade of animal life float in the air, waiting as spores do, till they find a nidus fit for their development.

M. Pasteur, Director of the Normal School in Paris, in a series of lectures published in the 'Comptes Rendus,' has not only proved that the atmosphere abounds in the spores of cryptogamic fungi and moulds, but with infusoria of the form of globular monads, the Bacteria, and vibrios, which are like little rods round at their extremities and extremely active. The Bacteria mona and especially the Bacteria terma, are exceedingly numerous. These minute beings are the principal agents in the decomposition of organic matter. They are more numerous in dry than in wet weather, in towns than in the country, on plains than on mountains.

In a memoir read at the Academy of Sciences, Paris, Mr. J. Samuelson mentions that he had received rags from Alexandria, Japan, Melbourne, Tunis, Trieste and Peru. He sifted dust from the rags from each of these localities respectively through fine muslin into vases of distilled water. Life was most abundant in the vases containing dust from Egypt, Japan, Melbourne, and Trieste. The development of the different forms was very rapid, and consisted of protophytes, Rhizopods and true Infusoriæ. In most of the vases monads and vibrios appeared first, and from these Mr. Samuelson traced a change first into one then into another species of infusoria. In the dust from Japan he followed the development of a monad into what appeared to be a minute

Paramœcium, then into Lexodes cucullus, and finally into Colpoda cucullus. From these and other experiments it is proved that many infusoria now classed as distinct types are really one and the same animal in different states of development. That appears to be the case also with the Amœbœ. In the dust from Egypt Mr. Samuelson found a new Amœba whose motions were very rapid; as to shape and mode of motion he compared it to soap bubbles blown with a pipe. He traced the gradual changes of the globular form of this Amœba until its pseudopodia were in full action, its increase by conjugation, and other circumstances of its life. In the same dust and in that only, the development of the Protococcus viridis was seen, and that in such abundance that at last the water was tinged green by that plant. In the dust from Egypt a vibrio was changed into a vermiform segmented infusoria of an entirely new type. Its length varied from the $\frac{1}{180}$ to $\frac{1}{100}$ of an inch, each ring was ciliated, and the whole series of cilia extending along the body acted in concert; a circlet of them surrounded the anterior segment; a canal seemed to extend throughout the body. It was propagated by bisection; the two parts remained attached to one another; an independent ciliary motion was observed in each which did not interfere with the motion of the whole. It was supposed to be a larval form or series of forms. Mr. Samuelson's observations show, that the atmosphere in all the great divisions of the globe is charged with representatives of the three kingdoms of nature, animal, vegetable, and mineral: that the animal germs not only include the obscure types of monads, vibrios, and Bacteria, but also the Glaucoma, Cyclides, Vorticella, and other superior Infusoriæ, and occasionally though very rarely germs of the Nematode worms.

It has been already mentioned that many of the

microscopic fungi are ferments, aiding greatly in the decomposition of organic matter. They however are by no means the only agents in decomposition. The moment life is extinct in an animal or vegetable, Infusoria of the lowest grade seize upon the inanimate substance, speedily release its atoms from their organic bond, and restore them to the inorganic world whence they came. The ferment which transforms lactic acid into butyric acid is a species of vibrio which abounds in the liquid, isolated or united in chains; they glide, pirouette, undulate, and float in all directions, and multiply by spontaneous division. Vibrios possess the unprecedented property of living and propagating without an atom of free oxygen; they not only live without air, but air kills them. This singular property forms an essential difference between the Vibrios and the Mycoderms: the former cannot live in oxygen; the latter cannot live without it, and as soon as it is exhausted within the infusion, they go to the surface to borrow it from the atmosphere.

There are also two groups of Infusoria which possess these opposite characters, one being unable to live in oxygen, while the other cannot live without it; sometimes they even inhabit the same liquid. When the tartrate of lime is put into water along with some ammoniacal and alkaline phosphates, a Monad, the Bacteria terma, and other Infusoria appear after a time. These little animals bud rapidly in an infusion of animal matter, then a slight motion is produced by the appearance of the Monas corpusculum and the Bacterium terma, which glide in wavy lines in all directions in quest of the oxygen dissolved in the liquid, and as soon as it is exhausted they go to the surface in such numbers as to form a pellicle, where by aid of the oxygen they form the simple binary compounds water, ammonia, and carbonic acid. In the meantime the Vibrios, which are without oxygen, are developed below, and keep up the fermentation, and between the two, the work of decomposition is completed.

It is not the worm that destroys our dead bodies; it is the Infusoria, the least of living beings. The intestinal canal of the higher animals, and of man, is always filled during life not only with the germs of vibrios, but with adult and well-grown vibrios themselves. M. Leewenhoeck had already discovered them in man, a fact which has since been confirmed. They are inoffensive as long as life is an obstacle to their development, but after death their activity soon begins. Deprived of air and bathed in nourishing liquid, they decompose and destroy all the surrounding substances as they advance towards the surface. During this time, the little Infusoria, whose germs from the air had been lodged in the wrinkles and pores of the skin, are developed, and work their way from without inwards, till they meet the vibrios, and after having devoured them, they perish, or are eaten by maggots.

Of all the Infusoria and ferments the Vibrios are the most tenacious of life; their germs resist the destructive effect of a temperature of 100° Cent. The spores of the Mucedines are still more vivacious; they grow after being exposed to a heat of 120° Cent., and are only killed by a temperature of 130° Cent. As neither spores of the fungi nor the germs of the Infusoria are ever exposed to so high a temperature while in the atmosphere, they are ready to germinate as soon as they meet with a substance that suits them.

M. Ehrenberg has estimated that the Monas corpusculum is not more than the $\frac{1}{24,000}$th part of an inch in diameter; whence Dr. M. C. White, assuming that the ova of the Infusoria and the spores of minute fungi are only the $\frac{1}{10}$th part in linear dimensions of their parent organisms, concludes that there must be an incalculable amount of germs no larger than the $\frac{1}{240,000}$th or $\frac{1}{100,000}$th part of an inch in diameter; and since according to MM. Sullivant and Wormley, vision with the most powerful microscope is limited to objects of about the $\frac{1}{80,000}$th part of an inch in diameter, we need not be surprised if Infusoria and other organisms appear in putrescible liquids in far greater numbers than the germs in atmospheric dust visible by the aid of microscopes would lead us to expect.

The ferments are the least in size and lowest in organization of all the Infusoria. The higher group which abounds in stagnant pools and ditches are exceedingly numerous, and their forms are varied beyond description. They are globular, ovoid, long and slender, short and thick, many have tails, one species is exactly like a swan with a long bending neck, but whatever the form may be, all have a mouth and gullet. Although the skin of the Infusoria is generally a mere pellicle, that of the red Paramœcium and some others resembles the cellulose covering of a vegetable cell, engraved with a pattern; but in all cases respiration is performed through the skin.

Whatever form the cell which constitutes the body of the Infusoria may have, the highly contractile diaphanous pellicle on its exterior is drawn out into minute slender cilia which are the locomotive organs of these creatures. Vibrating cilia form a circlet round the mouth of some of these animalcules, a group of very long ones are placed like whiskers on each side of it, as in the Paramœcium caudatum, and in some cases there is a bunch of bristles in front. Certain Infusoria have cilia in longitudinal rows, and in many the whole body is either partially or entirely covered with short ones. In some Infusoria their vibrations are constant, in others interrupted, and so rapid that the cilia are invisible. These delicate fibres which vary from the

$\frac{1}{500}$th to the $\frac{1}{15,000}$th part of an inch in length, move simultaneously or consecutively in the same direction and back again, as when a fitful breeze passes over a field of corn. These animalcules seize their prey with their cilia, and swim in the infusions or stagnant pools, in which they abound, in the most varied and fantastic manner; darting like an arrow in a straight line, making curious leaps and gyrations, or fixing themselves to an object by one of their cilia and spinning round it with great velocity, while some only creep.

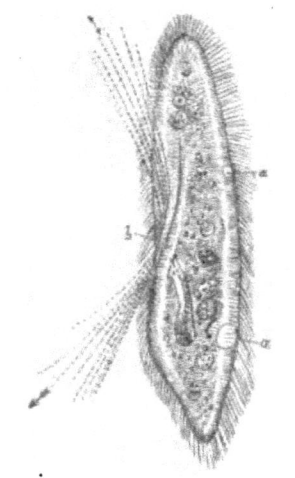
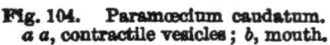
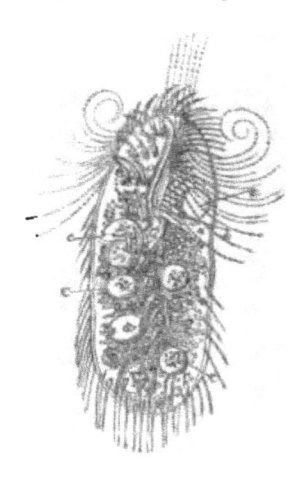

Fig. 104. Paramœcium caudatum. *a a*, contractile vesicles; *b*, mouth.

Fig. 105. Kerona silurus.—*a*, contractile vesicle; *b*, mouth; *c c*, animalcules which have been swallowed by the Kerona.

These motions, which bring the animalcules into fresh portions of the liquid, are probably excited by the desire for food and respiration.

None of the Infusoria have regular jointed limbs, but certain families of the higher genera have peculiar and powerful organs of locomotion partly consisting of strong ciliary bristles placed on the anterior in rows, used for crawling or climbing, and partly consisting of groups of strong processes which serve as traction feet, generally trailing behind the animal while swimming, or used to push it forward. When the bristles or cilia of this high group of Infusoria are used for crawling their motions may be traced to the contraction of the skin; but in the Infusoria that are never fatigued though their cilia vibrate incessantly night and day, it may be presumed that these motions are altogether independent of the will of the animal, in as much as there are innumerable cilia in the human frame that are never at rest during the whole course of our existence, nor do their vibrations cease till a considerable time after death—a striking instance of unconscious and involuntary motion.

The cell which constitutes the body of the Infusoria is filled with sarcode, which is the receptacle of the food, and in that substance all the internal organs of the animalcule are imbedded. In the higher genera it is full of granular particles of different sizes and forms, and it contains a nucleus in its centre, characteristic of cellular protozoa generally. The nucleus is of a dull yellow colour, and is enclosed in a transparent capsule, which in the smaller Infusoria reflects light brilliantly. It is generally of an ovoid form and single, but in several species the nucleus is double, and in others there are several nuclei.

The Infusoria have a distinct mouth and gullet, and for the most part another aperture for ejecting the indigestible part of their food, though some discharge it by the mouth, others through any part of their surface. A few of the larger Infusoria devour the smaller; others feed on minute vegetable particles, chiefly diatoms. Solid substances that are swallowed are collected into little masses mixed with water, and enter into clear ·spherical spaces called vacuoles in various parts of the sarcode, where they are partially digested. When the animal has not had food for some time, clear spaces only filled with a very transparent fluid are seen, variable both in size and number. It was on account of the digestive vacuoles that the Infusoria were called Polygastria by Ehrenberg.

Transparent contractile vesicles of a totally different nature from the vacuoles are peculiarly characteristic of such Infusoria as have a digestive cavity. They exist either singly or in even numbers, from 2 to 16, according to the species, and never change their places; but they dilate and contract rhythmically at pretty regular intervals. When dilated, they are filled with a clear, colourless fluid, the product of the digestive process which they are supposed to diffuse through the body of the animal.

The Euglena, a very extensive genus of Infusoria, have smooth bodies and green particles imbedded in the sarcode, which fills their interior; and M. Wöhler discovered that the green mantle covering the saline springs at Rodenberg and Königsborner, which consists of three species of these green Infusoria, gives out bubbles of pure oxygen; thus indicating a respiratory process in these animals, the same with that in plants, namely, fixing the carbonic acid of the atmosphere and exhaling oxygen, a singularly close analogy, if not identity, of action. The Euglenæ are also distinguished by an irregular oblong space in the head filled with a red liquid; but, as it does not contain a crystalline lens, it can only be regarded as the very earliest rudiment of an eye, totally incapable of distinguishing objects, though probably sensible to the influence of light. They swim with a smooth gliding and often rotatory motion, producing a kind of flickering on the surface of the water by the lashing of a long filament attached in front, and supposed to be their only organ of locomotion; nevertheless, Mr. Gosse thinks that they are covered with most minute cilia from their manner of swimming. The Euglena acus is one of the prettiest of these little animals; it is long and slender, of a sparkling green with colourless extremities, a thread-like proboscis, and a rich crimson spot. When it swims it rotates, and a series of clear, oblong bodies are seen towards the head, and another at the tail, as if they were imbedded in the flesh round a hollow.

The Loxades bursaria, which is a giant among its fellows, has an ovoid body with green particles imbedded in its interior. The outer skin is spirally grooved, so as to form a kind of network, the elevated points of which support the cilia with which its body is beset. It has a mouth and gullet lined with cilia, which force the food in balls into the soft matter in the interior, where both the food and the green particles circulate, being carried along by a gyration of the gelatinous matter in which they are imbedded.

A species of Peridinium, which is luminous at night, and occasionally covers large portions of the Bay of Bengal with a scarlet coat by day, nearly approaches the character of the unicellular Algæ. Mr. J. H. Carter observed that at first, when these animalcules were in a state of transition, their nearly circular bodies were filled with translucent green matter, closely allied, if not identical with, chlorophyll, which disappeared when the animal approaches its fixed state, and a bright red took its place: the Infusoria were then visible to the naked eye, and the sea became scarlet. The scarlet state only lasts for a few days, for each of these innumerable Infusoria becomes encysted or capsuled, and either floats on the water, or sinks to the bottom and remains motionless. The Euglena sanguinea has a scarlet state analogous to that of the Peridium. It is so minute and versatile that it is difficult to ascertain its true form, which, however, seems to be a spindle shape, with a pointed and blunt round head. In general it is of a rich emerald green, with perfectly clear, colourless extremities; but it sometimes occurs of a deep red, and in such multitudes as to give the water the appearance of blood.[1]

The Noctiluca miliaris, a luminous inhabitant of the ocean, and the most beautiful of the Infusoria, is distinguished by its comparatively gigantic size, and by its brilliant light, which makes the sea shine like streams of silver in the wake of a ship in a warm summer evening, when they come to the surface in countless multitudes. It is a globular animal like a minute soap bubble, consisting of gelatinous matter, with

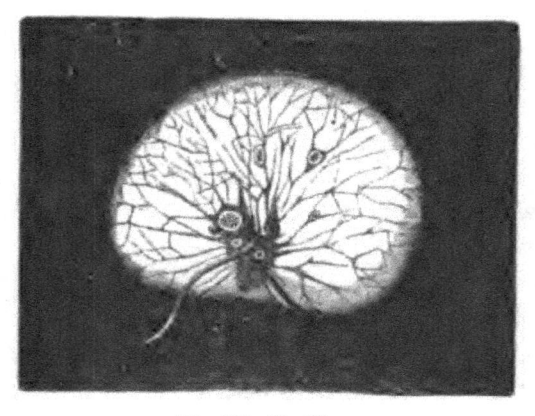

Fig. 106. Noctiluca.

a firmer exterior, and being about the thirtieth of an inch in diameter, it is visible to the naked eye, when a glass in which it is swimming is held to the light. On one side of the globe there is an indentation, from whence a tail of muscular fibre springs striped with transverse rings, which aids the animal in swimming. At the root of the tail lies the mouth, bordered on one side by a hard dentile lip leading into a funnel-shaped throat, from whence a long flickering cilium is protruded, supposed to be connected with respiration. The throat

[1] Mr. Gosse.

leads into a large cavity in the gelatinous substance, from whence the rudiments of an alimentary canal descend. From the internal surface of the globe sarcode fibres extend through the gelatinous matter, so as to divide it into a number of irregular compartments, in which vacuoles are often seen. They give buoyancy to the animal, and enable it to rise and sink in the water, but seem to disappear when the food is digested. The sarcode fibres constantly change their form and position, and the electric light emitted by a direct exertion of nerve power, which seems to be constant to the naked eye, really consists of momentary scintillations that increase in rapidity and intensity by the dash of an oar or the motion of the waves.

The Noctiluca is propagated by spontaneous division, a line appears bisecting the globe, which becomes more and more constricted till the animal is like a dumb-bell; the slender thread separating the two parts is then broken by their efforts to get free; the two new creatures swim off in different directions, and soon assume their adult form. But in many individuals there are clear, yellow globules with a well-defined nucleus, of a rich reddish-brown, which are the germs of the animal.

Most of the Infusoria multiply by continuous bisection, like the unicellular Algæ. The division generally begins with the nucleus, and is longitudinal or across, according to the form and nature of the animal, and is accomplished with such rapidity, that, by the computation of Professor Ehrenberg, 268,000,000 of individuals might be produced from one single animalcule of the species Paramœcium in a month. The Paramœcia are reproduced too by gemmation, and, as they are male and female, they are reproduced also like the higher classes.

The Infusoria have another mode of increasing. The animalcules either draw in or lose their cilia, and consequently come to rest. The animal then assumes a more globular form, and secretes a gelatinous substance from its surface, which hardens into a case or cyst, in which its body lies unattached and breaks up into minute ciliated gemmules, which swim forth like zoospores as soon as they come into the water by the thinning away of part of the cyst. In fact the animal is resolved into its offspring, which, as soon as free, gradually acquire the parent's form, though at first they may bear no resemblance to it. The scarlet Peridium seen by Mr. Carter in the Bay of Bengal is propagated in this manner. For the parent Peridium is broken up within its cyst into from two to four new ones, each of which when set free and grown up might undergo the same process.

The Loxades bursaria increases by three distinct methods, and sometimes by two at a time. In autumn, or the beginning of winter, six or eight germs containing granular matter and one or more hyaline nuclei are formed within the animal, each enclosed in two contractile cysts: they lie freely in the cavity of the body, and come one by one into the water through a canal ending in a protuberance in the skin. During this time the pulsations of the vesicles within the Loxades are continued, but the gyration of the green particles is suspended till all the germs are excluded and swim away, and then it is renewed as vigorously as ever. At first the young are totally unlike their parent, but by degrees acquire its form. The Loxades is also increased by division, sometimes across, sometimes longitudinally, and, in the latter case, one half is occasionally seen to contain germs which have been excluded before the other half had separated, so that the two distinct systems of propagation are simultaneous.[2]

The Vorticella nebulifera and some others of the

[2] 'Lectures on Comparative Anatomy,' by Professor Owen.

Infusoria are remarkable for the diversity of their reproductive powers ; for, besides division and gemmation, they are reproduced by a kind of alternate generation, accompanied by singular metamorphoses. The Vorticella, one of the most beautiful animals of its class, lives in pools of fresh water : groups of them are found on almost every mass of duckweed like little blue bells upon slender stalks, creating active currents in the water by the vibrations of long and powerful cilia with

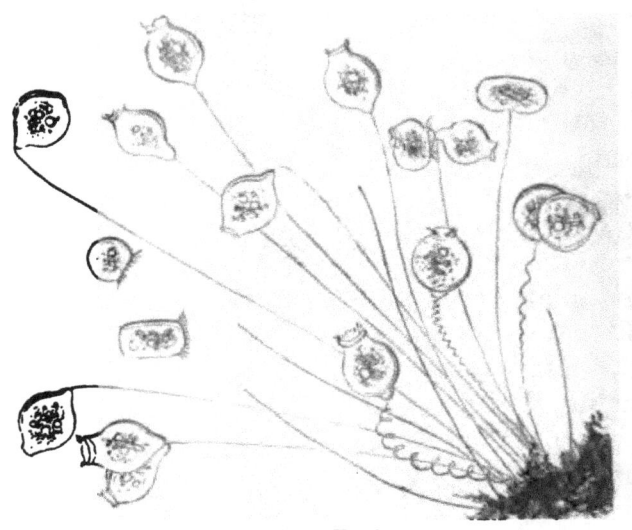

Fig. 107. Vorticellæ.

which the margin of the bell is fringed. The lip or edge of the bell is bent outwards into a permanent rim, and a deep groove cleaves the rim on one side, in which a wide cavity forming the mouth is placed. The mouth, the short throat or gullet, and the whole bell, are bristled with vibratile cilia.

The Vorticellæ feed on vegetable organisms, chiefly diatoms, and are exceedingly voracious. The cilia round the rim of the bell entangle the food, draw it into the mouth, and those in the gullet force particle after particle mixed with water into vacuoles which they make in the interior of the soft sarcode which fills the bell, and there the particles undergo rotation till digested and absorbed, and, if refuse remain, it is ejected through a softer part in the outer layer of the bell.

The stem that fixes the animal to a solid object is a tubular continuation of its outer membrane, containing a highly contractile filament; and, as the creature is extremely sensitive to external impressions, it folds up the ciliated rim of its bell, and its stalk shrinks down in a spiral on the slightest alarm, but the bell opens and the stalk stretches out again as soon as the alarm is over. When a Vorticella is reproduced by division,

Fig. 108. Acineta.

the bell separates longitudinally into two parts; one is often smaller than the other, and separates from its parent, swims about till it gets a stem, and fixes itself to an object. When the two parts are of equal size, the division extends to a greater or less distance down the stalk, and as each of these become perfect bells, and do not fall off but subdivide in the same manner, it follows that, by successive divisions, a whole group of these beautiful animals may spring from the same stem, as in fig. 107.

The Vorticella has a most wonderful mode of reproduction common to a few other Infusoria. A gelatinous substance is secreted by the bell, which hardens and envelopes it in a cyst; the encysted bell then separates from its stalk, and is transformed into an infusorial animal called an Acineta (fig. 108), closely resembling the Actinophrys sol with radiating filaments which it continually stretches out and draws in. A motile ciliated embryo, or Vorticella bud, is then formed within the Acineta, which, after a time, comes out at a slit in its side, swims about, gets a stem, fixes to some object, and is developed into a Vorticella. The slit closes again, and the Acineta keeps moving its filaments as usual, and another motile embryo is formed within it, which is emitted by a slit in the same manner, and is also developed into a Vorticella. As these young Vorticellæ, or bell animals, may undergo the same transformations, there may be an indefinite alternation of the two forms. The Vorticella-bud, when it issues from the slit in the Acineta, has an oval form, with a circlet of long cilia at its narrow end, a mouth at the more obtuse, a nucleus, and contractile vesicles, and, after swimming about till it finds a suitable place, it becomes fixed by one end of its oval body, a style or stem is formed, which rises rapidly, and the adult shape is developed. The Acinetæ are said to live upon Infusoria : they apply the dilated apex of their rays as sucking discs to the animal, and suck its contents till it dies. The Tricoda linceus undergoes metamorphoses analogous to those of the Vorticella, but more numerous and complicated.[3]

Most of the Vorticellæ, and probably the majority of

[3] Described in 'The Microscope,' by Dr. Carpenter.

Infusoria, remain unchanged for a time within their cysts, being then in a state analogous to the hybernal sleep of some of the reptiles. The cyst shelters them from cold and draught, and, when heat and moisture are restored, they resume their active vitality. The motions of the Infusoria are probably automatic, and in some instances consensual; they have neither true eyespecks, though their whole body seems to be conscious of light and darkness; nor have they ears; and, with the exception of touch, which the Vorticellæ have in a marvellous degree, it may be doubted whether the Infusoria have any organs of sense whatever, though they avoid obstacles and never jostle one another. The vibrations of their cilia are involuntary as in plants, an instance of the many analogies which perpetually occur between the lowest tribes of the two great kingdoms of nature. In both there are examples of propagation by bisection, conjugation, budding, and the alternation of generation, which occurs more frequently among Protozoa than among any other class of animals. There is a perfect resemblance between Zoospores and Protozoa; they both cease to move, the Zoospore when it secretes its cellulose coat and becomes a winter or resting spore, the Protozoon previous to encysting, a process presumed to be universal among that class of animals, before subdivision or reproduction begins. It is the dried cysts or germs of the Infusoria that float in the atmosphere as winter spores do, and it is believed that, like the fungi, the same germs may develope themselves into several different forms according to the nature of the liquid into which they may chance to be deposited; consequently, it is not necessary that the variety of germs should be very great, although the Infusoria themselves are of numerous forms.[4]

The Infusoria, the smallest of beings, apparently so insignificant, and for the most part invisible to the

---

[4] 'Lectures on Comparative Anatomy,' by Professor Owen.

unaided eye, have high functions assigned to them in the economy of nature. They 'are useful for devouring and assimilating the particles of decaying animal and vegetable matter from their incredible numbers, universal distribution, and insatiable voracity—they are the invisible scavengers for the salubrity of the atmosphere. They perform a still more important office in preventing the gradual diminution of the present amount of organic matter upon the earth. For, when this matter is dissolved or suspended in water in that state of comminution and decay, which immediately precedes its final decomposition into the elementary gases, and its consequent return from the organic to the inorganic world, these wakeful members of Nature's invisible police are everywhere ready to arrest the fugitive organic particles, and turn them back into an ascending stream of animal life. Having converted the dead and decomposing matter into their own living tissues, they themselves become the food of larger Infusoria, as the Rotifera and numerous other small animals, which, in their turn, are devoured by larger animals as fishes, and thus a pabulum fit for the nourishment of the highest organized beings is brought back by a short route from the extremity of the realms of organized matter.'[5]

[5] 'Lectures on Comparative Anatomy,' by Professor Owen.

SECTION III.

HYDROZOA, ZOOPHYTES.

ZOOPHYTES are animals of a much higher organization than the Protozoa, inasmuch as they are furnished with special organs of prehension, offence and defence, of attachment, and in many of locomotion. For the most part they consist of numerous individuals called Polypes, united in a community, and living together in intimate sympathy and combined action, so as to form one single compound animal.

Zoophytes are divided into two groups, namely the Hydrozoa, whose type is the common fresh-water Hydra, and the Actinozoa, which are composite animals, including the reef-building corals, whose polypes are formed according to the type of the Actinia, or common Sea Anemone. The Hydrozoa consist of seven orders, the first of which are the Hydridæ, inhabitants of fresh water; the next constitute the oceanic Hydrozoa, some of which, though extremely varied in form, are connected by the most wonderful relations.

The solitary Hydra that lives in fresh-water pools and ditches, consists of a soft cylindrical muscular bag, capable of being stretched into a slender tube, shrunk into a minute globe, or widely distended at will. At one end there is a circular mouth, which is highly sensitive, opening, closing, or protruding like a cone, and surrounded at its base by six long flexible arms called tentacles, arranged symmetrically. The mouth opens into a cavity extending throughout the length of the body, which is the stomach ; the other end of the sac is narrow, and terminates in a disk-shaped sucker, by which the Hydra fixes itself to aquatic plants, or floating objects, from whence it hangs down, and the tentacles float in the water.

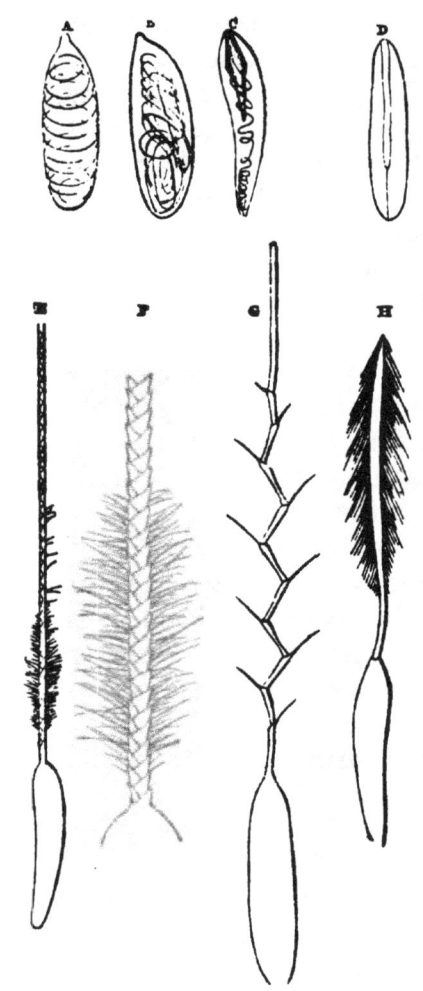

The sac or body is formed of two layers, an inner and an outer layer, of firmer texture, formed of cells imbedded in a kind of sarcode, and the space between the two layers is filled with a semifluid substance, mixed with solid particles and full of vacuoles. The inner and outer layers are united at the mouth, and the tentacles are closed tubes in communication with the cavity of the stomach. The exterior layer of the tentacles is beset with wart-like excrescences, formed of clusters of cells, with a larger one in the centre filled with a liquid. In

Fig. 109. Thread-cells and darts.—A, B, C, D, Thread-cells at rest ; E, F, G, H, appearance of the darts when projected.

all of them a long spicula, or sting, often serrated at the edge, is coiled up like a thread, and fixed by one end to a kind of tube, like the inverted finger of a glove, that the animal can dart out in an instant.

Thus armed, the tentacles are formidable weapons; they are highly contractile and wonderfully strong, tenaciously adhering to the small worms and aquatic insects on which the Hydræ feed, and they are aided by the roughness of their surface. They transfix their prey, and are believed to infuse a liquid poison from the dart, or thread-cells, into the wound, then twisting their other tentacles round the victim, it is instantly conveyed to the mouth, and slowly forced into the digesting cavity, where it is seen through the transparent skin to move for a short time, but as soon as the nutritious juice is extracted, the animal ejects the refuse by its mouth. In the inner layer, enclosing the cavity of the stomach, there are cells containing a clear liquid with coloured particles floating in it, which is supposed to perform the part of a liver; and, as the Hydræ have no respiratory organs, their juices are aërated through their skin. They have no perceptible nerves nor nerve centres, yet they are irritable, eminently contractile, and are attracted towards the light—all these being probably sympathetic motions.

Though in general stationary, the Hydra can change its place; it bends its body, stretches to a little distance, and fixes its anterior extremity firmly by its tentacles; then it detaches its sucker and brings it close to its mouth, fixes it, and again stretches its fore part to a little distance along its path, and repeats the same process, so that it moves exactly after the manner of certain caterpillars. It can even move along the water by attaching the expanded disk of its sucker to the surface, where it soon dries on being exposed to the air, and becomes a float, from whence the Hydra hangs down with its tentacles extended like fishing lines, as in fig. 110; or it can use them as oars to row itself along under the surface of the water.

On account of their simple organization, the Hydræ are endowed with the most astonishing tenacity of life.

As the whole animal is nourished from the surface of the digestive cavity, they appear to suffer no inconvenience from being turned inside-out, the new cavity performing all the functions of digestion as well as the old one. They may be cut into any number of pieces, and, after a little time, each piece becomes a perfect Hydra. The head may be cut off and they get a new one; or it may be split into two or three parts or more, and the animal becomes many-headed; and, what is still more marvellous, two Hydræ may be grafted together direct, or head and tail, and they combine into one animal.

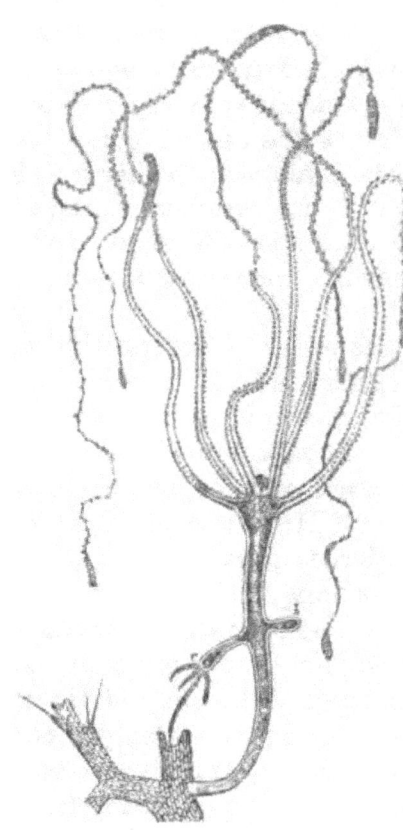

Fig. 110. Hydra fusca.

These singular and voracious creatures increase like plants by budding. A little protuberance rises on the body by the bulging out of the double skin or wall, so that the interior of the bud is a clear cavity in communication with the stomach of the Hydra (fig. 110, *b*). The bud increases in length, opens at its extremity into a mouth, and gradually acquires the size and form of its parent (fig. 110, *c*); the communication is then by degrees closed, and at last the matured bud drops off and becomes an independent Hydra. Dr. Carpenter observed that this process, which so closely resembles the budding of plants, must be regarded as a modification of the ordinary nutritious process. The same may be said of the power of reparation, which every animal body possesses in a greater or less degree, but which is most remarkable among the lower tribes, for when an entire member is renewed, or even when the whole body is regenerated from a small fragment, which is the case in many polypes, it is by a process exactly analogous to that which takes place in the reparation of the simplest wound in our own bodies, and which is but a modification of the process that is constantly renewing, more or less rapidly, every portion of our frame.

There is but one species of the single colourless Hydra, but there are four compound fresh-water Hydræ in England—the rubra, viridis, vulgaris, which is of an orange brown, and the fusca. They have coloured particles, either imbedded in their external coat, or immediately under it. The Hydra viridis and H. vulgaris have short tentacles, whilst H. fusca, which is a rare animal, has arms from seven to eight inches long, and so contractile, that they can shrink into the space of small tubercules. All these four Hydræ are compound and permanently arborescent animals; each springs from one individual hydra of its own race, which increases in length and forms the stem, while young ones spring from it and from one another consecutively, like the compound branches of a tree. The numerous tentacles that hang down like fishing lines, thickly covered with thread-cells and their envenomed darts, catch prey for the whole colony, because the communication between the stomachs of the young polypes or Hydræ and that of their parent is never cut off, as it is when the offspring is deciduous; but tubes from the base of each individual Hydra or polype, passing through the stalks and branches of the living tree, unite their stomachs with the stomach or assimilating cavity in the main stem. Each individual polype, sometimes to the number of nineteen, after having digested its food or prey, ejects the refuse from its mouth, and the nutritious juice traverses the labyrinth of tubes to that general reservoir.

Since every portion of the bodies of the Hydræ is nearly of the same kind, and as every part of their surface inside and outside is in contact with the water in which they live, and from whence they derive oxygen to aërate their juices, no circulation is necessary in these simple animals, either for nutrition of their tissues, or to furnish them with oxygen.

If the Hydræ only produced deciduous buds which are developed into facsimiles of their parent, their race would become extinct, since they die in winter, unless kept artificially in water of mild temperature; but the animals are hermaphrodite, so that each individual produces fertilized eggs in autumn, which are hatched in spring, so that the Hydra is alternately propagated by deciduous buds and by eggs. The fresh-water hydræ are the only hydroids that are locomotive, all the others being fixed to some solid substance.

The oceanic Hydrozoa comprehend the three families of Corynidæ, Tubulariidæ, and Sertulariidæ. They are chiefly compound animals, numerous in genera and species, and have great variety of form. They may be simple and slender, they may be creeping or like a bush or tree, more or less compound and regularly branched according to the form of the polypary or tubular substance which unites their numerous hydra-form polypes into one animal. In general they are exceedingly small; three or four inches in height is quite gigantic. There is scarcely a still clear pool left by the retiring tide among the rocks along the British coasts, that does not abound with these beautiful creatures attached to stones, old shells, or sea-weeds. But they must be sought for amidst the luxuriant marine vegetation and profusion of animal life which adorn these rocky pools, otherwise they would escape notice; and even when large enough to be conspicuous, the eye must be aided in order to see the wonderful minuteness and delicacy of their structure. The aquaria have furnished an opportunity to study their forms, habits, and the marvellous circumstances of their lives and reproduction.

The compound oceanic Hydrozoa are essentially the same in structure as the compound fresh-water Hydræ. They differ, however, from them in often having a greater number of tentacles, and in being defended by a firm and flexible horny coat; notwithstanding which they increase in size by budding from the base of a single primary polype. The horny coat covers the bud and grows with it; but as soon as the polype is formed within it, the top of the bud opens and the young polype protrudes itself, so that a separation is effectually prevented; and while the stem and branches are being formed, and increase by the continual development of new buds, the communication between the stomachs of the whole brood of polypes with that in the parent stem is maintained by tubes from their bases passing through the interior fleshy matter in the branches.

In short these marine Hydrozoa consist of a ramified tube of sensitive animal matter, covered by an external flexible and often jointed and horny coat or skeleton, and they are fed by the activity of the tentacles and the digestive powers of frequently some hundreds of hydra-formed polypes, as in the Sertularia cupressina. The common produce of their food circulates as a fluid through the tubular cavities, for the benefit of the whole community, while the indigestible part is ejected from the mouth of each individual. The stomach of each polype has a more or less ciliated lining, containing cells with nutritive juices, which are supposed to perform the part of a liver. The liquid which circulates in these animals is colourless, with solid particles floating in it; and there is reason to believe that sea-water is admitted into the tubes, and that, mixed with the juices prepared by the polypes, it circulates through the ramified cavities, is sent into the hollow prehensile tentacles, and returns back into the digesting cavity after having contributed to respiration by its oxygen. The movements of this fluid appear to depend upon the delicate ciliated fibre which lines the cavities of the tentacles and those of the stem and branches of the compound animal, possibly aided by vital contraction. The soft skin of the tentacles contains cells full of liquid, with a thread and its sting or dart coiled up within it. These thread stings are protruded when the skin is irritated, which frequently gives the tentacles the appearance of being beset with bristled warts. In many instances these kinds of Hydrozoa are covered with a gelatinous substance, either as a film or thick coat.

The reproduction of many of these arborescent or compound Hydrozoa is one of the most unexpected and extraordinary phenomena in the life-history of the animal creation. For besides the system of consecutive budding from a single polype which builds up the compound animal, peculiar buds are formed and developed, which bear no resemblance whatever to the polype buds: on the contrary, when mature, they assume an organization exactly the same as that of the common jelly-fish or Medusoid Acalephæ, and swim freely away from their fixed parent as soon as they are detached. These medusiform zooids, which are extremely small, consist of a cup or umbrella-shaped bell of colourless transparent matter, which is their swimming apparatus; it is contracted and expanded by a muscular band under the rim, the water is alternately imbibed and forcibly ejected, and by its reaction the zooid is impelled in a contrary direction. From the centre of the bell a stomach hangs down in the form of a proboscis, with a mouth at its extremity, either with or without tentacles and sting-cells. Four canals, or a greater number, which begin in the stomach, radiate through the transparent matter of the bell, and are united by a circular canal round the rim; they convey the nutritious liquid from the stomach throughout the system. This general structure may be traced in the zooids of the three great families of the oceanic hydraform-zoophytes, in a greater or less degree, from deciduous perfect medusæ to such as are imperfect and fixed.

These medusiform zooids are male and female, and when detached from their parent they are independent creatures, each of them being furnished with nutrient and locomotive organs of its own. They produce fertilized eggs, which are developed into ciliated locomotive larvæ; after a time these lose their cilia and acquire a rayed sucking disc, with which they fix themselves permanently to a solid object, and, after various changes, each gets a mouth and tentacles and becomes a perfect young hydra. Thus a brood of young hydræ is produced, each of which acquires the compound form of its parent by budding, and as each of these compound animals in its turn gives off medusa-buds, there is a cycle of the alternate forms of hydra and medusa or jellyfish, showing a singular connection between two animals which seem to have nothing in common. The analogy which so often prevails between plants and animals obtains here also, for the medusa-buds bear the same relation to the hydra or polype-buds that the flower-buds of a tree do to the leaf-buds: the flower-buds contain the germs of future generations of the tree, while the leaf-buds contain only the undeveloped stems, stalks, and leaves of the individual plant on which they grow.

The Corynidæ form the first of the three families of the oceanic hydra zoophytes. They comprise six genera, and many species of compound animals of various forms, each derived from a single animal by budding ; and although they possess a thin flexible coat, the polypes are sheathed either in a thin membrane or bone. Their club-shaped tentacles form either a single or double circlet round the base of their conical mouth, and are also scattered over their bodies when bare.

The zooids are developed at once in the Syncoryna Sarsii, which is a long, thinly branched, and horny

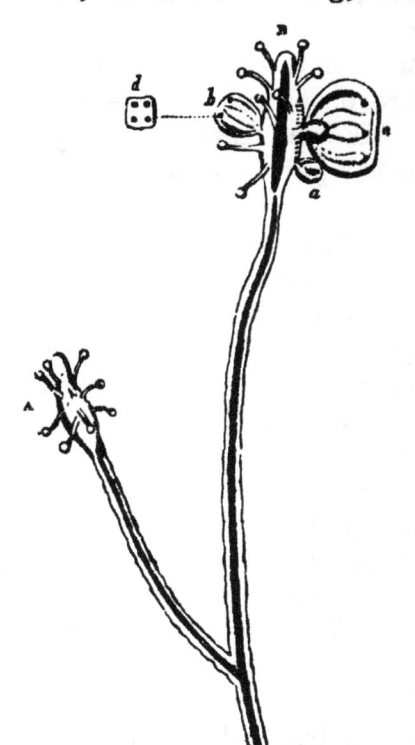

zoophyte, with a single naked, spindle - shaped polype at the extremity of each branch, as in fig. 111, A. The bodies of the polypes are studded with numerous tentacles, among which buds appear (fig. 111, *a*, *b*) ; these gradually expand into bell-shaped medusa-zooids (fig. 111, *c*), some being masculine and others feminine. They drop off their parent, swim away by the contraction of their bell, and their fertilized eggs are developed into single hydræ, which become arborescent like their parent by budding.

Fig. 111. Syncoryna Sarsii with Medusa-buds.

The family of the Sertulariidæ take branching forms, sometimes of perfect symmetry : they have a firm, horny coat, which not only covers the stem and branches, but becomes a cup for the protection of the polype.

The most common form of the family of the Tubularia has no branches : it has an erect, hollow stem like a straw, sometimes a foot high, coated by a horny sheath. The polype which terminates each plant has a mouth surrounded by alternately long and short tentacles. The stomach of the polype is connected with the hollow in the stem by a muscular ring, by whose alternate dilatation and contraction, at intervals of eighty seconds, the fluid is forced up from below, enters the stomach, and is again expelled. Another liquid carrying solid particles circulates in a spiral through the whole length of the stem. Some of this family are propagated by perfect deciduous medusæ, others by imperfect fixed ones; both are developed on the polypes or among their tentacles. Like the fresh-water Hydræ, these creatures can restore any part of their bodies that is injured.

Numerous instances might be given to show that the minute medusiform zooids are only a stage or phase in the life of an oceanic hydra : conversely it will now be shown, that the single simple hydra is but a stage in the life-history of the highly organized medusa, jelly-fish, or sea-nettle of sailors, the Acalepha of Cuvier.

The medusæ vary in size, from microscopic specks that swim on the surface of the sea in a warm summer day to large umbrella-shaped jelly fish almost a yard in diameter. They abound in every part of the ocean and in all seas, often in such shoals that the surface of the water is like a sheet of jelly. Their substance is transparent, pure, and nearly colourless; chiefly consisting of water, with so little solid matter, that a newly caught medusa, weighing two pounds, dries into a film scarcely weighing thirty grains.

The Pulmograde Medusæ, which swim by the contractions of their umbrella-shaped respiratory disc, form two distinct groups, the naked-eyed medusæ and the covered-eyed group. Both are male and female;

each has its own form of thread-cells; and the stinging power or strength of the poison is nearly in proportion to the size of the animal and the coarseness of its threads.

The disk, or umbrella-shaped swimming organ, in both groups consists of a large cavity included between two layers of gelatinous matter, which unite at the rim. The interior membrane, called the sub-umbrella, is encircled at its edge by a ring of highly contractile muscular fibre like the iris of our eyes, by which this swimming organ is expanded and contracted. From the centre of the sub-umbrella a stomach, in the form of a proboscis, is suspended, which is of a very different structure in the two groups.

The Thaumantia pilosella, a member of the naked-eyed group, is like an inverted watch-glass (fig. 112), less than an inch in diameter. The roof of this umbrella is much thicker than the sides, and gradually thins off towards the rim. The proboscis, or stomach, descends from the centre of the sub-umbrella, but not so far as to the edge of the rim: it ends in a mouth with four sensitive fleshy lips. Four slender canals, which originate in the cavity of the stomach, radiate from the centre of the roof of the umbrella and extend to its margin, where they unite at the quadrants with a canal which encircles the rim, and are prolonged beyond it in the form of tentacles armed with numerous thread-cells containing poisonous darts. These tentacles must be formed of muscular fibre, for they are very irritable: each of them may be extended and contracted separately or along with the others; they guide the medusa through the water, and can anchor it by twisting round a fixed object.

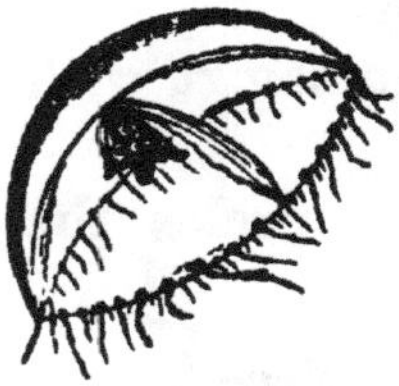

Fig. 112. Thaumantia pilosella.

The prey caught is digested in the stomach, the refuse is ejected by the mouth, and the nutritious fluid that has been extracted is carried up through the base of the stomach into the four radiating canals, to supply the waste and nourish the system. The digestive cavity and canals are lined with a soft membrane, covered with cilia, whose vibrations maintain the circulation of the juices and perform the duty of a heart; for the medusæ have none, nor have they any special respiratory system: their juices are aërated through the under-surface of the rim of the umbrella, while passing through the circular canal lying either within the water or on its surface.

A fringe of filamental tentacles hangs down into the water from the rim of the disc or umbrella, which is studded at equal distances by fleshy bulbs, each of which has a group of fifty dark eye-specks, being the rudiment of an eye; and if the animal be disturbed when in the dark, each eye-speck shines with a brilliant phosphoric light, and the umbrella looks as if it were begirt with a garland of stars.

Close to the edge of the canal which encircles the

Fig. 113. Otolites of Magnified Thaumantias.

margin of the umbrella, there are eight hollow semi-oval enlargements of the flesh, two in each quadrant formed by the four radiating canals: they are the eight ears of the medusa, for in these hollow organs there are from thirty to fifty solid, transparent, and highly refrac-tive spheres, arranged in a double row, so as to form a crescent, those near its centre being larger than the more remote. The solid spheres are analogous to the otolites in the ears of the more highly organized animals.

Mr. M'Cready has discovered nerve-centres behind each tentacle, and under each marginal coloured speck in several species of the open-eyed medusæ, which places this group of Acalephæ in a higher grade than any of the preceding orders. The medusæ swim by the muscular energy of their umbrellas: at each rhythmical contraction the water, which enters by the mouth and fills the great central cavity within the umbrella, is forced out again through an orifice at the other end, and by its reaction the medusa is impelled with considerable velocity in the contrary direction, so that the top of the umbrella goes first, and all its tentacles are dragged after it.

The medusæ are diœcious: in the males four reproductive cells full of reddish or purple granular matter surround the cavity of the stomach, and appear like a coloured cross through the top of the gelatinous umbrella. In the females, at a point just before the four radiating canals enter the marginal canal, the flesh on the exterior of the umbrella swells out into bulbs, containing vessels full of clear eggs with minute globular yolks. These eggs, when fertilized, are hatched, and the young are developed within these ovaries, so that they come into the water as a kind of infusorial ciliated animalcule destitute of a mouth. One end of the creature acquires a suctorial disc, fixes itself to an object, and uses its cilia. The other end opens into a mouth, round which tentacles like fishing lines spring forth; the central part is converted into the cavity of the stomach, and thus a perfect hydra is formed, capable of being propagated naturally by budding, or artificially by being cut in pieces, each piece becoming a perfect hydra, differing in no respect from a common simple fresh-water Hydra.

From one of these, numberless successive generations of simple hydræ may be produced by budding, all catching their prey with their tentacles and digesting it in their stomachs. The limits to this budding-system seems to be indefinite: years may pass in this stage, but at length it ceases, and either the original hydra, or one of its descendants, undergoes a series of remarkable changes. The body of the hydra lengthens into a cylinder; it is then marked transversely by a number of constrictions beginning at the free end; these become deeper and deeper, till at length they break up the body into a pile of shallow cups, each lying in the hollow of the other, and leaving a kind of fleshy wall at the point of suspension or fixture. The edges of the cups are divided into lobes with a slit in each, in which the coloured rudiment of the eye is sunk. The cups are permanent, and characteristic of the group of naked-eyed medusæ. After a time, the cups begin to show contractile motions, which increase till the fibre of their attachment is broken, and then the superimposed cups are detached from the pile one after another, and swim freely away by the contractions of their lobes as young medusæ, leaving what remains of the parent hydra to repair its loss and

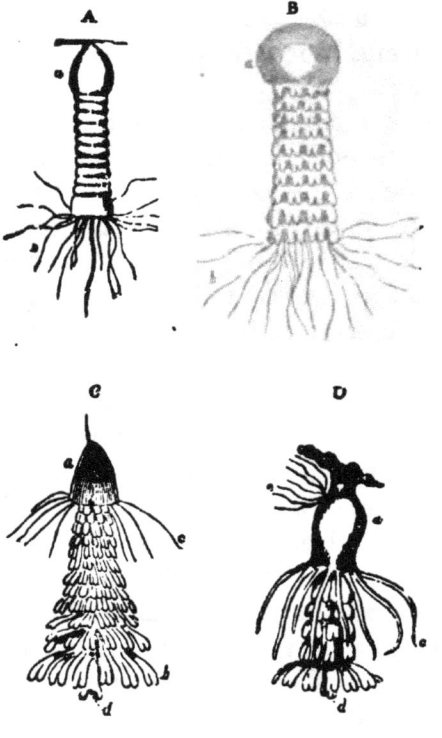

Fig. 114. A, B, C, D, development of Medusa-buds; *a*, polype-body; *b*, tentacles; *c*, a secondary circle of tentacles *d*, proboscis; *e*, new polype-bud.

again repeat this singular process. However, the young medusæ are not yet perfect. As they increase in size the divisions on the edge of the cup fill up; a proboscis-shaped stomach, with its four coloured cells and its square mouth, is developed from the centre of the sub-umbrella; the radiating canals extend from the central cavity, the encircling canal and fringe form round the umbrella-shaped cups, and the result is a highly organized Thaumantia pilosella, in whose life-history a simple hydra forms a singular stage.

Thus hydræ produce medusæ whose offspring are hydræ, and perfect medusæ produce hydræ whose offspring are perfect medusæ. However, the law of the alternation of generation is by no means peculiar to the Thaumantiæ. Many species of medusæ are subject to it, as the Turris neglecta, a beautiful little medusa not larger than a hempseed, common on the British coasts. It has a white muscular pellucid umbrella, a large proboscis of a rich orange colour at its upper part: in the orange-coloured flesh of it there are ovaries containing rose-coloured eggs, which are hatched within them, and come into the water as ciliated gemmules, which, after swimming about for a time, become fixed and are developed into small hydræ of a rich purple colour with sixty-four tentacles. From these hydræ others bud off indefinitely till the time comes when one of them becomes lengthened, constricted, divided into cups which drop off, and finally become a brood of the Turris neglecta.

The naked-eyed medusæ are extremely numerous. There are six orders of them and many genera, chiefly distinguished by the position and nature of their ovaries and the number of canals which radiate through their swimming organs. Both of the medusæ that have been described have four radiating canals; yet they belong to different orders, for the ovaries of the Thaumantia are in the edge of the umbrella, while those of the Turris are in the substance of the proboscis. Neither of these kinds have more than four ovaries, but some other kinds have eight ovaries and eight radiating canals. Most of the canals are simple, but in one genus they are branching. All are furnished with tentacles, some of them having stings, others none.

The covered-eyed group consists only of two natural divisions—the Rhizostoma, or many-mouthed medusæ, and the Monostoma, or one-mouthed medusæ. In both the coloured eye-specks at the margin of the umbrella are larger and more numerous, than in the naked-eyed group, and they are covered with a hood. The proboscis of the one-mouthed order terminates in a square mouth, the four angles of which are prolonged into tentacles with a solid hyaline axis. They have a fringed membrane along their under-surface, containing numerous stinging thread-cells. Sixteen canals, connected with the stomach or cavity of the proboscis, radiate over the flattish, cup-shaped umbrella; eight of these are branched, and terminate in the circular canal which runs round its fringed edge, and they form the nutrient and respiratory system of the animal, while the eight simple and alternate canals terminate in eight openings at the rim of the umbrella, through which the refuse or indigestible part of the food is discharged, thus forming an exception to the other pulmograde medusæ, and indeed to the Hydrozoa in general, which eject it at the mouth. All the canals are lined with cilia, whose vibrations maintain the circulation of the fluids, and perform the duties both of a heart and respiratory apparatus. Dr. A. Krohn has observed that in three species of the genus Pelagia belonging to the covered-eyed medusæ, the young are at once developed as medusæ without the intervention of the hydra form.

The disk of the Rhizostoma, or root-mouthed medusæ, is rather flat, and the large proboscis is unlike any other of the tribe. In the naked-eyed medusæ digestion is performed in the cavity of the proboscis; but in this order the proboscis is divided into four very long branches ending in club - shaped knobs (fig. 115), and nutrient tubes extend to their extremities from the great central cavity in the umbrella. Their broadish frilled borders are divided and subdivided along their whole lengths, and the nutrient canals, which follow all their ramifi-

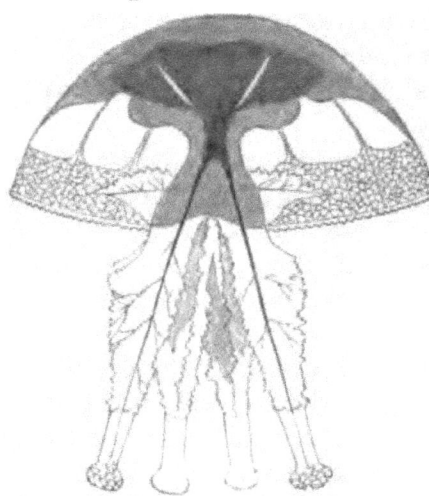

Fig. 115. Rhizostoma.

cations, end in numerous fringed pores upon their edges and upon the club-shaped ends of the quadrifid proboscis. These numerous pores are mouths; they absorb minute animalcules, which are digested while passing through the united canals to the great central cavity of the umbrella, which receives the products of digestion. Eight canals radiate from that great cavity and traverse the umbrella; and the nutrient fluid, mixed with the sea-water, passes from the great cavity through these canals into an elegant network of large capillary tubes spread on the under-surface of the margin of the umbrella, which is always in contact with the water; and in this beautiful respiratory organ the carbonic acid gas is exchanged for the oxygen in the water of the sea. The indigestible part of the food is discharged through the mouths or pores, whose edges are prolonged into solid tentacles containing thread-cells, with their usual weapons of offence and defence. Besides these armed tentacles, which are very numerous in the covered-eyed group, the gelatinous umbrella has a multitude of oval thread-cells on its external coat, in each of which a very long filament is spirally coiled, which darts out to a considerable distance on the smallest touch, and stings severely.

A few only of the British pulmonigrade medusæ sting: the Cyanea capillata, one of the single-mouthed covered-eyed family, is most formidable. It has very long tentacles, which it can throw off if they get entangled, but they continue to sting, even after they are detached from the medusa.

This is one of the most remarkable instances of the inherent irritability of muscular fibre still in full force after the tentacles have been separated from the living animal. In many of the lower animals, as in the Hydra itself, vitality is so far from being extinguished in the severed members that it repairs the injury. Since the covered-eyed medusæ have eyes, ears, and very sensitive tentacles, it may be inferred that they possess nerves of sight, hearing, and touch, though none have been discovered, probably on account of the softness and transparency of their tissues. The stinging power by which they kill their prey and defend themselves may be classed among the consensual powers prompted by the sympathetic sensations of hunger or danger.

In all latitudes the medusæ are highly luminous, especially in warm seas. Professor Vogt remarked that flashes of light passed over their disk when they touched one another in swimming, and they appear at intervals like globes of fire among the lesser lights of the Noctilucæ; if from involuntary nervous contraction, as is most likely, the light must be electric.

The medusæ are infested by many parasites. Entozoa are often abundant in their gelatinous substance, and crustaceans of various kinds and colours, such as shrimps, sand-hoppers, and a galæmon of glassy transparency, move about in the substance of their disc and arms, entering unscathed by the poisonous darts which inflict instant death on others of their class. The Libanea crab, of gigantic size compared with its host, is in the habit of taking up its abode between the four columns of the Rhizostoma. But the most singular intruder is the Philomedusa Vogtii, which is a polype with twelve thick short tentacles, its whole body and tentacles being covered with cilia and thread-cells. These polypes live in the disk, arms, and stomach of the medusæ, and, when taken out, their stomachs are found to contain fragments of the tentacles of their host, and even the thread-cells with their stings. The larger polypes devour the smaller ones, and the latter live for weeks within the larger ones without apparent inconvenience to either.[6]

Mr. M'Cready mentions that the larvæ of the medusa Cunina octonaria swim as parasites in the cavity of the bell of the medusa Turritopsis nutricula, which not only furnishes a shelter and dwelling-place to the larvæ during their development, but it also serves as a nurse, by permitting the parasites, which adhere by their tentacles, to take the food out of its mouth by means of their long proboscides. They undergo many transformations, and become nearly perfect medusæ while within their nurse.

Medusæ of different species are met with in every sea from the equator to the poles. They are eminently social, migrating in enormous shoals to great distances. The largest shoal of young sea nettles on record was met with in the Gulf Stream, off the coast of Florida, by a vessel bound for England. The captain likened them to acorns; they were so crowded as completely to cover the sea, giving it the appearance from a distance of a

[6] Dr. F. Müller, of Santa Caterina.

boundless meadow in the yellow leaf. He was five or six days in sailing through them, and in about sixty days afterwards, on returning from England, he fell in with the same school, as the sailors call it, off the Western Islands, and was three or four days in sailing through them again. Mr. Piazzi Smyth, when on a voyage to Teneriffe in 1856, fell in with a vast shoal of medusæ. With a microscope he found part of the stomach of one of these creatures so full of diatoms of various forms — stars, crosses, semicircles, embossed circles and spirals—that he computed the whole stomach could not have contained less than 700,000. The flinty shells of the diatoms ejected in myriads by the medusæ, accumulate in the course of ages into siliceous strata, which, heaved up by subterranean fires, at length become the abode of man. Thus gelatinous transparent beings indirectly aid in forming the solid crust of the earth by means of the microscopic vegetation of the sea.

Ciliograde Hydrozoa.

The ciliograde Acalephæ, which form four orders and many genera, and which swim by means of symmetrical rows of long cilia, are represented on the British coasts by the Cydippe pileus and the Beroë Forskalia (fig. 116), little delicately tinted, gelatinous, and transparent animals that shine in the dark.

The Cydippe pileus is a globe three-eighths of an inch in diameter, like the purest crystal, with eight bands of large cilia, stretching at regular distances from pole to pole. A mouth, surrounded by extremely sensitive tentacles, is situated at one pole, the vent at the other. The Cydippes poise and fix themselves to objects by means of two very long tentacles, fringed on one edge by cirri, that is, short curled tentacles. These cirrated tentacles, which in some species stretch out to more than twenty times the length of the animal, can be instantaneously retracted into cavities at the posterior end of the body, while, at the same time, the marginal filaments are as rapidly coiled up in a series of close spirals. The whole of these complex organs are enclosed within the limits of a pin's head.

The manner in which these little gems swim is beautiful; sometimes they rise and descend slowly, like a balloon, and when they glide along the surface of the water in sunshine, the cilia on the eight meridional

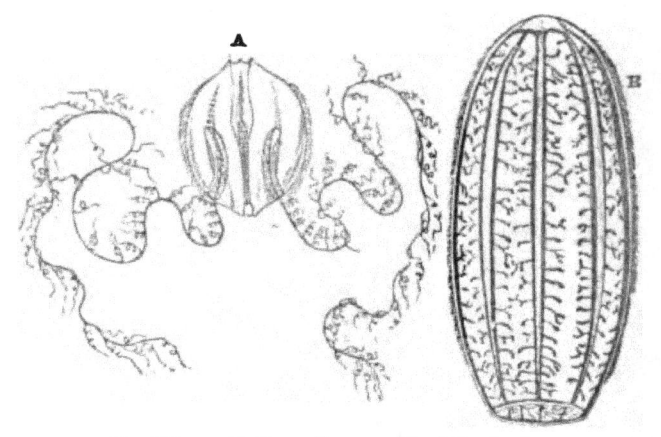

Fig. 116. A, Cydippe pileus; B, Beroë Forskalia.

bands exhibit the most brilliant iridescence. The long cirrated tentacles follow all their motions in graceful curves, or hang indolently down, and sometimes they are suddenly stretched to their full length, and as suddenly retracted, and in all their varied convolutions the cirri that fringe them are in constant vibration, and exhibit all the tints of the rainbow. Sometimes these creatures whirl round their axis with great rapidity, but, active as they are, no nervous system has yet been discovered in them.

The common Beroë is like an elongated melon, ob-

PRAYA DIPHYS

tusely octangular, with eight rows of cilia, extending from a mouth at one end to a kind of ciliated star at the other.   The Beroës are of a gelatinous transparent substance, which expands and contracts with great facility : it is always expanded when they swim.

The Cestum Veneris belongs to another genus of the same .family.   It is like a blue ribbon, the mouth and vent being on the opposite sides in the middle of the band, which is furnished throughout its whole length with active cilia for swimming. The ciliograde Hydrozoa are monœcious, and do not produce medusa-zoids.

Campanograde Acalephæ.

There is a group of oceanic Hydrozoa, consisting of several families, which are fed by numerous suctorial organs called polypites, with tentacula and thread-cells attached to their bodies, so that they are analogous to the marine hydræ, in being colonies of individuals united into a compound animal.   Some have air-vessels, which enable them to float on the surface of the water ; but the locomotive organs of this group are bells, so that they may be called Campanograde Acalephæ.

The family of the Diphyidæ are colourless, and of such transparency that they are all but invisible when in the water, and are gelatinous masses clear as crystal when taken out of it.   They are chiefly inhabitants of the warmer parts of the Pacific and Atlantic Oceans, but many fine specimens are found in the Mediterranean. Of these the Praya diphys is one of the most extraordinary (fig. 117).   It has two large swimming-bells, their mouths turned backwards, with which the whole community is connected.   They are nearly equal in size, soft, gelatinous, transparent, and colourless, rounded in front, open and truncated behind.   The adjacent sides are parallel, with a groove between them, into which one end of the long tubular filiform body of the animal is fixed by slender tubes, through which a nourishing liquid passes into radiating canals in the bells, and from them into a circular canal at their margins, which are surrounded by a muscular contractile iris, like that in our eyes, which shuts and opens the bells. By the alternate absorption and ejection of the water the bells go head foremost, and regulate the motions of the whole compound animal. When both bells are active it goes straight forward; when the right hand bell is alone in action, it goes to the left, and *vice versâ*; in fact, the bells act as a rudder.

The slender cylindrical body or axis of the Praya is so transparent, that the cavity and muscular fibres of its walls are distinctly seen. These animals are extremely contractile. Professor Vogt mentions an individual he met with at Nice more than three feet long, when extended on the surface of the water, which could contract itself into little more than a finger length. It was said to have had a hundred isolated groups of polypites with their appendages attached to it; but in general the Prayæ are not so long, and seldom have more than thirty or forty of these isolated groups, which are attached to the under-side of the long flexible body, and hang down like a rich and beautiful fringe. In the figure, the position of the numerous groups of polypites and their appendages are merely indicated by round marks and lines.

In the body of the Praya diphys (fig. 117), as in that of the whole family, there is a nutritious liquid, which, by means of cilia, flows on its interior surface in two directions: it enters the canals in the two large bells, and supplies them with nourishment.

The polypites which digest the food are vermiform double sacs communicating at one end by a valve with the canal in the body of the animal; and at the free end they are prolonged into a mouth with an everted lip, and the digesting apparatus lies in the centre. Each polypite is supplied with food by its own fishing-line descending from a point close to where the polypite is fixed to the long axis. It is a long, tubular, branched tentacle, each branch ending in a coloured, pear-shaped, or fusiform battery of thread-cells with their stings. A gelatinous plate is placed on the upper side of the common axis immediately over the isolated groups, to protect and separate them.

Such are some of the most general characters of the family Diphyidæ: the Praya diphys has something peculiar to itself.

In the Praya, each individual group has a swimming-bell of its own adjacent to the polypite, and lying parallel to the axis of the animal, with its mouth turned backwards. It is connected by tubes both with the general central canal, and with a helmet-shaped protecting plate. On the other side of the polypite, there is a tuft of vermiform buds with spiral terminations, bristled with thread-cells. From the centre of this tuft a tentacle, or fishing-line, descends with numerous branches, the whole forming a tubular system connected with the common canal in the axis. Each of the branches of the tentacle terminates in a vermilion-coloured tendril, coiled up into a minute capsule. The inside of the tendril is not only bristled with the points of sabre-shaped darts, but it conceals a filament crowded with thread-cells. On the slightest touch, the tendril stretches out like a corkscrew of red coral, and every dart springs forth. Such is, more or less, the complicated structure of the offensive and defensive weapons of many of this order of oceanic Hydrozoa, which appear to the naked eye as merely brightly-coloured points. The use of these tentacles, or fishing-lines, is the same in all; they seize, kill, and carry their victims to the mouth of the polypite by contracting their long lines.

In the Praya, the groups are individualized in the highest degree consistent with union; for, when the animal is at rest, each of the individual groups, amounting to thirty or forty, swims about by means of its little bell independent of the rest. Their motions can be compared to nothing but a troop of jugglers performing gymnastic exercises round a cord represented by the common body of the animal; except for adherence to which the life and will of each group are so perfectly independent, that the mutual dependence of the whole is only seen when the common trunk contracts to bring all its appendages towards the two principal bells, which then begin to move.[7]

Thus each group has a special life and motion, controlled by a general life and motion; strong individual muscular power controlled by general muscular power; yet no nervous system has as yet been discovered, so this animal activity must for the present be attributed to a strong, inherent, contractile power in the muscular fibre. The Praya is seldom complete, on account of the ease with which it casts off its great bells.

None of the Diphyidæ have special organs for respiration; their juices are aërated through their delicate tissues. They are diœcious, and invariably produce perfect male and female medusiform zooids; they are situated among the groups of the polypites and their appendages, and are attached to the axis of the animal. When free, they swim away by the contraction of their bells; the eggs are fertilized, and produce young Diphyidæ, male and female; so these animals, like most of the oceanic Hydrozoa, have two alternate stages of existence.

[7] 'Recherches sur quelques Animaux inférieurs de la Méditerranée,' par C. Vogt: *Mémoires de l'Institut National Génevois*, tom. i.

Physograde Acalephœ.

The Galeolaria lutea (fig. 118, frontispiece) is similar to the Praya diphys in having a slender, tubular body, with groups of sterile polypites and their appendages hanging at intervals along its under-side like a fringe, and also in having two swimming-bells at its anterior extremity; but it has no special small bells. The large ones differ from each other in size, form, and position. The largest is nearly cylindrical, its mouth is turned upwards, and its rim is elevated at one part into two stiff organs like the blinkers that are put over horses' eyes: besides these, it has six salient points, which nearly close the mouth of the bell at each contraction of the muscular iris that lines the margin of the cavity. The small bell, which goes first in swimming, is thicker and shorter, and its side rises in a hump, upon which the closed end of the large bell rests, and in the cavity between the two the anterior extremity of the filiform body is fixed. Each of the groups of polypites, with their tentacles, lies immediately under its spathe-shaped protecting plate. The polypites are very contractile, and on their protuberant part, containing the digestive cavity, there is a large circular space, which, as well as the whole tissue of the polypite and the stinging capsules at the extremities of the tentacles, are of an orange colour, and are akin in structure to those described.

When very young the Galeolaria and its congeners have only their swimming-bells and one polypite group affixed to the end of a short tubular axis; by and by a second group is developed from buds between the bells and the first group; then a third is developed between the bells and the second group, and so on; the length of the body and the number of groups continue to increase indefinitely. It is only when the animal is full grown and complete in all its parts, that reproductive organs are developed towards its posterior end. Buds then appear upon the hollow stems of the polypites towards the posterior end of the body. But as the Galeolaria is diœcious, male and female buds are never on the same individual. The female buds become medusiform zooids, like those of the Praya diphys, only the transparent cup, with which it swims away from its parent, has two projections like ears on its rim.

The development of the buds in the male Galeolaria is similar. At first they are pale, but they assume an orange red colour as they advance towards maturity, and, when complete, the sac which hangs down from the centre of the transparent cup becomes of a brilliant vermilion. These male and female medusa-zooids swim about for several days, and the fertilized eggs are hatched into young Galeolariæ, male and female.

Thus the Galeolaria lutea has two kinds of polypites, both nutritive, but one is sterile, the other prolific. The latter are similar to the prolific individuals of the syncorine Hydræ, in which the anterior part is a digestive organ, while on the base or stalk true medusa-zooids are found. It is curious that the spathe-protecting plate of the Galeolaria appears in the egg as a globe of such size that the other parts seem to be merely the appendages.

The Apolemia contorta (fig. 119) unites the most graceful form to the utmost transparency and delicacy of tissue. It has a double float, the first small and globular, the second long and oval. The neck is short, the rose-coloured body is flat as a ribbon, and covered with thin, curved, pointed, and imbricated plates, like tiles on the roof of a house, but so minute that they are only perceptible to the naked eye by a slight iridescence. At the extremity of the short neck buds, semi-developed buds, and perfect swimming cups are arranged in vertical series; and as the flat body is twisted into a spiral to its farthest end, the cluster of bells forms a perfect

APOLEMIA CONTORTA.

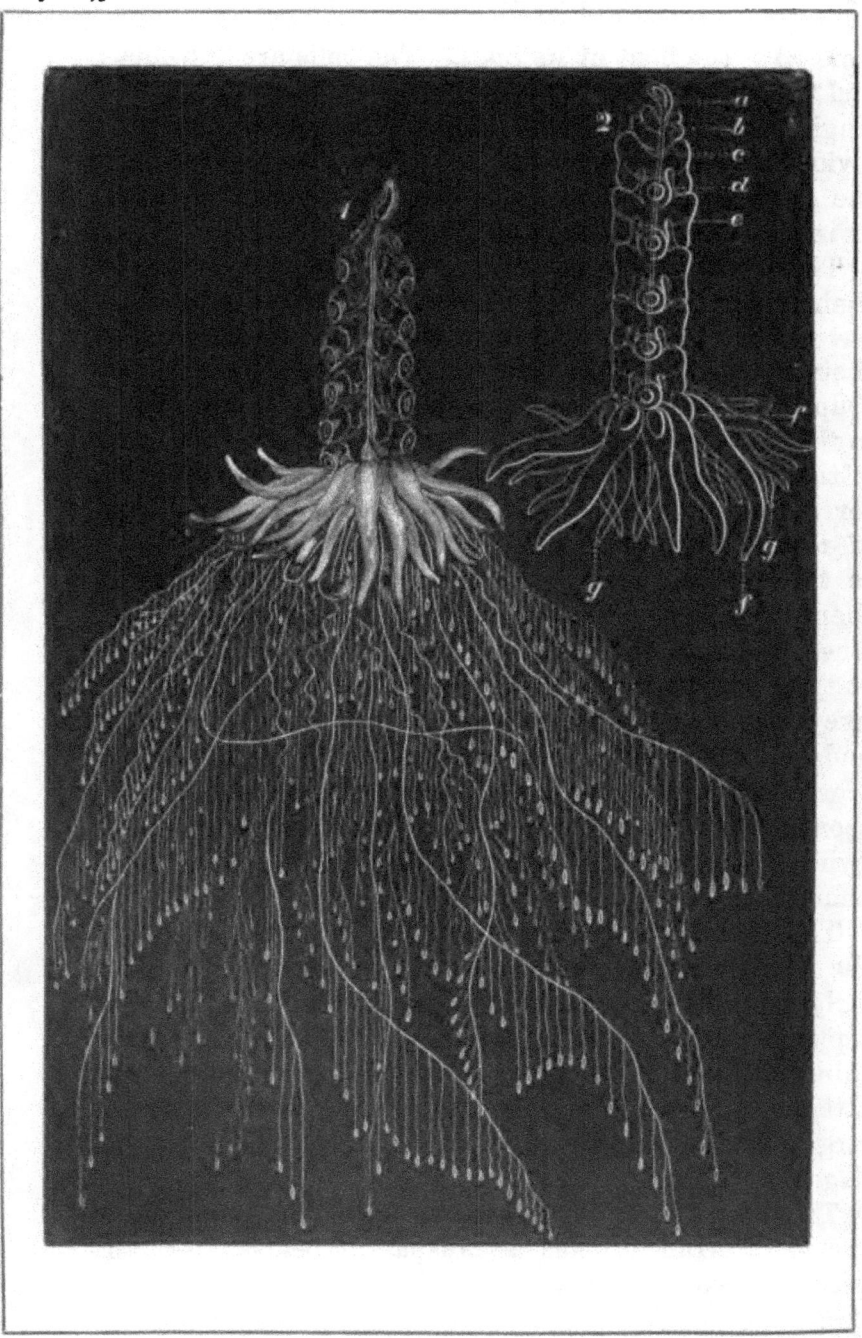

PHYSOPHORA HYDROSTATICA.

cone with the float at its apex. The bells are flattened; and there is always in their more solid posterior part a single canal rising directly from the general trunk which divides into four branches; and these, having traversed the swimming cavity, unite anew in a circular canal, or iris, destined to shut and open the cup.

. The sterile polypites that are attached at intervals by their hollow stems to the twisted body of the Apolemia, have twelve rows of cells inserted in the bright lining of their digestive cavities; their anterior part has a trumpet-shaped mouth full of thread-cells. The tentacles affixed to their stems and their secondary lines are like those of the Diphyidæ. Besides these sterile polypites, which serve only to feed the animal, the Apolemia has a kind of mouthless prolific organs, which do not contribute to the general nourishment: each group has a pair of them attached to the extremity of a branching stem. They resemble polypites in being long and contractile at their extremities; the interior is full of a substance like sarcode, and encompassed by a red ring. Female buds yielding eggs appear on the stem of one of these organs, while male buds are developed into medusiform zooids on the stem of the other, which become detached, swim away, and the fertilized eggs yield young Apolemiæ.

The natural position of an individual of the family of the Physophoridæ when at rest is to hang perpendicularly from its air-vessel. The body, which begins with a pyriform float, descends in a slender filiform scarlet tube with a number of hyaline natatory cups or bells attached on each side. The lower end of the body enlarges into a bulb or disk supporting various appendages.

The Physophora hydrostatica (fig. 120), common in the Mediterranean, has a transparent pear-shaped air-vessel tipped with red, from which the slender cord-like tube of the body descends. Immediately below the air-vessel, a number of buds and young bells are attached, followed by a series of perfect three-lobed swimming bells, placed on each side obliquely one below the other; and as they alternate and embrace the body with their deeply excavated sides, they give it the appearance of a crystal cone. Four canals spring from the hollow stalks of the bells, traverse them, and end in a circular canal close to the membranaceous iris which surrounds the margin of the internal cavity. Below the cone the tubular body expands, and is twisted into a flat spiral, so as to form a hollow disk or bulb, to which three different circlets of organs are appended. The first and uppermost is a coronet of red, worm-like, closed sacs, in constant motion, with large thread-cells at their pointed extremities. They are attached to the upper surface of the bulb by their broad bases, and communicate with its tubes by a small valve. Male and female capsules follow either in a circle, or mixed with the third and undermost circlet of organs, which consist of sterile nourishing polypites, fixed by hollow stems to the bulb, each of which has a long branching tentacle fixed to the base of its digesting cavity.

There are as many polypites on the under-side of the bulb as there are red worm-like sacs on its upper edge. Each polypite consists of three distinct parts. The posterior part is a hollow red stalk inserted under the circumference of the disk; the second part is a bright yellow globular expansion containing the digestive cavity lined with cilia; the third and anterior part, which ends with the mouth, is quite colourless and transparent, and assumes various shapes by constant expansion and contraction.

At the limit between the red stalk and the yellow globular part of the polypites there is a tuft of cylindrical appendages, from which a long tentacle descends with its secondary tentacles and red nettle-bulbs. All

the canals of this Physophora are connected, and their
walls are lined with muscular fibres, either circular,
longitudinal, or both, which give a marvellous contractile and motive power. When the animal is suspended
from the surface of the sea by its float, every member is
in motion, especially the numerous tentacles, which are
perpetually in search of food, and are so extremely sensitive that even a sudden motion of the water makes
them shrink under the red worm-like organs on the edge
of the disk. This animal is generally from one to three
inches long.

All the preceding members of the physograde group
are really campanograde, for the action of the wind upon
the floats of the Physophoridæ must be small, otherwise
they would not be furnished with so many swimming
cups. The Physaliidæ and Velellidæ are the only two
orders that are truly physograde, for the wind is their
only locomotive power.

The Physalia, or 'Spanish man-of-war' of sailors, is by
far the most formidable animal of the Acalephæ tribe ;
its poisonous stings, which burn like fire, inflict instant
death on the inferior animals, and give painful wounds
to man himself. Its body, as it floats, is a long horizontal double sac (fig. 121), which begins with a blunt
point, gradually enlarges, and becomes cylindrical about
the middle; then it somewhat suddenly widens in a
transverse or lateral direction. Along the upper surface
of the pointed half the membrane or wall of the sac is
raised into a transversely placed crest, which dies away
at the enlarged end. The greater part of the body is
smooth, but the under-surface of the transversely enlarged end swells into lobes, from whence numerous
tentacles and other organs descend.

Almost the whole of the body of the Physalia is filled
by an air-vessel, so that it floats on the surface of the
sea, and is wafted to and fro by the wind. The bladder
containing the air is enclosed in two membranes, the

outer one dense, thick, and elastic, the inner formed of delicate fibres and lined with cilia. The air-sac is only attached to one part of the interior; and there it communicates with the exterior by a small aperture, which may be seen at about half an inch from the pointed apex. of the animal. The body is several inches long, of a

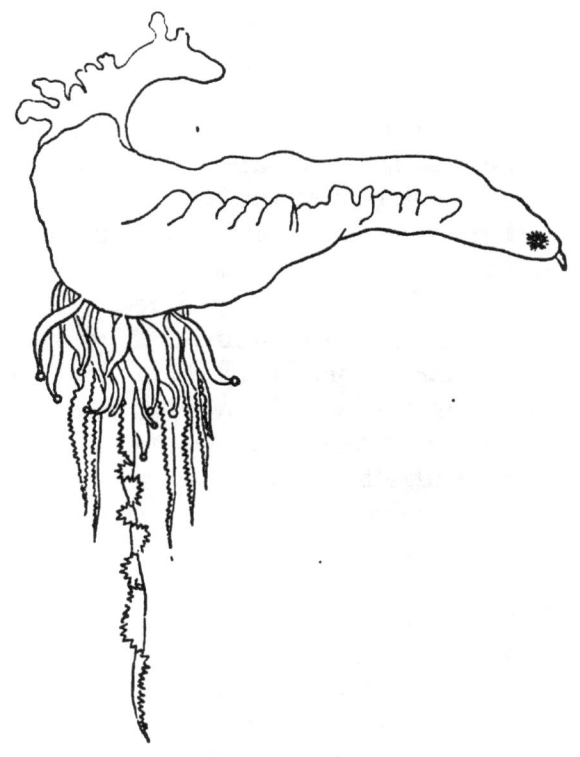

Fig. 121. The Physalia.

delicate pale green colour, passing gradually into dark indigo blue on the under-surface; the ridge of the crest is tipped with dark crimson, and the pointed end is stained with deep bluish green.

The appendages, which hang down from the inferior and thick part of the body, are large and small branchless tentacles of various lengths, and sterile polypites in different stages of development. In some individuals the tentacles are nine or ten feet long, of a deep blue colour at their origin, and formed of two distinct parts, which have a common base. One is a long conical bag, formed by an extension of the under-surface of the body lined with cilia, and ending in a pointed apex full of stinging thread-cells. It is flat on one side, attached throughout its length to the tentacle, and is supposed to furnish poison for the stings. The tentacle itself is a closed tube whose canal communicates with the cavity of the long sac, and consequently with that in the animal's body. The interior of the tentacle is ciliated, its upper part is gathered into folds; and the rest, which hangs straight down, is like a delicate narrow ribbon, highly contractile from muscular fibres, of which the most conspicuous are longitudinal. The tentacle is marked at regular intervals by blue kidney-shaped masses, containing myriads of powerful thread-cells, in which the threads of the darts are coiled in a spiral, and contain muscular fibres, that serve to contract and extend them. The smaller tentacles vary as much in length as the large ones; they are of similar structure, but of a paler colour, and are indiscriminately mixed with the other appendages.

The polypites, which are direct processes from the under-surface of the body, are crowded in groups of various sizes round the base of the large tentacles and mixed with the small; they are of a deep blue at their base, frequently of a bright yellow at their extremities, and on an average about three-fourths of an inch long. They are as irritable and contractile as the tentacles, and are in constant motion. Their mouth is large, with an everted lip armed with thread-cells; it sucks in the prey caught and brought to it by the contraction of the tentacles, and which is speedily dissolved by the powerful solvent juices in its digesting chamber.

Among the numerous appendages attached to the under-surface of the Physalia, there are bluish-green velvety masses fixed to extremely small branching processes from the body of the animal, which seem with a microscope to consist of tentacles, polypites in various stages of development, male reproductive capsules which are never detached, and female buds that are developed into medusiform zooids, and are presumed to become free as in other cases. The Physaliidæ are social animals, assembling in numerous shoals in the warm latitudes of the Atlantic and Pacific. They naturally have their crest vertical, kept steady by their tentacles, which drag down in the water; but Professor Huxley has seen them at play, in a dead calm, tumbling over and over. The Physalia does not possess the power of emptying and refilling its float with air: it is doubted whether any of the physograde animals have that power, but the subject is still in abeyance.

The Velellidæ are little sailing members of the physograde group. The Velella spirans (fig. 122), a Mediterranean species, has a body or deck consisting of a hollow horizontal disk, of a firm but flexible cartilaginous substance, surrounded by a delicate membranous fringe or limb half the width of the body. A triangular vertical crest, formed of a firm transparent plate, also encompassed by a delicate limb, is fixed diagonally from one angle of the disk to the other, but not on the fringe; and as the natural position of the Velella is to float horizontally on the surface of the water, the crest is exposed to the wind and acts as a sail.

The float or air-vessel is flat, horizontal, and nearly fills the whole body of the animal: it consists of two thin, firm, and rather concave plates joined at their free edges, and united also by a number of concentric vertical partitions, between which there is a series of concentric chambers or galleries filled with air. The chambers communicate with one another by apertures in the dividing membrane; they also communicate with the exterior by perforations through the surface of the body. Very long pneumatic filaments, that is tubes filled with air, descend from the inferior surface of the float, and pass through the lower plate of the disk into the water.

The disk is transparent, and appears to be white from the air within it; and it is marked by concentric rings

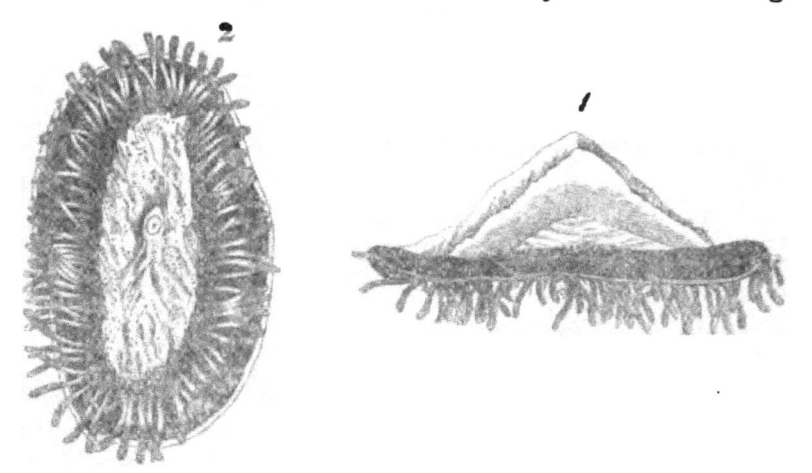

Fig. 122. Velella spirans:—1, upper side; 2, under-side.

corresponding to the divisions in the air-vessel below. The fringe-like limb that surrounds it is flat, flexible, semi-transparent, and of the richest dark blue passing into green, with a light blue ring; it is very contractile, and moves in slow undulations. The sail or crest is thin, firm, and transparent, covered by a bluish membrane; its limb is dark blue, crossed by waving yellow lines.

An irregular microscopic network of vascular canals, containing yellow matter, is seen in the soft substance which covers the sail; it ends in a canal round its margin. A similar system exists both in the upper and under-surface of the disk. All these systems are connected with one another, and with organs pending from the inferior side of the disk, which are hid when the Velella is in its natural horizontal position. These organs consist of a large central sterile polypite, which supplies the whole system with elaborated juices; it is surrounded by smaller polypites, which are both nutritive and reproductive; and the whole is encircled with a ring of prehensile and armed tentacles fastened to the rim of the disk, immediately adjoining to the underside of the limb. The pneumatic filaments already mentioned are mixed with these different organs.

In the Velellidæ caught by M. Vogt, he invariably found the stomachs of the large as well as of the small polypites, full of the carapaces of minute crustacea, shells, the bones of small fishes, and larvæ, so as even to be swelled out with them. The indigestible parts are thrown out at the mouth, and the elaborated juices are transferred to the various systems of canals to be distributed through all the members of the animal. The mouths of the small polypites take various forms; sometimes they are wide and trumpet-shaped, with everted lips, sometimes they are contracted. These small polypites consist of a double sac, fastened to the disk by a hollow stem with many rounded elevations on their surface full of thread-cells. The tentacles of the Velellidæ are strong, thick, club-shaped tubes, completely closed at their extremities, which abound in thread-cells; their cavity is filled with a transparent liquid, supposed to play an important part in their elongation.

Medusiform zooids are formed on the slender stems of the small polypites. It is presumed that they lay fertilized eggs which yield Velellidæ, so that this animal has probably alternate states of existence; but nothing is known of its earliest stages of development. The youngest form yet discovered is that described by Prof. Huxley, in his excellent monograph on 'Oceanic Hydrozoa.'[8] The Velellidæ are inhabitants of warm and tropical seas, but are occasionally found on the coasts of Great Britain, being carried by the Gulf Stream to the Bay of Biscay, and thence wafted northwards by the prevalent winds.

Although the Porpita, a genus of the Velellidæ, has no sail, it is akin to the Velellæ in size and structure. The body of the Porpita consists of two circular cartilaginous disks, united at their edges and surrounded by a blue membranous limb. On the surface of the upper disk there are beautifully radiating striæ, each of which ends at the circumference of the disk in a little protuberance, which gives it the appearance of a toothed wheel. A large sterile polypite occupies the centre of the under-surface of the body, surrounded by a zone full of smaller ones; and the space between the zone and the blue limb is occupied by a narrow area of a reticulated appearance, to which numerous circles of tentacles are fixed, that spread out and radiate all around the margin of the animal. The interior circular rows are simple, short, and fleshy, not extending much beyond the edge of the limb: the succeeding circles are gradually longer, while the exterior row, which extends far beyond the limb, are branched and beset with slender filaments, ending in minute globes, sometimes filled with air, so that a Porpita is like a floating daisy, though differently coloured. The Porpita glandifera, a pretty little inhabitant of the Mediterranean, which only appears in calm weather, is not more than eight lines in diameter; somewhat convex, white, marked by radiating striæ, and encompassed by a dark blue limb. The central polypite and those next to it are whitish,

---

[8] Published in 1858, by the Ray Society.

the rest become of a darker blue towards the limb; the tentacles are pellucid and bluish, and the three last rows have little dark blue globes attached to them by slender filaments.

The Porpita has a horizontal air-vessel divided vertically into air-chambers like the Velella, but they are much more numerous. In a middle-sized Porpita, four or five lines in diameter, there are twenty-three or twenty-four air-chambers surrounding a central one, and eighty or ninety pneumatic filaments, so that the animal is extremely buoyant. Brown matter, supposed to be a liver, lies directly below the undermost wall of the air-vessel, through which, as well as through the base of the animal, all the pneumatic filaments penetrate; the greater number go straight down into the water, but a portion of them terminate in the walls of the polypites.

A complete system of canals, ciliated internally, traverses all parts of the animal; and it may be presumed that the cilia maintain its juices in a state of circulation similar to that in the Velella; and the functions of the polypites, great and small, that are in connection with the liver, are also similar to those of the Velella. The Porpita is armed with thread-cells like all the class. The central polypite is sterile and nutritive; the small ones are both nutritive and reproductive: buds spring from their stems, which become independent male and female medusiform zooids, swim away from their parent and produce abundance of eggs, whence a new generation of Porpitæ arise.

In this singular class of fresh-water and oceanic Hydrozoa, the internal cilia, aided by the contraction of the walls of the body, are the sole means provided by nature for the circulation of the fluids.

SECTION IV.

ANTHOZOA ZOOPHYTES.

THE life-history of the oceanic Hydrozoa, which may be regarded as one of the triumphs of microscopic science, would have been incomplete had it been separated from that of the Pulmograde Acalephæ and the Physograde groups: but the most important part of that numerous race of animals are the Anthozoa zoophytes, which include the builders of the coral reefs and atolls of the Indian and Chinese seas. The coral polypes, though feeble and inconspicuous individually, when united in large communities acquire a power which enables them to build the most stupendous structures in the midst of a tempestuous ocean.

The Anthozoa zoophytes, or living flowers, form two extensive groups—the Asteroids, or Alcyonian zoophytes, whose polypes have six or eight hollow prehensile tentacles radiating round their mouth like a star or the petals of a single blossom, and the Actinian or Helianthoid zoophytes, which have ten, twelve, or more hollow tentacles encircling their mouth in several rows, like the blossom of a double sun-flower.

Alcyon Zoophytes.

The Alcyon zoophytes comprise the Alcyons, Gorgons, and Pennatulidæ, or sea-pens. The polypes are of the same form in all, and are united by a fleshy or horny substance into large communities, so connected and mutually dependent as to constitute one compound

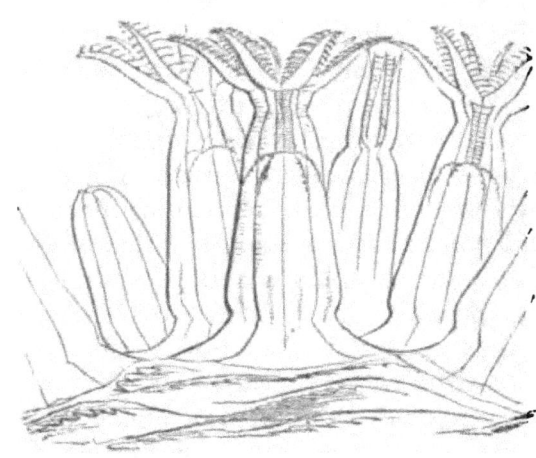

animal. Figure 123 represents a highly magnified group of Alcyonian polypes in different stages of expansion. The body of the polype is soft, contractile, and composed of thin, delicate transparent tissues. It has the form of a cone resting upon its

Fig. 123. Alcyonian polypes highly magnified.

base, which is generally of a firm material. Its upper extremity presents a central orifice, which serves both

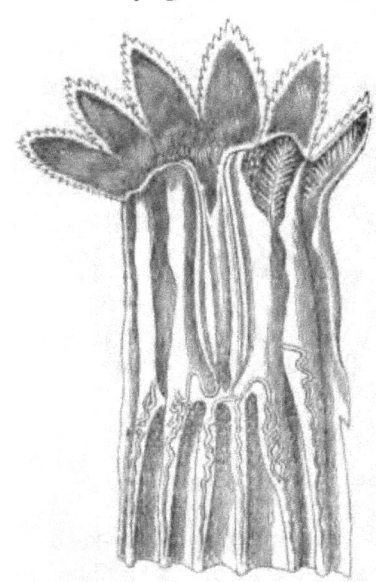

for a mouth and vent, and is encompassed by six or eight broad, short, hollow tentacles, enlarged towards their base so as to meet, and their edges are seen with a lens only to be fringed with minute hollow tubes or pinnæ closed at their free end.

The narrow slit of the mouth opens into the stomach, which is a flat, short sac hanging down in the central cavity of the polype's body, with an orifice at its lower end. The stomach is fixed to the internal walls of the body by eight vertical

Fig. 124. Polype of Alcyonidium elegans.

folds forming so many longitudinal chambers open at their lower extremity. The whole of the surface of the interior, the walls, the stomach, and the septa or divisions, are covered with fine cilia, by whose vibrations constant currents are maintained in the water which bathes every part of the cavity freely entering at the mouth. The polypes are carnivorous, living upon infusoria and minute particles of animal matter floating on the water, which they seize with their mouth, or arrest with their flexible and contractile tentacles. The food is digested by the solvent juices in the stomach, and the refuse is ejected at the mouth.

The eggs of these polypes are formed and fertilized among the vertical folds adjacent to the stomach. When hatched, the larvæ pass through the stomach and come out at the mouth as active ciliated creatures, so like eggs that the Alcyon zoophytes were believed to be oviparous. However, in some of the genera they are discharged through pores between the bases of the tentacles.

The Alcyon polypes have multitudes of needle-like spicules, rough with projecting knots. They are collected into triangular groups at the foot of each tentacle; the central and largest point runs up into the tentacle. Towards the lower end of the polype, spicules again occur scattered through the skin and crowded into groups, as in fig.

Fig. 125. Spicula of Alcyonium digitatum.

125. These, however, form short thick cylinders, each end being dilated into a star of five or six short branches. The spicules always contain an organic base hardened by

carbonate of lime, for when Dr. Carpenter dissolved the
lime with dilute acid, a gelatinous substance remained,
which had the form of the spicules. Fig. 125 shows
those of the Alcyonium digitatum, or Dead Man's Fingers, generally assumed as the type of this numerous
order, which contains sixteen genera and many species,
differing much in form but connected by a similarity of
digitate structure.

The Alcyonium digitatum, when torn from the rock to
which these animals are attached, shrinks into a cream-
coloured fleshy mass of somewhat solid texture, rough
and hard to the touch, and studded all over with hollow depressions or pits. When put into sea-water,
these lumps, from the size of a pea and upwards, expand,
become semi-transparent, and from each depression a
polype protrudes its beautifully symmetrical eight-
petalled blossom. Their tentacles are short, broad, and
prehensile; and the slender pinnæ, which fringe their
edges arching outwards, are seen with a high magnifying
power to be rough with prickly rings, discovered by Mr.
Gosse to be accumulations of thread-cells with their
darts.

These Alcyons, when expanded, are about an inch-
and-a-half high and two-thirds of an inch thick, but
individuals are met with two or three times as large,
and much divided into blunt finger-like lobes. The
sarcode mass of these compound animals is channelled
like a sponge, by branching canals, the orifices of which
open into the stomachs of the polypes; and, by bringing
them into communication with each other, unite the
whole into one compound animal, which is maintained
by the food caught and digested by each individual
polype. Currents of sea-water mixed with the nutritious juices are made to circulate through the branching
canals by the vibrations of cilia with which they are
lined; they flow round the stomachs of the polypes,

supply their juices with oxygen, and carry off the carbonic acid gas and refuse of the food. In this case, as in many others, the cilia may be regarded as respiratory organs.

The unarmed Alcyons are generally thick, short, and rough; some form a crust on rocks from whence lobes rise. With the exception of the Xenia, a tropical species, the polypes of the unarmed Alcyons can retreat within their polypary, so as to be entirely or partially out of sight.

The polypary, or mass, of the armed Alcyons is either membranous or leathery, and is entirely bristled with large spicules similar to the very small ones in the tentacles of its polypes. It forms branching masses terminated by prominent tubercules thickly beset by spicules. The polypes retreat into the mass when they are in a state of contraction.

The Gorgons, which form the second family of Alcyonian zoophytes, are compound animals, consisting of a solid stem or axis either simple or branched, adhering by its base to a rock or some submarine body, and coated by a layer of a softer fleshy or horny substance exactly in the same manner as the bark covers the stem and branches of a tree. This bark or fleshy substance is filled with polypes similar to those described; however, they are shorter, their base is a little enlarged, and is turned towards the axis of the stem and branches of the Gorgon. The softer substance or bark is much developed between the polypes, and is full of spicules, of forms varying with the genera. A system of almost capillary canals traverses the soft coating and opens into the lower part of the cavity containing the viscera of the different individuals, thus affording a passage for the circulation of the nutritive juices.

The larvæ of the Gorgons are like ciliated eggs; they swim with their thick end foremost, and are perfectly soft.

That state, however, is transitory; for no sooner do they lose their cilia and settle on a submarine substance than their lower part becomes hard, forms a solid layer on the substance, and constitutes the base for a Gorgon's stem. A small elevation rises on it, and at the same time the upper part of the larva assumes a fleshy consistence and surrounds the elevation. These two grow simultaneously; the small elevation rises higher and higher, and its coat containing the polypes grows proportionally with it, and continues to cover it whatever form it may take, whether a branching or plumage stem, or a simple slender rod. The stem and branches are increased in thickness by successive concentric layers of horny or calcareous matter between their surface and the soft bark.

The Gorgoniidæ are divided into three natural groups, the Gorgons, Isidæ, and Corallines, according to the nature of their axis. The two first agree in having stems either of a substance like cork or horn entirely or partly flexible; but the stem of the Gorgons has no joints, while that of the Isidinæ is jointed. The stem of the Corallines has no joints, and is entirely stony and branching.

The Gorgonia verrucosa, so common in the Mediterranean, British Channel, and the intermediate seas, is like a small shrub a foot high, with numerous branches: the cup-shaped tubercules inhabited by the polypes are irregularly distributed, and not very salient, yet enough to give the white encrusting coat a rough warty surface. In this Gorgon there is an ovary at the base of each polype: the eggs are discharged through eight small pores placed between the bases of the eight tentacles. These animals are wonderfully prolific: a Gorgon, six inches high, produced ninety eggs in one hour.

The Gorgonia graminea, found on the coast of Algiers, instead of being arborescent, is thin and cylindrical throughout its whole length. The covering is white, and nearly smooth; the cups containing the polypes either have no salient border, or are deeply sunk in the coat.

The Gorgons known as sea-fans live in warm seas, and are of numerous species. Not only all their branches, but all their branchlets and twigs, spread in the flat form of a fan, are soldered together so as to form a net with open meshes; the coating is thin, and the polypes are placed bilaterally.

The stems and branches of the Isidæ, which form the third group of Gorgoniidæ, are composed of a series of calcareous cylinders, separated by either horny or cork-like nodes; the polypes are only born in the bark of the former. In the genus Isis the calcareous cylinders are deeply striated by straight or wavy lines. This race of animals are mostly inhabitants of warm seas; but they once lived in a colder climate. Some species of them are preserved in a fossil state in the cretaceous earth in Belgium, and in the plastic clay near London.

There is but one genus of the Coralline Gorgon, and the type of that is the common red ornamental coral of commerce found in the Mediterranean Sea only. Dr. Carpenter has discovered that the solid calcareous stem of the Corallium rubrum is made up of aggregations of spicules closely resembling those of the other Alcyonian zoophytes, but of an intense red, sometimes rose colour or whitish. The stem and branches are delicately striated along their length, and covered with a soft substance of the same colour as the stem, into which the polypes retreat when alarmed; but when fishing for food, with their eight white tentacles expanded, the red stem and branches appear as if they were studded with stars. Prof. de Lacaze Duthiers, who was appointed by the French Government to investigate the natural history of the red coral with a view to the regulation of the fishery at

Algiers, found that the individual polypes are either male or female, but that the males and females are on different branches of the same coral, one branch being almost exclusively the abode of male polypes, and another of female. The eggs are fertilized by the intervention of the water. After an egg is fertilized, it is transferred to the stomach of the female, which thus serves both for digestion, incubation, and transformations of the egg. At first the egg is naked and spherical; afterwards it becomes elongated and covered with cilia. A cavity is formed in it, which opens externally,

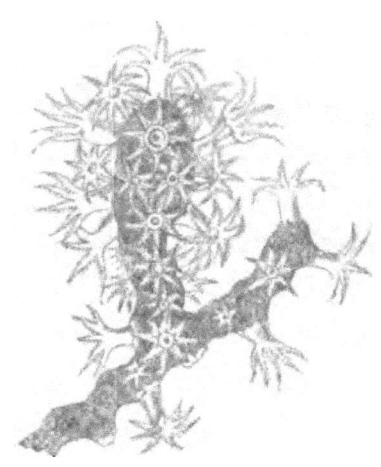

Fig. 126. Red Coral Branch.

and finally becomes the mouth; it then acquires the form of a little white worm, and when it comes into the water it is very active, swimming in all directions, avoiding its comrades when they meet, rising and descending in the water with its hinder end foremost. It loses its cilia after a time, fixes itself to a rock, and acquires the form of its parent in the manner described as to other Gorgons.

The red coral generally grows on the under-side of ledges or rocks, in a pendent position, and at considerable depths. It is not found at 15 or 20 fathoms; they only begin to fish for it at from 30 to 60 fathoms; and it is brought up from even 100 or 120, while the strong reef-building corals cannot exist below 25, or at most 30 fathoms; being immensely superior in vigour, these require a greater supply of air, light, and heat. The red coral is generally fished for along the coasts of Algiers and Tunis; it is also found in the seas round

Sicily and Sardinia, and in the Grecian Archipelago. The red coral is always irregularly branched. The

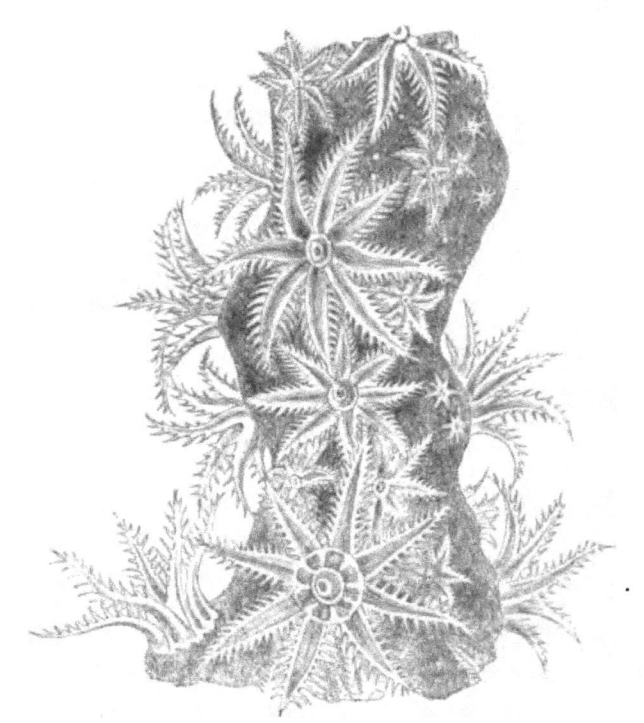

Fig. 127. Red Coral (greatly magnified), from ' Histoire Naturelle du Corail,' par M. Lacaze Duthiers.

branches are sometimes white, supposed to be from disease ; the white coral of commerce is a species of Caryophyllia, an Actinian, and not an Alcyon, zoophyte.

The Corallium Johnstoni, a native of the Atlantic, has a white axis, with branches spreading flatly and horizontally like a fan from the rock to which it is attached ; it is entirely covered with a yellowish flesh, but the polypes only inhabit the upper surface, as if they could not live in shade. The Corallium secundum, a similar zoophyte, was discovered by Professor Dana near the Sandwich Islands, with a white or rose-coloured fan-shaped stem and branches, covered by a scarlet coat, having the polypes also only on the upper surface.

The Pennatulidæ, or sea-pens, which are the third family of the Alcyon zoophytes, bear a great resemblance to a goose's feather. The genus Pennatula has a flatly-feathered, upright, calcareous axis, the bare part of which is analogous to the quill; but, instead of being fixed like the stem of a Gorgon, it is merely stuck into sand or mud at the bottom of the seas, while the upper feathered part, containing the polypes, remains in the water. The axis decreases in thickness upwards, and the pinnules, which diverge from it transversely like wings, are angular, thin, membranaceous, and strengthened by spicules. The whole animal is covered with a soft fleshy tissue; the polypes, which have eight pinnated tentacles, are arranged in a single row along the edges of the pinnules, with their visceral extremities prolonged into the soft tissue, so as to give it a tubular structure, through which the nourishing juice prepared by the polypes is carried for the maintenance of the general envelope, the refuse being thrown out at their mouths. When the sea-pens leave the mud or sand, they do not swim actively with their pinnules, but move languidly at the bottom. The Pennatulæ are phosphorescent; they are of a dull reddish brown during the day, but at night they shine with the most brilliant iridescence. In the tropical seas they occasionally exceed a foot in length; in the cool latitudes they are not more than five or six inches. The Pennatula phosphorea, found on the British coasts, has a hollow axis, occupied by a well-developed stylet; long pinnulæ symmetrically disposed on each side of the middle and upper part of the axis; the polypes, which are very contractile, are arranged transversely on their upper and anterior edges; the pinnæ of the wings are scythe-shaped, and furnished with a vast number of sharp spicules, and these combine in bundles at the base of the cells, in which the polypes live. The back of the pen, lying between the feathery wings, is sometimes smooth, sometimes crowded with scales, arising from the development of the spicules with which it is filled. The eggs of this animal are yellow, and have the size and form of poppy seeds. They are developed into ciliated larvæ within the polypes, which come out at their mouths, and swim away; but their activity is much diminished when they have acquired their mature form. These Pennatulæ increase also by a kind of budding. There are species of phosphorescent sea-pens in all the European seas and Indian Ocean.

The Virgulariæ are sea-pens which have long slender stems, with short transverse pinnules, on both sides of their extremity: they have no spicules, and are remarkable for the contractile power both of their axis and polypes. Mr. Darwin mentions a species he met with during his voyage in the Southern Ocean, which seems to be akin to the Virgularia juncea common in the Indian Seas. They were long and slender, projecting in vast numbers like stubble above the surface of muddy sand. When touched or pulled, they suddenly shrunk down with such force as to disappear partly or altogether. Sensitive as these animals are, they have no nerves; hence their motions must be owing to the irritable nature of muscular fibre. The eggs of the Virgularia mirabilis, native on the Scotch and Norwegian coasts, are formed in the fleshy coat at the base of each polype. As soon as they acquire their yellow colour and ciliated surface they enter into its body, and revolve in it for a little time before they come out at its mouth.

The family of the Tubipora, inhabitants of warm seas, are the most beautiful of the Alcyons. They consist of rounded masses of considerable size, formed of fragile, hollow, and nearly parallel calcareous tubes. The tubes do not touch one another, but they are united at intervals by horizontal plates, formed of an extension of their bases, dividing their mass into stages. In the

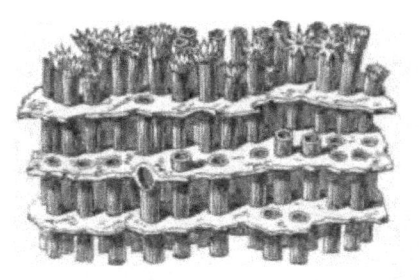

Fig. 128.   Tubipora musica.

Tubipora musica, a native of the Indian Ocean, there are several superincumbent series of equal and parallel tubes, exactly like the pipes of an organ. The whole compound fragile mass is of the richest crimson, and the polypes spread their white tentacles like stars over the mouths of the uppermost pipes, or retreat into them. Buds spring from the upper part of the tubes, and the result is the death of the parents, which are succeeded by a young living race a stage above them. The Tubipora purpurea lives in the Mediterranean and Red Seas. The polypes of a species found by Professor Dana, at the Feejee Islands, have their centre and mouth of a brownish red, and their tentacles yellow, edged by a double fringe of violet-coloured pinnules.

Actinian Zoophytes.

The great family of the Actinian zoophytes abounds in genera and species. The common Sea Anemone, or Actinia, of which there are more than seventy species on the British coasts, is the model of the minute polypes which inhabit the stony corals, and build the coral reefs and atolls of the tropical Pacific.

The Sea Anemone has a cylindrical body, attached at one end by a sucker to rocks or stones at no great depth, and a flat circular disk at the other, with the mouth in its centre: the mouth, which is surrounded by a series of tubular, smooth-edged, radiating tentacles, resembles a blossom. The soft smooth body consists of two layers, as may be seen in the sections of an Actinia (fig. 129). The outer layer generally contains red matter, the inner one is of muscular fibre, and contains a great cavity, in which a somewhat globular bag or stomach is suspended. The space between the stomach and the cylindrical body of the animal is divided into chambers by perpendicular radiating

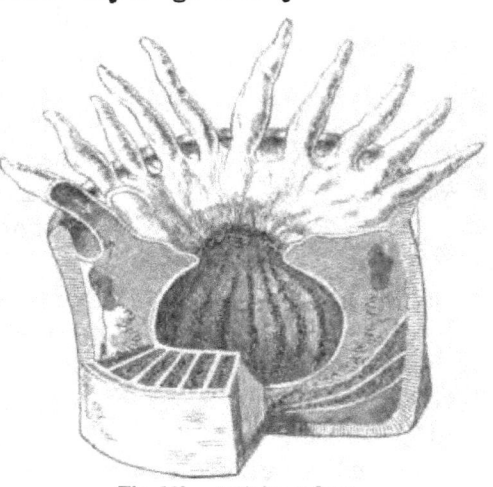

Fig. 129. Actinian polype.

partitions, consisting of thin plates or lamellæ. The mouth, which opens at once into the stomach, imbibes sea-water ; and the hollow tentacles surrounding it being perforated at their extremities, and in communication with the chambers immediately below them, also imbibe the sea-water and convey it into the chambers ; and the vibrations of the innumerable cilia, with which all the cavities of the animal are lined, keep them perpetually bathed with the respiratory medium mixed with nutrient juices from the coats of the stomach.[9]

The Sea Anemone is monœcious and oviparous; the eggs are formed and fertilized in the lower parts of the perpendicular lamellæ or radiant plates; but they are hatched within the visceral cavity, and the larvæ issue from the mouth. The Actiniæ are also propagated by buds. They have as great a power of repairing injuries as the Hydræ, and like them too, though generally fixed,

[9] 'Lectures on Comparative Anatomy,' by Professor Owen.

they can creep about by means of their expanded suctorial disk, and even float on the surface of the water. In many species the tentacles, as well as the body, are brightly coloured. The Actinia sulcata, an inhabitant of the British Channel, is of a deep crimson, with from 100 to 200 grass-green tentacles. The tints are owing to coloured particles in minute globules, that lie under the transparent skin of the animal and its tentacles.

With the exception of some of the Acalephæ, the thread-cells of the Sea Anemone are more highly developed than in any other animals. They not only differ in the various Actinian zoophytes, but sometimes even in the same individual. The complicated structure and action of this warlike apparatus was unsuspected previous to the microscopic observations of Mr. Gosse on the Actiniæ in general, and especially on the little scarlet fringed Sagartia miniata, a native of the British coasts. Like all the Anemones, it is highly sensitive ; on the slightest touch it draws in its scarlet blossom, and shrinks into the form of a hemispherical bulb. While in the act of contracting, white filaments like ribbons shoot out from various parts of its surface, and new ones appear on every fresh effort, streaming out to the length of several inches, irregularly twisted and tangled. As soon as the contraction is finished, these fine white filaments begin to be recalled, and gradually retire in small irregular coils into the interior chambers between the stomach and the wall of the body, where they are stored up when not in activity.

Each filament makes its egress and ingress through an almost imperceptible transverse slit, discovered by Mr. Gosse, in the middle of an oval depression in the wall of the animal's body. The slits, which are called cinclides, are very numerous, and resemble a pair of inverted eyelids, which can be opened and shut at pleasure. When the animal is irritated it contracts, and the water which fills the perpendicular chambers is forced in a stream through the slits, and carries with it the white filaments lodged within them; and then these quivers, which are full of deadly weapons, are ready for action.

Under the microscope, the white filaments are like narrow flat ribbons with their edges curled in, and thickly covered with cilia. They have not the slightest trace of muscular fibre, even when viewed with a microscopic power of 800 diameters; yet they extend, contract, bend, and coil in every direction; they bring together the margins of the ribbon so as to form a tube, and open them again; and the filaments perform all these motions even when severed from the animal, no doubt by the contractile nature of the clear jelly or sarcode, of which their bases are composed, as in the tentacles of the Acalephæ.

Innumerable oblong dart or stinging-nettle cells, closely packed together, lie under the folded edges of the ribbons, throughout their whole length, especially at their tips.[1]

The polypes of the stony corals, though extremely small, are essentially the same in structure as the Sea Anemone, but they have no sucker at their base. The Sea Anemone is of soft tissue throughout its whole body. In the polypes of the madrepore corals, on the contrary, the whole of the perpendicular lamellæ which divide the interior of the body into chambers become hard, from being consolidated by particles of carbonate of lime; and their upper edges, which appear as rays round the mouth of the animal, give that starry appearance to the surface of dead madrepores after the soft part of the polypes has been destroyed.

Most of the coral polypes are unarmed; but in some, as, for example, the Caryophyllia Smithii, there are multitudes of dart-cells in the tentacles, besides numerous

---

[1] 'Evenings at the Microscope,' by P. H. Gosse, Esq.

pellucid filaments or ribbons, full of thread-cells, lying in coils within the chambers which surround the stomach.

We are indebted to Mrs. Thynne's interesting observations on the Caryophyllia Smithii in her aquarium for the life-history of the animals armed with this formidable artillery. This madrepore, which inhabits many parts of the European seas, at various depths, is a species of the only lamelliform genus of corals which range beyond the tropics. It is a solitary individual polype, with an external calcareous cylindrical coat, wider at the base, when it is fixed to a rock; and the mouth, which has several rows of tentacles, is in the centre of the disk of the cylinder. The tentacles are delicate, transparent, granular tubes, about an inch long, tapering to their extremities, and ending in an opaque white knob full of chambered thread-cells with their darts; but the thread-cells are of a larger size in the ribbons coiled in the chambers round the stomach of the animal. These madrepores are described by Mrs. Thynne as of various tints, from a pure white to a bright apricot colour. At intervals they eject from the mouth a whitish blue fluid, resembling wood smoke, in a stream three or four inches long, sometimes containing a few eggs. But the eggs, though no doubt formed at the base of the lamellæ, become densely packed like fine dust in the hollows of the tentacles, from whence they are expelled by contractions, and escape by the mouth. The eggs lie quiet for a few days in the place where they are deposited: by and by they begin to rotate, slowly at first, then more rapidly, and finally they are developed into most minute madrepores, with the star and colour of the parent. In a few months they become as large as a crown piece, with a very wide mouth and a membranous integument or covering, for they do not get their hard calcareous coat till they are two years old. While in that soft state they propagate by spontaneous division, which always begins at the mouth, and is repeated every few weeks during the second year of their lives. When they split into segments, the broken ends of each segment bend round and unite; and the mouth, which at first is on one side, being a portion of the old one, comes to the centre of the disc, and in addition to the few old tentacles that remain, new ones are added, with their interior chambers, till they amount to five rows, and in this manner a brood of young Caryophylliæ is formed.

During the second year of their soft state, these madrepores increase by budding. The buds spring from the base of the membranous covering, they expand, get a mouth and tentacles, aid in feeding themselves by greedily taking any small particles of animal food offered to them, and seem also to share in the sustenance provided by the mother, as they dilate when she is fed; ultimately they separate from her. These madrepores have patches of a milk-white fluid substance, which unite and almost cover the space between the mouths and the rows of tentacles: in others of the madrepore tribe these patches are purple, green, yellow, or ultramarine blue. The Caryophylliæ have locomotion while their skin is soft, but no activity; they merely avoid obstacles, and move away from one another; but, as soon as they get their hard calcareous

Fig. 130. Lobophylla angulosa.

coat, they become permanently fixed, and no longer undergo division or gemmation, but lay eggs.[2]

[2] 'Observations on the Caryophyllia Smithii,' by Mrs. Thynne, in the *Annals and Magazine of Natural History.*

The European Caryophylliæ never have more than one star, but sometimes a great many individuals are united in a spreading bunch, as in the madrepore Lobophylla angulosa (fig. 130), or in a branched or tufted mass. Their exterior is invariably striated, and each terminates in a star, with the polypes, mouth and tentacles in its centre. These compound madrepores are inhabitants of warm seas.

The number of tentacles possessed by the Actinian polype varies with the species of the coral. When full grown they have twelve, twenty-four, even forty-eight, or more. When young, they have only four or six, but in general the number increases rapidly as they advance in age. The perpendicular hard lamellæ, which divide the cavity round the stomach of the polype into perpendicular chambers, as in fig. 129, and form stars round the mouth, consist of thin sheets or plates, either applied or soldered together; and for every new tentacle that is produced at the mouth, a corresponding new chamber is formed immediately below it, between the sheets or leaves of the lamellæ; so that the number of chambers and perpendicular plates is always equal to the number of tentacles, and so the circulation of the fluids is maintained. Since the upper edges of the lamellæ form the rays of the stars round the mouth of the polype, it is clear that the number of rays in a star must always be equal to the number of lamellæ. The new tentacles are always produced exterior to and between the adjacent old ones, so as to form an outer circle, and consequently a new circle of rays will be added to the star round the mouth exterior to the old ones. There may be two, three, or more concentric circles of tentacles round the mouth of the polype, the last being the shortest. However, some polypes never have more than twelve tentacles during the whole course of their lives. The first formed rays of a star are generally, though not always, the longest and most prominent; and sometimes the edges of the lamellæ rise high above the hollow or cup which is the centre of the star, and contains the mouth of the polype. In some families of corals these edges, which form the rays, are toothed or spined.[2]

A horny column in the axis of the polype, hardened by sulphate and carbonate of lime, and called the columella, generally shows its top in the centre of the star, and varies in structure in the different genera. Thus the Actinian polypes may be said to possess an internal skeleton, and as they approach maturity they also acquire an external one in the form of a cylindrical coat, or stony wall, which surrounds them, and into which most of them can withdraw the soft upper part of their bodies and tentacles, so as to be partly or altogether concealed. The perpendicular lamellæ are sometimes extended through the stony walls of the polype, so as to form a series of broad, well-developed ribs on its exterior surface.

The stony substance of corals is chiefly carbonate of lime, which the polypes have the power of abstracting from the sea-water, combined with a small quantity of animal matter, and a still smaller quantity of phosphate of lime, with a trace of silver and magnesia. This stony substance takes the crystalline form of needles. By the successive deposition of these needles, a network is formed round the body of the animal, which by a series of these deposits is condensed into a hard impervious coat or wall. During this formative process many characteristic forms may be produced by division and building, depending upon the genus and species of the polype; but they do not lay eggs till they come to maturity.

Some corals increase both by budding and division, but by far the greater number grow in size by budding,

---

[2] 'Histoire des Corallines,' par Professeur Milne-Edwards.

as the Astræa, which constitutes a portion of the reef-building corals of the tropical seas. They form groups, in which the whole of the polypes, except their starry summits, are soldered or pasted together by a living viscous substance, consolidated by carbonate of lime, abstracted from the sea-water, so that the resulting coral frequently becomes a rounded mass, the surface of which is more or less covered with stars, which may be circular or angular, large or small, deeply set or prominent, according to the genera or species, both of which are exceedingly numerous. In fact the forms produced vary according as the buds spring from the base of the polypes, from the sides of the cylindrical body, from the summit or disk, from the limits of these three parts, or from the whole animal. In all these varieties the buds are the result of a superabundance of vital activity in the part. When the buds proceed from the sides of the polypes the corals are rounded masses ; but when they spring from the disk or cups of the star, the consequence is the death of the parent polypes, and the development of a new layer of living individuals above the dead ones. No part of the new polypes is seen except their stars, their bodies being enclosed in the common tissue. As this process may be continued indefinitely, the coral may increase to any size ; but the size becomes still greater when successive buds are formed over every part of the polypes, and when all the successive generations are soldered together by the common tissue. In every case the polypes are alive only on the surface where they have free access to light, heat, and air, which is furnished by the sea-water in which they live.[4]

In the reef-building corals the living viscous substance that covers the surface and connects the polypes into a mass, is in process of time so completely consolidated by

[4] 'Histoire des Corallines,' par Professeur Milne-Edwards.

abstracting the small quantity of carbonate of lime that the sea-water contains, that little if any animal matter remains; and as this process is continually repeated, one generation of polypes perishes after another, the inert matter increases indefinitely, and the surface at which the consolidation is actually going on is the only part that is alive.

The surfaces of the dense convex masses of many of these Astræan corals are entirely covered with deep hexagonal stars, whose rays extend upwards all round, and end in narrow, sharp, and elevated lines formed by the junction of the rays of the adjacent stars; in other species the rays are often crowded together, and the columella only shows a few points in the deep hollows. Through these deep cups the polypes protrude their circular disks and tentacles in quest of food, the nutritious products of which maintain the polypes as well as the general living fabric which unites them, and the refuse is ejected from their mouths; for each polype has an independent life of its own besides the incidental life that it possesses as part of a compound being. In many of the corals the polypes show great sensibility, shrinking into their cells on the slightest touch, yet no nervous system has been discovered.

The variety of compact and branching corals far exceeds description: 120 species are inhabitants of the Red Sea alone, and an enormous area of the tropical Pacific is everywhere crowded with the stupendous works of these minute agents, destined to change the present geological features of the globe, as their predecessors have done in the remote ages of its existence.

Four distinctly different formations are due to the coral-building polypes in the Pacific and Indian Oceans, namely, lagoon islands or atolls, encircling reefs, barrier reefs, and coral fringes, all nearly confined to the torrid zone.

An atoll is a ring or chaplet of coral, enclosing a lagoon or portion of the ocean in its centre. The average breadth of that part of the ring which rises above the surface of the sea is about a quarter of a mile, often less, and it is seldom more than from six to ten or twelve feet above the waves : hence the lagoon islands are not visible even at a very small distance, unless when they are covered by the cocoa-nut palm or the pandanus, which is frequently the case. On the outside, the ring or circlet shelves down for a distance of one or two hundred yards from its edge, so that the sea gradually deepens to about twenty-five fathoms, beyond which the sides of the ring plunge at once into the unfathomable depths of the ocean with a more rapid descent than the cone of any volcano. Even at the small distance of some hundred yards no bottom has been reached with a sounding line a mile and a half long. All the coral on the exterior of the ring, to a moderate depth below the surface of the water, is alive ; all above it is dead, being the detritus of the living part washed up by the surf, which is so heavy on the windward side of the tropical islands of the Pacific and Indian Oceans, that it is often heard miles off, and is frequently the first warning to seamen of their approach to an atoll.

On the inside, these coral rings shelve down into the clear calm water of the lagoon by a succession of ledges of living corals, but of much more varied and delicate kinds than those on the exterior wall and foundation of the atoll. The corals known as Porites are the chief agents in building the exterior face of the ring : they form great rounded irregular masses, like the Astræa, but much larger, being many feet in thickness ; and as the polypes are only alive on the surface, numberless generations must have lived and died before they could have arrived at that size. The rays of the stars are toothed at the edges, so that they present rows of little points ;

in some species the rays are almost invisibly slender, the interstitial matter is full of pores, and the polypes have twelve tentacles.

The Millepora complanata or palmipora is very commonly associated with the Porites; it is the largest coral known. It grows in thick vertical plates, intersecting each other at various angles, and forms an exceedingly strong honey-combed mass, generally affecting a circular form, the marginal plates alone being alive. Instead of stars, the polypes live in simple pores: myriads of these small cylindrical pores penetrate the surface of the plates perpendicular to their axes; sometimes they are so minute as to be scarcely visible.

Between the plates, and in the protected crevices of the outer circle of the ring, a multitude of branching zoophytes and other productions flourish; but the Porites, Astræans, and Milleporæ seem alone able to resist the fury of the breakers, essential to the very existence of these hardy corals, which only obtain their full development when washed by a heavy sea. The outer margins of the Maldive atolls, consisting chiefly of Milleporæ and Porites, are beat by a surf so tremendous that even ships have been thrown by a single heave of the sea high and dry on the reef. The waves give innate vigour to the polypes by bringing an ever-renewed supply of food to nourish them, and oxygen to aërate their juices: besides, uncommon energy is given and maintained by the heat of a tropical sun, which gives them power to abstract enormous quantities of solid matter from the water to build their stony homes, a power that is efficient in proportion to the energy of the breakers which furnish the supply.

The Porites and Milleporæ, which are the chief reef-building corals, cannot live at greater depths than fifteen or twenty-five fathoms: not for want of heat, for the temperature of the ocean in these latitudes does not sink to 68° Fahr. till a depth of 100 fathoms, but light and abundance of uncombined air are essential, and these decrease as the depth increases. The polypes perish if exposed directly to the sun even for a short time, so they build horizontally between these limits. The actinian polypes in the corals, which live at different depths in the crevices of the atolls, have the same general structure; their disks and tentacles are sometimes tinted with brilliant colours; some sting, others have a considerable diversity of individual character.

On the margin of the atolls, close within the line where the coral is washed by the tide, three species of Nullipores flourish; they are beautiful little plants, very common in the coral islands. One species grows in thin spreading sheets, like a lichen; the second in stony knobs as thick as a man's finger, radiating from a common centre; and the third species, which has the colour of peach blossom, is a reticulated mass of stiff branches about the thickness of a crow's quill. The three species either grow mixed or separately, and, although they can exist above the line of the corals, they require to be bathed the greater part of each tide: hence a layer two or three feet thick, and about twenty yards broad, formed by the growth of the Nullipores, fringes the circlet of the atolls and protects the coral below.

The lagoon in the centre of these islands is supplied with water from the exterior by openings in the lee side of the ring, but as the water has been deprived of the greater part of its nutritious particles and inorganic matter by the corals on the outside, the hardier kinds are no longer produced, and species of more delicate forms take their place. The depths of the lagoon varies in different atolls from fifty to twenty fathoms or less, the bottom being partly detritus, partly live coral. In these calm and limpid waters the corals are of the most varied and delicate structure, of the most charming and dazzling hues.   When the shades of evening come on, the lagoon shines like the milky way with myriads of brilliant sparks.   The microscopic medusæ and crustaceans invisible by day form the beauty of the night, and the sea-feather, vermilion in daylight, now waves with green phosphorescent light.   This gorgeous character of the sea bed is not peculiar to the lagoons of the atolls; it prevails in shallow water throughout the whole coral-bearing regions of the Pacific and Indian Oceans.

Encircling reefs differ in no respect from the atoll ring, except in having islands in their lagoons, surrounded also by coral reefs.   Barrier reefs are of the same structure as the atoll rings, from which they only differ in their position with regard to the land.   They form extensive lines along the coasts, from which they are separated by a channel of the sea of variable depth and breadth, sometimes large enough for ships to pass.   A very long one runs parallel to the west coast of New Caledonia, and stretches for 120 miles beyond the extremities of the island.   But a barrier reef off the north-eastern coast of the Australian continent is the grandest coral formation existing.   Rising at once from an unfathomable depth of the ocean, it extends for a thousand miles along the coast with a breadth varying from 200 yards to a mile, and at an average distance of from 20 to 60 or 70 miles from the coast, the depth of the channel being from 10 to 60 fathoms.   The pulse of the ocean, transcendently sublime, beats perpetually in peals of thunder along that stupendous reef, the fabric of almost microscopic beings.

SECTION V.

ANNULOSA, OR WORMS.

THE Annulosa, which are the lowest grade of articulated animals, consist of four distinct orders: the Entozoa, which are muscle and intestine parasites; the Turbellariæ, fresh and salt-water animals covered with cilia; the Annelida, or Worms; and the Rotifers, or Wheel animalcules.

Entozoa.

There are three genera and numerous species of Entozoa. Every animal has one or more species peculiar to itself; fourteen infest the human race. They have a soft, absorbent body of a white or whitish colour, in consequence of being excluded from light, and living as they do by absorbing the vitalized juices of the animals they infest. Their nutritive system is in the lowest state of development; yet there are some of a higher grade. All are remarkable for their vast productiveness.

The Tænioïdæ, which belong to the inferior group, are intestinal, many-jointed worms, which have neither mouth nor digestive organs; and what is called the head has only hooks and suckers to fasten it to the internal membrane of the animal at whose expense it lives. The common Tænia, or Tape-worm, sometimes ten feet long, which is the type of the order, has four suckers and a circle of hooklets round a terminal proboscis to attach it to its victim. Though destitute of the organs of nutrition it is extremely prolific, for each segment of its long flat body is a reproductive monœcious zooid, which forms and lays its own eggs exactly as if it were a single independent animal, thus furnishing a very remarkable instance of the law of irrelative repetition, which is a series of organs performing the same functions independently of one another. Two pairs of canals containing a clear colourless liquid extend throughout the body of the worm.

Bags, or vesicles called cysts, had been found in the glands and muscles of various animals, afterwards discovered to contain young worms, which attain their perfect development within such creatures as eat the flesh containing the cysts. Under circumstances so unprecedented, it required no small skill and patience to determine the life-history of these singular creatures. The cysts differ in size and form according to the genera, and are embedded singly or in groups in the flesh of their victim, on whose ready prepared juices they live.

The greater number of the Tænia genus begin their lives as sexless cysted larvæ, and on entering their final abode, segments are successively added till the worm has arrived at its adult state. The tape-worm of the cat has its origin in the encysted larvæ found in the livers of the mouse and rat. One species of Entozoa, while in its primary state, inhabits the stomach of the stickleback, and only comes to perfection within the aquatic birds that feed on this fish. Another species infests the livers of the salmon tribe, and gets its perfect form in the pike and perch.

Sheep and the hog are more tormented with cysted worms than any other domestic animals used for food. If introduced into the human intestines by eating raw ham or sausages, the larvæ soon acquire the perfect form. The eggs of the Tænia may be introduced into the human or animal stomach; for dogs and other carnivora which eat raw unwholesome meat are infested by full grown tænia, which fix themselves to their entrails by their hooks and suckers, while at the same time egg-bearing segments separate successively from their posterior extremity, and being voided scatter the eggs far and wide on land and in water.

The young of some Entozoa undergo various transformations, as those of the Distoma of the Lymnæa. When full grown that entozoön is like a sole, flat, broad, and long, with a kind of head at the broad end, and two suckers on its under-surface, in one of which there is a pore serving as a mouth, whence an alimentary canal extends, which spreads in branches almost throughout the whole body. This animal has a filamentary nerve round its gullet, from which minute fibres pass to the mouth, and two filaments extend backward on each side as far as the second sucker. The eggs which occupy the whole margin of the body are developed into worms, each of which seems to be merely a mass of structureless cells enclosed in a contractile case. By a second change each of these cells is transformed into a freely swimming ciliated zooid endowed with eyes. Having escaped from their contractile case, they remain for a time in that state, and then imbed themselves in the mucus on the foot of the fresh-water mollusk Lymnæa, or pond snail, where they are transformed into true Distomata, and ultimately enter into the body of the Lymnæa itself, where they lose their eyes and cilia, which are no longer of use in their dark and permanent abode. The Fluke found in the livers of sheep that have the rot is a Distoma.

The Nematoid order, or thread-worms, that live in the muscles of men and animals, are long, smooth, and cylindrical, with a structureless skin covering layers of longitudinal and circular fibres, by means of which they can stretch and contract themselves. They are generally pointed at both ends with a mouth at one extremity and an orifice at the other. The Filariæ are slender, sometimes of great length, as the Guinea worm, which varies in length from six inches to two, eight, or even twelve feet. In Persia they are believed to be introduced into the system by drinking water in which their eggs have been deposited. This worm may grow in the muscles of a man to the size of five or six feet without giving much annoyance, but when its head bores through the skin it produces a painful sore unless extracted. In Persia, where the worm is common, the natives seize it by the head, draw it carefully out, and wind it round a bit of wood, an operation which may require several days to accomplish. It has a numerous viviparous progeny, which come out through the mouth. There are certain very small slender species of Filaria which attack the eyes both of men and horses; some bury themselves close to the eye, and a very minute kind enters the ball itself.

The Ascaris lumbricoïdes, a common intestinal threadworm of the hog, ox, and the human race, is sometimes of great length. The sexes are distinct, and their fertility enormous. The ovaries are two tubes sometimes several feet long, in each of which the eggs are arranged in whorls round a central stem, like the flowers of a plantago. By counting the number of microscopic eggs in a whorl, and the number of whorls, Dr. Eschricht ascertained that in a full grown female the average number of eggs amounted to sixty-four millions. In this species of worm the embryo is not developed from the egg while within the victim, so that most of the eggs perish.

Different species of Anguillulæ, which are minute eel-like worms slender as a hair, inhabit the alimentary canal of fresh-water snails, frogs, and fishes, but many species are not parasitic. These are often united in swarming masses that nestle in mud, wet moss, wet earth, and aquatic plants. One species causes the cockle in wheat, appearing like a living tuft of white wool in the blackened grains. They appear in sour paste and in other decomposing substances, and are so tenacious of life that, after being completely dried for months, and apparently dead, they revive on being moistened.

Turbellariæ.

The Turbellariæ are fresh- and salt-water animals, distinguished by having the whole surface of their bodies covered by cilia, under which in some species there are thread-cells containing six, eight, or a greater number of darts. Most of the members of this tribe have elongated flattened bodies, and move by a sort of crawling or gliding motion over the surface of aquatic plants and animals. Some of the smaller kinds are sufficiently transparent to allow their internal structure to be seen by transmitted light. The mouth, which is situated at a considerable distance from the rounded end of the body, opens into a sort of gullet leading into the stomach, which has no other orifice, but a great number of branching canals are prolonged from it, which carry its contents into every part of the body. A pair of oval nerve-centres are placed near the rounded end of the animal, whence nerves extend to various parts of the body; and near to these there are from two to forty rudimentary eyes according to the species, each of which has its crystalline lens, its pigment layer, nerve bulb, and its cornea. The power of the Planaria to reproduce portions which have been removed is but little inferior to that of the Hydra.

Annelids.

The Annelids are the most highly organized of all the worm tribe. They are exceedingly numerous and varied; some are inhabitants of fresh water, others are terrestrial, but by far the greater number and most highly endowed are marine. They generally have a long, soft, and smooth body, divided or marked by transverse rings into a succession of similar segments. In many the first and last segments are alike; in others the first segment can scarcely be called a head, though it exercises several functions, while in the highest two orders the head is the seat of several senses. On each side of the bodies of the Annelida there are one or two long rows of tufted bristles or feet, which may be regarded as the earliest form of symmetrical locomotive organs. Most of the Annelids have ocelli or eye-specks, and in many of them the head supports soft cylindrical tentacles, which are obviously organs of touch. These worms are divided into four orders, the Suctorial, Terrestrial, Tubercular, and Errantia, or Wandering Worms.[5]

The first order consists of Leeches of different kinds: their body is long, slightly segmented, with a suctorial disc at each end. Their skin is smooth, whitish, and translucent; beneath it are cells filled with brown or greenish matter, and three layers of muscular fibres follow; the first are transverse, the second cross one another diagonally so as to form a network, and the third are longitudinal. The mouth, which occupies the centre of the principal sucking disk, varies in form with the genera. In the common leech it has an enlarged lip, and opens into a short gullet leading into a capacious and singularly complicated stomach, divided by deep constrictions into eleven compartments, the last

[5] According to the system of M. Milne-Edwards, who made the Annulosa a particular object of investigation.

of which is connected with an intestinal canal, which ends in a vent in the middle of the terminal sucker.

Within the mouth there are three crescent-shaped jaws, presenting their convex edges towards the cavity of the mouth, beset with from seventy to eighty teeth, formed of a highly refractive crystalline substance resembling glass. The leech makes a vacuum with its sucker, which forces the part to which it is applied into contact with the three-toothed jaws, which are moved sidewise by strong muscles, and saw through the skin and small bloodvessels below it.

The leech, like the other Annelids, has two distinct systems of circulating liquids, one red, the other colourless. The red liquid or blood is kept in circulation by the pulsations of a heart, or rather a contractile vessel behind the head. It is carried away from the heart by a pulsating canal passing along the back of the leech, and is brought back to the heart by a similar canal extending along its ventral side. During this course, portions of the liquid are sent off through veins to different parts of the body. The respiratory organs of the leech are pores arranged at regular distances on each side of the body which open into little sacs having capillary bloodvessels distributed under the skin through which the blood is aërated.

The colourless liquid which contains many organic molecules, occupies the space between the alimentary canal and the inner wall of the body, from whence it passes into canals which ramify extensively, but are not furnished with returning passages. This liquid forms a support to the muscles of the skin, and is kept in circulation by the motions of the leech.

Fig. 131 shows the highly developed nervous system of the leech. From the double lobe of the brain ten optic nerves go to the bases of ten black eye-specks, which mark at equal distances the upper margin of the expanded lip. A nerve-centre below the gullet supplies the lip and jaws with strong nerves. A double longitudinal cord, united at equal distances by twenty-one double nerve-centres, extends from a ring round the gullet throughout the whole length of the body, supplies the different organs with nerves, and ends near the vent in a nerve-centre, from whence nerves radiate through the terminal sucker.

The circulation of the blood and of the colourless liquid, as well as the nerve system, prevail generally in the Annelids, modified by the structure of the individual.

The leech, though greedy of blood, lives in fresh-water ponds, wet grass, and damp places, where it never can meet with warm-blooded animals. It probably lives on minute aquatic insects.

The common Earth-worm, which is a principal member of the second order of Annelids, has a more important part assigned to it in the economy of nature than its humble appearance leads us to suspect. It has a long, soft, cylindrical body tapering to a point at both ends, divided into numerous rings. The mouth is furnished with a short proboscis, or snout, without teeth. A long salivary glandular mass surrounds a short wide

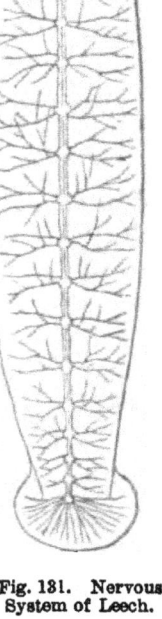

Fig. 131. Nervous System of Leech.

gullet, which leads to a digestive organ similar to a gizzard, whence a canal is continued to the vent. The circulation of the two fluids, and the nervous system modified at head and tail, are like those of the leech. Four rows of minute bristles extend longitudinally along the ventral surface of the worm, two on each side.

With a low magnifying-power they appear to be minute points regularly pushed out and drawn in; but when more highly magnified each point is seen to consist of two transparent glassy rods having their points bent backwards : on these feet the worm crawls very rapidly.

While making its cylindrical burrow a slimy mucus exudes from the body of the worm, which cements the particles of earth together and renders the walls of the burrow perfectly smooth and slippery. When the worm pierces the earth it stretches its snout into a fine point that it may penetrate more easily, and when it is fixed, it draws its ringed body towards its head by a muscular effort; and to prevent it from slipping back again, it fixes the hooks of its posterior feet firmly into the ground. Having thus secured a point of support it penetrates deeper into the earth, draws up its body, fixes the hooks of the posterior feet into the smooth surface of the burrow, and continues the same process till the burrow is deep enough. Thus the feet are employed as points of resistance for the exertion of muscular force. This worm swallows earth mixed with decaying animal and vegetable matter, assimilates the nutritive part, and casts out the refuse in the form of fine mould, which

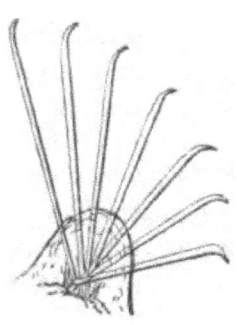

Fig. 132. Foot of Naïs.

may be seen in little heaps at the edges of their burrows. In fact, nearly all the fine vegetable mould so precious to gardeners and farmers has passed through the intestines of the common earth-worm.

There is a colourless little freshwater species of the genus Naïs, remarkable for the beauty of its bristled feet. There are two pairs on each ring of the worm, consisting of wartlike perforated protuberances, through which a number of microscopic bristles protrude, arranged in a radiating pencil like a fan. They are very slender, bent at the tip, and so transparent that they look like threads of spun glass; the worm thrusts them out and draws them in with extreme rapidity.

A blood-red Naïs lives in burrows in the mud at the bottom of springs and pools in immense multitudes; large tracts of the mud of the Thames are red with a species of them; half of their bodies stretched out of their burrows maintain a constant oscillating motion on its surface, but, like the earth-worm, they instantly shrink into their burrows on the least alarm. They have no respiratory organs; but their blood is aërated through their skin, which is so transparent that, with a microscope, the whole of the internal structure, the motions of the liquids, and the particles they contain are distinctly visible. The blood acts the part of internal gills, by aërating the colourless liquid contained in a set of vascular coils surrounding the organs of digestion.

The Tubicola are marine worms, forming the third order of Annelida, according to the system of M. Milne-Edwards. They live in tubes, either of a shelly calcareous substance, which forms naturally on the tenacious mucus of their skins, or in tubes artificially constructed by themselves of sand and particles of shell glued together. All the Tubicola can protrude their gills and the anterior part of their bodies, and some can leave their tube and return to it again. These worms, which form beautiful objects for the microscope, have ringed bodies with tubular bristled feet, and respiratory organs or gills fixed either on the head or near it. They have an alimentary canal loosely attached to the ventral wall of the body, and two systems of circulating liquids, one red, the other colourless. In the Tubular Annelids the principal organs of respiration are the contractile plumes on the head.

In the Terebella there are distinct organs for the

aëration of both liquids, which form a beautiful plume when expanded, as in fig. 133, which shows the animal when out of its tube. What may be called the head is fixed upon the first ring of the body. The mouth has a lip like a funnel-shaped cup with numerous long slender tubular tentacles ; and two delicate arborescent branches or gills are fixed immediately behind the head. The colourless liquid which occupies the space between the alimentary canal and the ventral wall of the worm, is sent by the contractions of the body into the slender tubular filaments round the mouth, which are covered by cilia, whose action continually renews the stratum of water in contact with them. The blood in its usual course enters the capillary tubes of the arborescent gills, where it is oxygenized, and, after being distributed to the different parts of the body, returns to the heart and gills again.

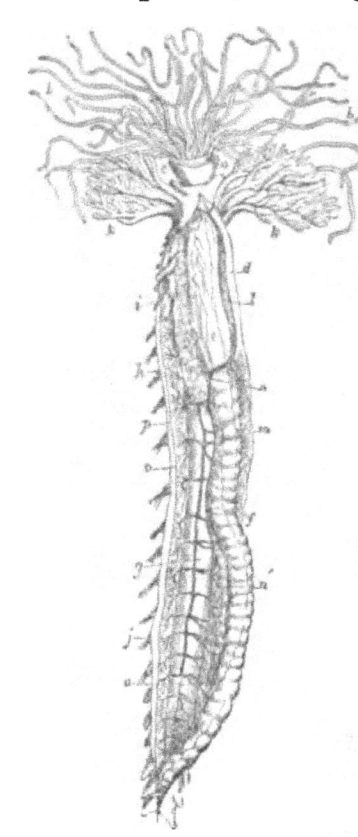

Fig. 133.   Terebella conchilega.—*a*, lip, surrounded by tentacles, *b b*, all placed upon the first segment of the body, *c* ; the skin of the back, *d*, is laid open, exposing the circulatory system ; *e*, pharynx ; *f*, intestine ; *g*. muscles of the belly ; *h*, gland, supposed to be the liver ; *i*, generative organs ; *j*, feet ; *k k*, gills ; *l*, heart ; *m*, dorso-intestinal vessel ; *n*, intestinal vessel ; *n*, venous sinus ; *o o*, ventral trunk, branching into smaller veins, *p*.

The slender filaments which radiate from the head of the tubicular worms are flattened, sometimes tortuous, always ciliated, and are often barred and variegated by bright purple, green, and yellow tints, forming a rich and gorgeous crown.

The mucus, which cements together the particles of sand and shell for the artificial tubes of this kind of worms, is believed to be secreted from glands in the first segment of the body; but the long slender filaments of the head are the active agents in the structure. The tentacles are hollow bands with strong muscular edges, which the worm can bring together so as to form a cylinder, at any point of which it can take up a particle of sand, or a whole row of particles, and apply them to its glutinous body. The fibres at the free ends of the tentacles act both as muscular and suctorial organs; for when the worm is going to seize a particle of sand or food, the extremity of the tentacle is drawn in by the reflux of the colourless liquid in its interior, so that a cup-shaped cavity is formed in which the particle is secured by atmospheric pressure, aided by the power of the circular muscular fibres at the extremity of the tentacle.

The Serpula and its allies are richly-coloured worms, living in contorted tubes with lids, frequently seen

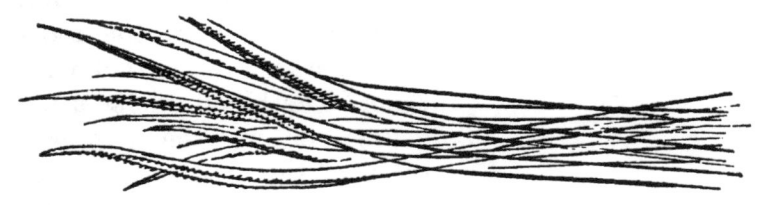

Fig. 134. Pushing poles of Serpula.

encrusting rocks, the shells of oysters, and other mollusca. By a peculiar mechanism of their bristly feet they can open the lid of their tube, push out their fan of gorgeous tentacles, pull it in again, and shut up the tube. As the protrusion of the worm from its tube is slow, cautious, and gradual, the retreat swift and sudden as lightning, there are two distinct sets of organs in the feet by which these motions are performed.[6]

---

[6] Dr. Thomas Williams on 'British Annelides,' British Association, 1852.

On the back of the worm there is a sort of shield, the sides of which bear seven pairs of wart-like feet, which are perforated for the working of protrusile microscopic bristles (fig. 134). Their upper parts are double-edged, with a groove between them, and serrated with close-set teeth. The organs of retreat are much more complicated and numerous. Mr. Gosse has computed that there are about 1,900 blades on the seven pairs of feet, each movable at the will of the worm, and that there are nearly 10,000 teeth hooked into the lining of the tube when it wishes to retreat. The manner in which it comes out of its tube and retires into it again is the same as that employed by the earth-worm.

There are twenty-four genera of the order Errantia, or wandering sea-worms. Multitudes swarm on every coast; they have considerable muscular strength, and are highly irritable; some are called sea-centipedes, from the number of their feet and length of their segmented bodies, which are slender, and vary from a few inches or less to thirty-five or forty feet. They are generally coiled up under stones, or wander by the slipperiness of their smooth skins through masses of sea-weeds or shells at low tide. In most of them the rings are decidedly marked; the first and last segments are unlike, while the rest are mere repetitions one of another. Their locomotive organs are a pair of perforated fleshy warts on each of their numerous segments, through which groups of rigid, simple or barbed bristles are protruded and retracted.

The Errant Worms have a distinct small head with a mouth, or rather an orifice, on the upper side of it, through which a cylindrical gullet is from time to time turned inside out, forming a kind of pear-shaped bag, whose surface is studded with secreting glands; and its extremity, which is perforated, is surrounded by a muscle that contracts strongly on whatever it is applied to, and holds it firmly while the re-inversion of the sac draws it into the body to be digested. This apparatus is unarmed in the genera Arenicola, Phyllodoce, and others, but in the Nereis it has one pair of strong curved horny jaws. In the Eunice there are three toothed jaws on one side and four jaws on the other side of the gullet, each pair having a different form, and the tiny Lombrinereis has eight little black hooks which are seen through its pellucid tissues, snapping like so many pairs of hooked scissors. The Errant Worms are voraciously carnivorous, and when the gullet is turned inside out the toothed jaws project, seize the prey, and drag it into a ciliated alimentary canal, for there is no proper stomach in these worms. The canal is generally straight, and terminates in a vent at the posterior end of the body.

The respiratory organs of the Errantia are external gills of great variety of forms: they are chiefly like branching trees, or filamentary bushes, traversed by capillary bloodvessels. They are sometimes small, and arranged on every segment along both sides of the back; sometimes they are large and fixed only at intervals. Like the lower Annelids, they have two liquid systems, one red and the other colourless, and the circulation of the blood is the same; but as the pulsations of the vessel behind the head are too feeble to send the blood through the labyrinth of capillary vessels in these long worms, there is a supplementary heart, or pulsating vessel, in each segment of the worm, which partakes in and facilitates the general circulation.

The Eunice and other very long worms may have hundreds of these centres of propulsion, which make the circulation rapid; and it is increased by the restlessness and activity of the worms themselves, which bring their gills perpetually into new strata of water.

The nervous system of the Errantia consists of a

double cord extending along the ventral side of the body, and united at equal intervals by double nerve-centres, as in fig. 131; but in the Annelids the two cords diverge below the gullet, surround it, unite again above that tube, and form a principal bilobed nerve-centre or brain. Each segment of the worm is occupied by a small double nerve-centre. In some of these marine worms there are hundreds of segments and as many nerve-centres. There are more than a thousand of these pairs of nerve-centres on the ventral cord of the Nemertes gigas, or Great Band Worm, which is sometimes forty feet long and an inch broad. The head is like a snake, and the bristled feet are jointed to enable it to move over hard surfaces.

The movements of the bristly feet of the Errantia are reflex, depending on the nerve-centres in their segments; but they are controlled and connected by the double cord which passes through them.

Every hair, cirrus, and tentacle on the bodies of the Errant Worms is a living organ of feeling, shrinking at the smallest touch, but enabling them to select their food, to move towards and retreat from objects, and to thread their way through the most intricate labyrinths with unerring certainty, which seems to render them independent of eyes; yet many of them have multitudes of eyes, or rather eye-specks, according to the genera. Some have but one eye-speck placed in the forehead; one genus has a double row throughout their whole length, two in each segment, while the Amphicora has two in its tail. All these eye-specks have their crystalline lens, pigment-layer, and nerve-bulb, so that the Errant Worms must see objects, and their motions show that they do; but we can form no idea of the kind of vision.

Besides the variety of organs on the skin of the Errantia, some of these worms have two rows of flat plates on their backs overlapping each other at their

edges like the scales of a fish. They are well developed
in the Aphrodita hystrix, or the Sea Mouse of fishermen, and its congeners. That Annelid, which is an
inhabitant of European coasts, is thicker and broader
than other sea-worms. The two rows of overlapping
shields on its back, and the quantity of iridescent
hairs, cirri, and other appendages covering the body,
is so great as to form a kind of felt or fur like the
skin of a mouse. The members of this genus of sea-
worms have no gills properly so called; the only external sign of respiration is a periodical elevation and
depression of the shields on their backs by the action
of a complex system of muscles. The thick covering of
felt on the body of the worm below the shields becomes
filled with water during their elevation, which is ejected
forcibly at the posterior end of the body during their depression. Although the water does not penetrate the
thin skin on the back of the worm, its oxygen does, and
is accumulated in the colourless liquid in which the
stomach floats; and from it the blood, which is of a pale
yellow colour, receives its oxygen. The feet of the worm
are fan-shaped groups of sharp glassy bristles enclosed
between two plates, which prevent them from hurting the
animal when it puts them out or draws them in. The
Aphrodita is male and female : the eggs escape through
pores in the female, and are received in a kind of pouch
beneath the dorsal shields till hatched. The embryo
is an oval locomotive mass, with groups of cilia, and
indications of an eye-speck: after swimming about for
twenty-four hours, the segments begin to be developed.

Worms of the genus Polynoë have also two rows of
shields on their backs, but they are studded with transparent oval bodies on short stems, supposed to be
organs of touch. The filiform tentacles and antennæ
that are developed between the shields, as well as the
cirri or curly bristles of the feet, are likewise covered

with similar sensitive organs. Fig. 135 shows the foot, cirri, and bristles of a Polynoë, which are enclosed in plates which preserve them from hurting the worm. These glassy bristles are beautiful objects under the microscope; still more so are the jointed feet, transparent as the purest flint glass, of the Phyllodoce viridis, one of the most beautiful Annelids on our coasts, where it threads

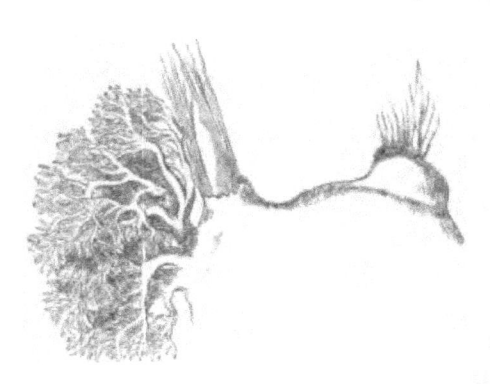

Fig. 135. Foot of a Polynoë.

its way among young mollusca like a slender green cord, exhibiting foliaceous gills in the highest perfection.

In the marine Annelids the embryo, on leaving the egg, is a gelatinous globular mass of cells furnished with strong cilia. In a few hours the mass elongates and divides into four parts, a head, a large ciliated segment, a smaller one without cilia, and a ciliated tail. After a time a succession of new segments are interposed, one by one, next to the tail segment, and the corresponding internal organs of each are developed till the worm arrives at its adult state. In many Annelids the embryo is highly developed within the parent; that of the Eunice has from 100 to 120 segments before it leaves her; and in the Nereis diversicolor the young, covered with cilia, come out by hundreds at an orifice in the side of the mother.

Many of the marine Annelids are luminous; electric scintillations are given out during the act of nervous contraction, which are increased in brilliancy and rapidity by irritation.

According to Professeur Quatrefages, the Annelida

Errantia and Tubicola have no zoological regions characterized by one or more special types like the other classes of animals; they have representatives in all seas. But it is exactly the contrary with regard to species. The number of species common to any two seas, or the shores of two continents, is very small; there is not a single species common to the Atlantic coasts of France and the Mediterranean. The sea-worms are not affected by climate, but they are said to be more abundant on granitic and schistose coasts than on the calcareous.[7]

With regard to fossil remains, worm-tracks are seen in the Forest marble, long calcareous tubes occur in the Upper Silurian and Carboniferous strata, and in all the later formations tubercular Annelids abound, especially of the genera Serpula, Spirorbis, and Vermilia.[8]

Tardigrada.

The Tardigrades are slow creeping animalcules, which seem to form a link between the Worms and the Rotifers, though they are more nearly allied to the former in having a vermiform body divided transversely into five segments, the first of which is the head, and each of the others has a pair of little fleshy protuberances furnished with four curled hooks. They resemble the Rotifers in their jaws, in their general grade of organization, and in the extreme length of time they can remain dried up without loss of life. When in the dried state they can be heated to a temperature of 250° Fahr. without the destruction of life, although when in full activity they cannot endure a temperature of more than from 112° to 115° Fahr. When alive the transparency of their skin is such as to show a complicated muscular system, the fibre of which is smooth; and as no respiratory organs

---

[7] 'Comptes rendus,' July 1864.
[8] 'Palæontology,' by Professor Owen.

have yet been found, their respiration must be cutaneous. These animalcules have no nerve-centre in the head, but they have one in each segment of the body ; and they are furnished with a suctorial mouth at the end of a retractile proboscis, on each side of which are two tooth-like styles, the rudiments of lateral jaws. The structure of these creatures is microscopic.

Rotifera.

Although the Rotifera are microscopic objects, their organization is higher than that of the Annelida in some respects. They are minute animalcules, which appear in vegetable infusions and in sea-water, but by far the greater number are found in fresh-water pools long exposed to the air: occasionally they appear in enormous numbers in cisterns which have neither shelter nor cover ; a few can live in moist earth, and sometimes individuals are seen in the large cells of the Sphagnum or Bog-Moss.

The bodies of the Rotifers have no cilia; they are perfectly transparent, elongated, or vermiform, but not segmented; they have two coats, both of which in some genera are so soft and flexible that the animal can assume a variety of forms; while in others the external coat is a gelatinous horny cylindrical shell or tunic enclosing the whole body except the two extremities, which the animal can protrude or draw in. The soft kind can crawl over solid surfaces by the alternate contraction and extension of their bodies like a worm, and the stiff Rotifers are capable of doing the same by the contractility of their head and tail. All can swim by means of cilia or lobes at their head. The greater number possess means of attaching themselves to objects by the posterior end of their bodies and of removing to another place.

The wheel-like organs from which the class has its

name, are most characteristic in the common Rotifer (fig. 137), where they consist of two disk-like lobes projecting from the body whose margins are fringed with long cilia. It is the uninterrupted succession of strokes given by these cilia, passing consecutively like waves along the lobes, and apparently returning into themselves, which gives the impression of two wheels in rapid rotation round their axes.

The Brachionus pala (fig. 136) affords another instance of the two-wheeled Rotifers. Though of unusually large dimensions in its class, it is just visible to the naked eye as a brilliant particle of diamond when moving in a glass of water. Its transparent horny tunic, when viewed in front with a microscope, is a cup of elegant form, bulging at the sides. One side of the rim is furnished with four spines, of which the middle pair are slender and sharp as needles, with a deep cleft between them; the other side of the rim is undulated but not toothed, and the bottom of the cup ends in two broad blunt points.

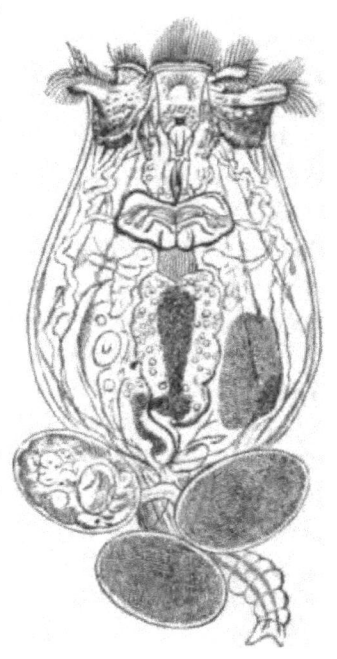

Between the terminal blunt points there is a round opening for the protrusion of the foot of the animal. The tunic is of glassy transparency, so that every organ and function of the animal can be traced with perfect distinctness.

Fig. 136. Brachionus pala, with three eggs attached to its foot.

The foot of the animal is long, rough and wrinkled, not unlike the flexible trunk of an elephant. It can be lengthened, shortened, drawn within, or pushed out of the tunic in an instant. It terminates in two short conical fingers or toes, which can be widely separated or brought into contact. By means of these, the Brachion has the power of mooring itself even to the smooth surface of glass so firmly, that it can stretch itself in all directions, shaking itself to and fro with sudden violence without letting go its hold. The Rotifers usually fix themselves before they set their wheels in motion in search of food.

From the anterior rim of the shelly cup, the Brachion protrudes a waved outline of limpid flesh which, as soon as it rises above the level of the sharp-pointed spines, spreads out into three broad flattish muscular lobes. On the edges of the middle one there are very strong cilia like stiff bristles, which do not vibrate, but are either erect or converge to a point, whereas the edges of the other two lobes are thickly fringed with long stout cilia, which, by striking the water in perpetual rapid succession, each cilium bending and rising again, produce the appearance of two circles of dark spots in rapid horizontal rotation, like wheels on their axis. It is merely an optical deception, for both the animal and its lobes may be at rest. The vibrations of the cilia can be instantaneously arrested, and the whole apparatus drawn out of sight, and as instantaneously protruded and set in motion.

In the flesh, on the ventral side of the Brachion, there is a deep cleft, the edges of which as well as the whole interior of a tube of which it is the orifice, are thickly covered with vibratile cilia. This tube leads to a mouth with powerful jaws of unwonted structure, which is so deeply sunk in the tissues of the body, that it never comes into contact with the water. It opens into a gullet leading to a stomach, intestine, and vent, at the posterior end of the body.

The vibrations of the cilia on the lobes of the animal's

head form two circular currents in the water, like whirlpools, which draw all floating particles into their vortices, and the streams from the two whirlpools uniting into one current, flow off horizontally and pass immediately over the slit on the ventral side of the animal. Some of the floating particles are arrested by the cilia on the edges of the slit, and are drawn into the sunken mouth by the vibrations of the cilia in the tube. The edges of the slit act like lips, and seem to possess the sense of taste, or of some modification of touch, which enables them to select from the particles presented to them, such as are fit for food; these are admitted into the mouth, where they are bruised by the powerful jaws. The mouth or masticating apparatus is the most extraordinary and complex part of this animal. It consists of two horny toothed jaws, acting like hammers upon an anvil. The two hammers, which approach each other from the dorsal sides of the body, are each formed of two parts united by a hinge; the first parts correspond to the handles; the second parts, which are bent at right angles to the first, resemble hands with five or six finger-shaped teeth united by a thin membrane. The teeth are parallel to one another when they meet on the anvil, and are seen through the transparent mass tearing the food into fragments. Some of the Rotifers resemble the Errant Annelids in being able to turn this complicated machine inside-out through the ciliated tube and slit, so as to bring it into contact with the water. When the food has been masticated it is sent into the stomach, where it is digested. The whole of this process is seen through the transparent and colourless body of the Brachion, because its favourite food is the Syncryn velox, a minute bright green plant, which from its active motions was at one time believed to be an animal.

The Brachion has four longitudinal muscular bands

transversely striated, which move the ciliated lobes of the head, push them out and draw them in. From these muscular threads are sent to the different parts of the body, to the mouth especially, two strong bands, which bend and unbend the joints of the hammer-like jaws. The vigorous motions of the long serpentine foot and the firm hold of its anchors are owing to muscular bands fixed high up on the interior wall of the body, which extend throughout the whole length of the flexible organ. As long as the Brachion is fixed, the vibrations of the cilia on its lobes only produce whirl-pools in the water, but the moment that it lets go its hold, these vibrations, in consequence of the reaction of the water, give the animal both a smooth progressive motion and a rotation round its axis.

Minute as the Brachionus pala is, it has several organs of sense. A sparkling, ruby-coloured, square eye-speck with a crystalline lens and crimson pigment layer is placed on a wart-like prominence on its back, and this prominence Mr. Gosse believes to be the brain of the animal. In the cleft between the spines and close to the eye-speck are two tubes, one within the other. The innermost tube, which can be protruded and withdrawn, has a bunch of bristles at its extremity that have the sensibility of antennæ. Nerves from the brain pass into these, to the various organs of the body, and to the lobes on the head.

The Brachion has no propelling vessel or heart to maintain the circulation of its liquids, but, like the Annelids, a colourless liquid occupies the general cavity between the alimentary canal and the internal wall of the body. It is believed to be connected with nutrition, and is furnished with oxygen by a complicated organism, and is kept in motion by the vibrations of long cilia. The determination of the whole structure and motions of a creature barely visible to the naked eye, is a won-

derful instance of microscopic research, and of the perfection of the mechanism exhibited in the most minute
objects of creation.

Fig. 137 represents the common Rotifer when its
wheels are expanded and when they are retracted. The
body is slender and flexible,
it is stretched out by longitudinal muscles, and its girth
is diminished by circular
ones. The internal struc-
ture is similar to that of
the Brachion, but there is a
prominence or head between
the wheels on which there
are two crimson eye-specks,
and the foot terminates in
three concentric movable
tubes that can be protruded
and drawn in like the tubes
of a telescope ; each has a
pair of claspers to enable
the Rotifer to fix itself to
any object.

The Rotifers are male and
female, but, like the greater
number of Infusoria, the
males are only produced at
intervals. The female Rotifers have their perfect form
when they leave the egg :
they even come out of the

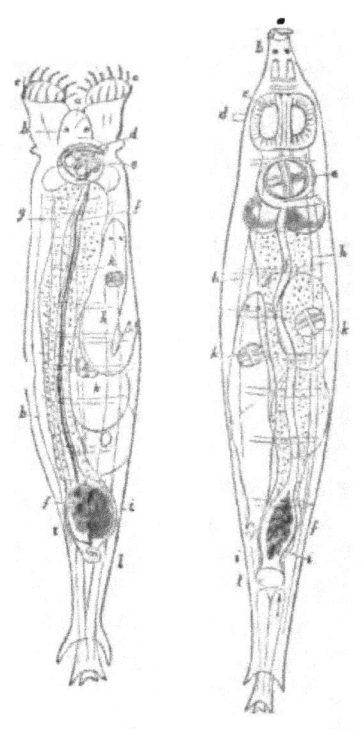

Fig. 137. Common Rotifer:—*a*, mouth ;
b, eye-spots ; *c*, wheels ; *d*, probably
antenna ; *e*, jaws and teeth ; *f*, alimentary canal ; *g*, glandular mass
enclosing it ; *h*, longitudinal muscles ;
i i, tubes of water-vascular system ;
k, young animal ; *l*, cloaca.

egg while it is attached to the tail of the mother, as
in the Brachionus pala (fig. 136). The males, when
hatched, have neither spines nor mouth, yet, during
their short lives, their motions are very fleet on account
of the vibrations of long cilia round their front.

Some Rotifers are remarkably fertile. Professor Ehrenberg estimated that, in the course of twenty-four days, the offspring of a single individual of the genus Hydatina might amount to seventeen millions. Female eggs laid in autumn are collected in heaps and covered with a gelatinous substance, which protects them from the cold in winter, though the Rotifers themselves are sufficiently protected by their great tenacity of life. They revive after being frozen; they may be dried for an unlimited time, but, as soon as they meet with warmth, moisture, and food, they resume their vitality.

SECTION VI.

ECHINODERMATA.

THIS class consists of five orders, all of which are marine. They are, with one exception, creeping animals, and the whole class is remarkable for having most of their members and general structure either in fives or multiples of five. Their skin is hardened by calcareous deposits, sometimes of beautiful microscopic structure: they have a digestive cavity, a vascular fluid system, and some distinct respiratory organs, so that they are comparatively of a high grade.

Echinodermata Asteroïdea.

The Asteroïdea, or Star-Fishes, which are the highest order, form two natural families, the Stelleridæ and Ophiuridæ, which comprise twenty-two genera.

The simplest form of the Stelleridæ is the common star-fish, with its flat regularly five-sided disk. A tough membrane, strengthened by reticulated calcareous matter, covers the back, and bends down along the sides, while the under-side of the body or disk, on which the animal creeps, is soft and leathery, with the mouth in its centre. In the other genera, although the body is still a flat, five, equal-sided disk, the angles are extended into long arms, broad whence they diverge from the disk, but decreasing rapidly in width to their extremities, so that the animal is exactly like a star with five long, equal, and flexible rays.

The backs of all the star-fishes are covered with most minute movable spines, and with microscopic organs like minute pincers, called pedicellariæ, which are diffused generally over the surface, and form dense groups round the spines. They have a slender, contractile, calcareous stem, and a head formed of two blades, which they continually open and shut, the whole being coated with a soft external tissue. They grasp anything very firmly, and are supposed to be used to free the star-fish from parasites. In some species of Goniaster the pedicellariæ resemble the vane of an arrow, and are so numerous as to give a villous appearance to the skin of the back.

On the under-side of each ray of a star-fish, a central groove or furrow extends throughout its whole length, and the semi-calcareous flexible membrane which covers the back and rays not only bends down round the sides of the rays, but borders both edges of the grooves. Upon these edges ridges of small calcareous plates beset with spines are placed transversely: they are larger near the mouth, and gradually decrease in size as they approach the point of the ray.

Interior to the spines, these ridges are pierced by alternate rows of minute holes for the long rows of feet, which diminish in size to the end of the ray. The feet are contractile muscular tubes communicating through the holes with internal muscular sacs, which are regarded as their bases. The sacs are full of a liquid, and when the animal compresses them the liquid is forced through the holes into the tubular feet, and stretches them out; and when the muscular walls of the hollow feet are contracted, the liquid is forced back again into the sacs, and the feet are drawn in. The liquid is furnished by a circle of small vascular tentacles, or sacs, surrounding the mouth, which are both locomotive and prehensile. From these a canal extends through the centre of each ray, which in its course sends off lateral branches to the bases of the feet to supply them with liquid. The whole of this system of vessels and feet are lined with vibratile cilia, which maintain a perpetual circulation in the liquid.

The toothless mouth on the under-side of the disk dilates so as to admit large mollusca with their shells. The short gullet and stomach are everted, protruded through the mouth, and applied round the object to be swallowed, which is then drawn in, digested, and the shell is discharged by the mouth. However, in three orders of this family there is a short intestine and vent. From the large stomach, which occupies the central part of the disk of the star-fish, a couple of tubes extend to the extremity of each ray, where they secrete a substance essential for digestion: the stomach is in fact a radiating organ, partaking the form of the animal it sustains.

A pulsatory vessel near the gullet propels the yellow blood into a system of fine tubes, that are spread over the walls of the stomach and its rays. Through these walls the blood receives a nutritious liquid, which it carries with it into a network of capillary vessels, widely extended throughout the body, being propelled by the contractile powers of the vessels themselves, and after having supplied the tissues with nourishment, it is carried by tubes to the point from whence it started, to begin a new course. The capillary network passes immediately under a portion of the skin of the star-fish, through which an exchange of the respiratory gases takes place. Besides, the star-fishes breathe the sea-water through numerous conical tubes, that project in patches from the back. Through these tubes, which can be opened and shut, the water is readily admitted into the cavity containing the digestive organs, with which they are in communication. The star-fish slowly distends itself with water, and then gives out a portion of it, but at no regular time. The cavity is never empty of water, and as its lining is densely bristled with cilia, their vibrations keep the vascular surface of the digestive organs perpetually bathed with the respiratory medium.

The star-fishes have a radiating system of nerves suited to their form. A ring of slender nerve-cords surrounds the mouth, from whence three nerves are sent off at the commencement of each ray: two of these, which are filaments, go to the organs in the central disk, while the middle one, which is a great trunk, passes through the centre of the rays, and terminates in a nerve-centre, or ganglion, placed under a coloured eye-speck at their extremity. The structure of the rays, the eye-specks, and the nerve-centres below them, are so similar, that they are merely repetitions of one another; hence no nerve-centre can control the others, but they are all connected by the ring encircling the mouth, which is a common bond of communication. How far the movements of these animals indicate sensation we have not the power to determine, but they feel acutely, for the mouth, the feet, and especially the pedicellariæ, are highly sensitive, and shrink on the least touch. The eye-specks are probably sensitive to light, and as the star-fishes often feed on putrid matter, they are supposed to be endowed with the sense of smell.

The family of the Ophiuridæ, or Snake Stars, are widely distributed in the ocean. The genus Euryales with branching rays, and that of Ophiura with simple rays, comprising the Brittle and Sand Stars, are abundant in the British seas. In the sand stars there are cavities full of sand at the points from whence the rays diverge, which appear like warts on the surface of the disk.

Their rays are exceedingly long, thin, and flexible; they have no central groove nor feet, but they are employed as organs of locomotion and prehension, for by their alternate strokes the sand stars can elevate or depress themselves in the water, creep on the bottom, and by twisting them round objects they can fix themselves, firmly aided by spines or bristles on their edges. The Ophionyx has the addition of movable hooks beneath bristled spines. The rays are bent by the contraction of internal muscles, and extended again by the elasticity of the external leathery coat. The Ophiuridæ, like the Luidia fragilissima belonging to the preceding order, cast off a ray if touched, and even all the five if rudely handled; but they can replace them with as much ease. If only a fragment of a disk remains attached to a ray the whole animal may be reproduced.

The Ophiuridæ have an internal calcareous skeleton or framework, in the form of spicules, scattered in their tissues. They have a capacious mouth with tentacles and ten small chisel-shaped teeth, five on each side, which meet and close the mouth. The mouth is separated from the stomach by a circular muscle that opens and shuts the passage, but no canal diverges from the stomach through the rays. The nervous system and the circulation of the blood are similar to those in the Stelleridæ; and respiratory organs, in the form of from two to four plates, or lamellæ, project from each of the spaces between the bases of the rays into the central cavity, by which sea-water has free access to bathe the digestive organs and aërate the blood.

The colour of the star-fishes, as well as of other marine invertebrate animals, seems to be independent of light. The Ophiuridæ that had been living at a depth of 1,260 fathoms in the North Atlantic were coloured, though not a ray of light could reach their dark home, and those dredged up from 100 to 300 fathoms on the coast of Norway were of brilliant hues—red, vermilion, white, and yellow. In general, both plants and animals of the lower kinds become of a sickly white when kept in darkness.

The Stelleridæ are male and female, and form fertilized eggs of an orange or red colour. These eggs are first converted into a mass of cells and then into larvæ, not radiating symmetrically like their parents, but of a bilateral form, the two sides being perfectly alike and bordered by a ciliated fringe nearly throughout their whole length. These two fringes are united by a superior and inferior transverse ciliated band, and between the two the mouth is placed. A stomach, intestine, and vent are formed; the creatures can provide for themselves, and swim about as independent zooids. A young starfish is gradually developed by a succession of internal growths, part of the original zooid is retained, and the rest is either thrown off or absorbed; then the starfishes having lost the power of swimming, crawl slowly away and acquire their full size. There is great diversity in the external form of the zooids of the different genera, as well as in the portion of them retained in the adult star-fish.

Fossil star-fishes have a very wide range. They are found among the earliest Silurian organic forms, but they scarcely bear any resemblance to existing genera. The Ophiuridæ, fished up from the bottom of the North Atlantic, come nearest to them. Five genera are found in the Oolitic formation, all extinct; three genera range from the Lias to the present seas; and five genera belonging to the Cretaceous period are represented by living species.

Echinodermata Crinoïdea.

The Crinoid Echinoderms, or Stone-Lilies, are like a tulip or lily on an upright stem, which is firmly fixed to a substance at the bottom of the sea. During the Jurassic period, miniature forests of these beautiful animals flourished on the surface of the Oolite strata, then under the ocean. Myriads of their fossil remains are entombed in the seas, and extensive strata of marble are chiefly composed of them. Their hollow joints are known in several parts of England as wheel stones, and as St. Cuthbert's beads on the Northumbrian coast, in honour of the patron saint of Holy Island, where they abound. The Crinoïdea are of two kinds : the Encrinites, which chiefly flourished in the Palæozoic period and are now represented by a minute species (Rhizocrinus Lofotensis) lately discovered on the coast of Norway by Professor Sars, have a smooth, cylindrical, jointed stem ; and the Pentacrinites, which began at the Lias, and have a five-sided jointed stem, the present representative of which is the Pentacrinus caput-Medusæ, found in the West Indian seas.

The hollow, five-sided, calcareous, jointed stem of the living Pentacrinite is filled with a spongy substance, and supports a cup on its summit, containing the digestive organs, mouth, and tentacles of the animal. The cup is formed of a series of calcareous plates, and from its margin five long many-jointed rays diverge, each of which is divided into two-jointed branches. Groups of curled filaments, called cirri, are placed at regular distances from the bottom of the stem to the extremity of the rays, while, on the opposite side of the rays, there are groups of feathery objects called pinnæ at each joint. Food is caught by the tentacles and digested by the stomach and viscera at the bottom of the cup, from whence vessels diverge through a system of canals in the axes of the rays, pinnæ, and down the stem, all of which convey sea-water mixed with nutritious liquid, for the nourishment of the animal.

The genus Comatula are star-fishes, believed to have

alternately a fixed and a free state.   Mr. J. V. Thomson
discovered that the Pentacrinus Europæus is merely the
fixed state of a Comatula.   These star-fishes have pairs
of pinnæ placed at regular distances along their long-
jointed rays, and in the pinnæ sacs containing eggs are
placed as far as the fifteenth or twentieth pair.   The
eggs yield active ciliated larvæ, which attach themselves
in the form of flat oval disks to corallines and sea-weeds.
By degrees they develop a stem, about three-fourths of
an inch high, with twenty-four distinct joints.   Its expanded top bears five sulphur-coloured bifurcating rays
with their pinnæ and dorsal cirri.   A mouth is formed
in the centre with its tentacles, and a lateral prominent
vent.   The actual change of a Pentacrine into a Comatula has not been seen, but as the small Pentacrinites
disappear in September, at which season the Comatulæ
appear, it is believed that when full grown the top of
the fixed Pentacrinite falls off and becomes a Comatula,
which swims backwards with great activity by striking
the water alternately with its long rays.   The Pentacrinus caput-Medusæ, which is fixed by its stem to sea-
weeds and zoophytes, forms a most beautiful object for
the lower magnifying powers when viewed in a fluid by
a strong refracting light.

Echinodermata Echinoïdea.

The family of Echinidæ, commonly known as Sea-Eggs
or Sea-Urchins, have a beautiful but complicated structure.   The calcareous shell of an Echinus is a hollow
spheroid with large circular openings at each pole.   In
the larger of the two, called the corona, the mouth of the
animal is situated; in the lesser circle the vent is placed.
The spheroid itself is formed of ten bands extending in a
meridional direction from the corona to the lower ring;
that is, from one polar circle to the other.   Each band
consists of a double row of pentagonal plates increasing

in size from the poles to the equator, nicely dovetailed into one another, and the bands are neatly joined by a zigzag seam. Every alternate band is perforated by a double series of minute double holes for the passage of the tubular feet of the animal. The five perforated or ambulacral bands have rows of tubercules parallel to the series of feet holes, supporting spines movable in every direction. The five imperforated bands are characterized by a greater number of spines, but there are none within the polar circles. The spines may be long rods, or merely prickles, or stout, club-shaped bodies, according to the genera.

The microscopic structure of the shell of the Echinus is everywhere the same; it is composed of a network of carbonate of lime, with a very small quantity of animal matter as a basis. In general, the network extends in layers united by perpendicular pillars, but so arranged that the open spaces, or meshes, in one layer correspond to the solid structure in the next.

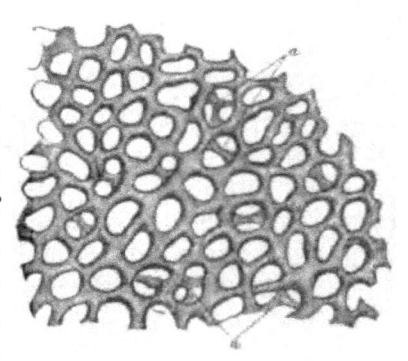

Fig. 138. Section of Shell of Echinus. *a*, portions of a deeper layer.

The spheroid of the Echinus is covered with spines, and both outside and inside by a contractile and extensile transparent membrane, which supports the shelly plates at the poles, and dips between the bands but does not penetrate them. Its extensile nature admits of the addition of calcareous matter to the edges of the plates when the animal is increasing in size. The membrane lining the interior of the shelly globe is tough; it encloses the digestive organs, and forms a muscular lip to the mouth, which is armed with five triangular, sharp-pointed, white teeth, and surrounded by five pairs of pinnate tubular tentacles. The outer margin of the lip is fringed with a circle of snake-headed pedicellariæ visible to the naked eye.

The five teeth, whose sharp tips meet in a point when closed, are triangular prisms, the inner edge is sharp and fit for cutting. Each tooth is planted upon a larger triangular socket, two sides of which are transversely grooved like a file, and as these two sides are in close contact with the sides of the opposite socket, the food when cut by the small teeth is ground down by the sockets, and a salivary secretion finishes the mastication. The sockets of the teeth are connected by ten additional solid pieces, placed two and two between them, which completes the pyramidal apparatus called Aristotle's lantern; it consists of forty solid calcareous pieces arranged in fives, and moved by forty muscles attached to five calcareous ridges, and five arches near the internal edge of the corona.

Five pairs of these muscles when acting together protrude and retract the teeth; when acting separately they draw them to one side or to the other; five pairs separate the five teeth, five pairs shut them, and the remaining five pairs work the bruising machine. The masticated food passes through a short gullet into the stomach, where it is digested, and the indigestible part is carried by an intestine to the vent in the smaller polar circle.

The smaller polar circle is formed of ten triangular plates, five are attached to the bands containing the feet holes, and five to the intermediate bands. The last five are perforated, and are the reproductive plates: the other five are also perforated for the discharge of the liquid that moves the tubular feet, and which, after having circulated in the body, is no longer of use. In five of these polar plates there are red specks, the rudiments of eyes, the only organs of sense these creatures seem to possess except that of touch and probably smell. The nervous system is a slender, equal-sided pentagon round the gullet, from the sides of which five nerves are sent to the muscles of the mouth, and others, extending along the ambulacral or feet bands, end in nerve-centres under the eye-specks.

Fig. 139. Sucker-plate of Sea-Egg.

The mechanism for extending and retracting the feet by a liquid, is the same with that in the star-fishes, but the pores which admit the liquid into the feet are double. The tubular feet swell at their extremity into a fleshy sucker, within which there is a thin glassy reticulated rosette (fig. 139), of which fig. 140 is a highly magnified segment. It is perforated in the centre by a large round opening. The sea-urchins can stretch their feet beyond the spines, and by means of the suckers they can attach themselves even to smooth objects, or

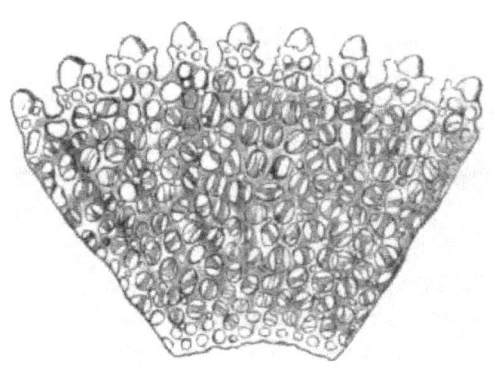

Fig. 140. Section of a sucker-plate.

aided and directed by their spines they roll themselves along with a rotatory motion head downwards.

The circulation of the bright yellow blood is like that of the star-fishes. It is aërated both internally and externally. The external respiratory organs are short, branched, and highly vibratile bodies attached in pairs to the oval extremities of the fine imperforated bands.

There are pedicellariæ scattered among the spines of the sea-urchins which are in constant motion, protruding themselves beyond the spines and withdrawing again, snapping their pincers, and grasping firmly anything that comes within their reach, or that is presented to them. The pedicellariæ vary much in form and position in the different genera of the Echinidæ; but they invariably consist of a long, slender, calcareous stem, and generally tripartite head, the whole coated with a gelatinous fibrous transparent substance. The head of the Pedicellaria globosa is a formidable weapon; at the apex of each of its three serrated and toothed blades there is a strong sharp spine directed horizontally inwards, so that the three spines cross each other when the blades close, which they do so energetically that nothing could escape from such a grasp. The pedicellariæ are curious microscopic objects; they are extremely irritable, and although their use is unknown, they must be essential to the well-being of the animals, since hundreds are scattered over their shells.

The spines of the Echinidæ vary in shape and structure in the different genera and species. Those of the Scutella form merely a velvety pile. On the common sea urchin the spines are simple, and shed twice in the year; those on the Amphidetus are both club and spoonshaped; and, on the Cidaris, they are large formidable clubs moved by a ball and socket. All the spines, whatever their form may be, are moved in that manner; for there are little tubercules on the surface of the shell on which a cup at the bottom of the spines is pressed down by the muscular skin which covers the shell and spines, and by its contractile power it enables the animal to move the spines in any direction.

The microscopic structure of the calcareous spines is often beautifully symmetrical. Those of the Acrocladia mamillata consist of concentric alternate layers of network and sheaths of pillars; so that a section of the spine perpendicular to its axis exhibits a succession of concentric rings like those of an exogenous tree. The cup at the bottom of the spine is very dense network, and the last of a sheath of encircling pillars form the ribs, sometimes seen on the exterior of the spines.

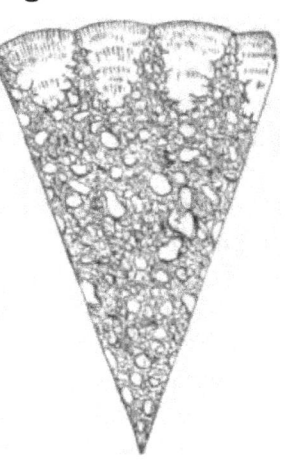

The spines of the Echinus miliaris, of which fig. 141 represents the segment of a section highly magnified, are fluted columns of calcareous glass, the grooves of which are filled with solid glassy matter curved on the exterior. The innumerable hairlike objects attached to the shells of some of the Echinidæ, the

Fig. 141.   Spine of Echinus miliaris.

almost filamental spines of others, and the pedicellariæ themselves, are formed of a regularly reticulated substance. When the Echinidæ are stripped of their spines and all their appendages, their shells show 2,400 plates united with the symmetry of a tesselated pavement.

The Echinidæ are male and female, and the eggs are excluded through the five perforated productive plates at the posterior end of the shell. According to the observations of Prof. Fritz Müller the embryo, soon after issuing from the egg, takes a form represented (magnified) in fig. 142.

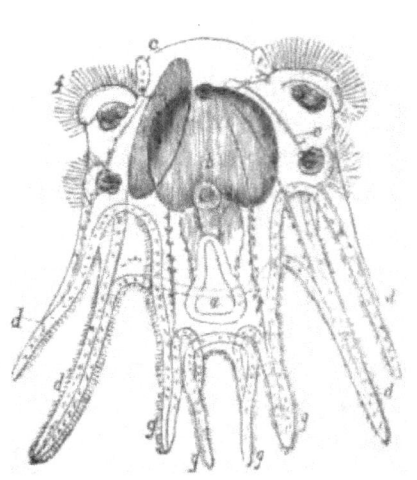

Fig. 142. Pluteus of the Echinus:—*a*, mouth; *b*, stomach; *c*, echinoid disk; *d d d d*, four arms of the pluteus-body; *e*, calcareous framework; *f*, ciliated lobes; *g g g g*, ciliated processes of the proboscis.

All parts of this creature, which is called a Pluteus, are strengthened by a framework of calcareous rods tipped with orange colour, all the rest being transparent and colourless. It swims freely, back foremost, by means of its cilia.

While in this active state a circular disk (*c*, fig. 142), covering the stomach (*b*, fig. 142), appears within it, which gradually expands, and sends through the skin of the Pluteus spines, pedicellariæ, and tubercules, ultimately developed into hollow feet. Then the feet are pushed out and drawn in, the pedicellariæ (D, fig. 143) snap their pincers; and while the half-formed Echinus is making these motions within the Pluteus, the mouth

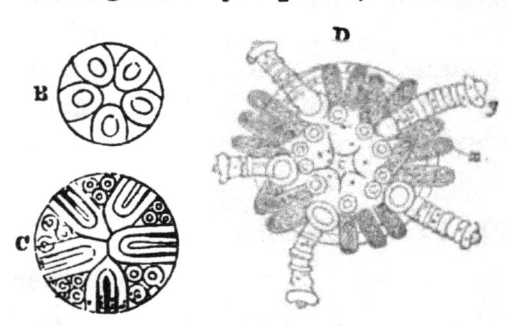

Fig. 143. Larvæ of Echinus in various stages of development within the Pluteus, which is not represented :—B, disk with the first indication of the cirrhi ; C, disk with the origin of the spines between the cirrhi ; D, more advanced disk with the cirrhi, *g*, and spines, *x*, projecting from the surface.

and gullet of the Pluteus itself are in constant activity; and, while it swims about, the unformed Echinus within it gets a globular shape, the shell is formed, and when the Echinus is complete, the rest of the Pluteus is thrown off, and the young animal rolls away.

The free swimming larval zooids of the Echinodermata are generally hyaline, and some are phosphorescent. The Pluteus is also the larval zooid of the ophiurid starfishes; they may be seen in great numbers on the surface of the sea in August and September. The young starfish is formed in them by a process analogous to that described. The motions of the Echinidæ are reflex; nothing indicates volition.

The fossil Echinidæ first appeared in the lower Ludlow limestone, and attained their maximum in the Cretaceous strata. A species of Diadema, with annulated hollow spines, common in the Chalk, still exists. Numerous species of the genus Clypeaster, remarkable for their flattened form, and known as lake urchins, are peculiar to the Tertiary strata and existing seas; and, lastly, five species of Spatangidæ, heart-shaped urchins, which lived in the Tertiary periods, still exist. In consequence of the porous texture of the solid calcareous parts of the Echinidæ, their fossil remains are commonly impregnated with pyrites or silex, without altering their organic structure, so that they exhibit a fracture like that of calcareous spar.

Echinodermata Holothuroïdea.

The Holothuridæ, or Sea-Cucumbers, are of a higher organization than the preceding Echinoderms. They are soft, worm-shaped, five-sided animals, covered by a flexible, leathery integument or skin, in which are imbedded a vast multitude of microscopic calcareous plates of reticulated structure. The mouth, which is placed at one end of the animal, is surrounded by ten bony plates forming a lantern, analogous to that of the Echinus; they support branching, tubular, and retractile tentacles, which encompass the mouth like a star. The tentacles are connected with sacs at their bases, and are extended and retracted by the injection of a watery liquid contained in them. Innumerable tubular, suctorial feet, precisely similar to those of the Echinus, are protruded and retracted through corresponding pores in the skin of the animal by a watery liquid, in sacs, at their bases. The water is supplied by a system of canals connected with an annular reservoir round the top of the gullet, which is supplied with water by a bottle-shaped bag at the mouth.

Besides transverse muscles, five pairs of muscles attached to the lantern at the mouth, extend throughout the whole length of the animal. Nerve-chords from the ring at the gullet accompany these, and such is the irritability of this muscular system, that the Holothuriæ eject their viscera when alarmed or caught; but they have the power of reproducing them: sometimes they divide their whole body into parts.

The respiratory organs are two very long and beautifully arborescent tubes veined with capillary blood-vessels. The circulation of the blood is similar to that of the star-fishes, but more complicated.

The minute calcareous particles scattered independently in the tough leathery skin of the Holothuridæ remain as fine dust when the flesh is dissolved and washed away; but, upon microscopic observation, Mr. Gosse found that the forms of these particles are remarkable for elegance, regularity, and variety of structure, but that the normal form is an ellipse of open work built up of five pieces of a highly refractive, transparent, glassy material, having the shape of dumb-bells.

The Holothuriæ found under stones at low spring tides, on the British coasts, are small; those dredged up from deep water are five or six inches long, and not unlike a well-grown warty cucumber; they do not form an article of food in Europe, but they are highly esteemed by the inhabitants of the Indian Archipelago and in China, where many shiploads of the trepang are imported annually. It is a species that swarms in the lagoons of the coral islands, the reefs of the coral seas, and at Madagascar. Some species are two feet long, and six or eight inches in circumference.

The order of the Holothuridæ form eggs like all the other Echinoderms; the larval zooid has the same form as that of the star-fishes, and changes its form twice, while the members of the Holothuria are forming within it; at last they combine with those of the zooid, and no part is cast off.

Echinodermata Synaptidæ.

The Synaptidæ are five-sided creatures, similar in structure to the Holothuriæ, though more worm-like. The whole order, which consists of the two genera of Synapta and Chirodota, have twelve calcareous plates round the mouth, five of which are perforated for the passage of the vascular water canals, which convey the liquid for the protrusion of the feet.

The calcareous particles imbedded in the skin of the genus Synapta are anchor-shaped spicules fixed to elliptical or oval plates, (fig. 144). The plates are reticulated and sometimes leaf-shaped, and the flukes of the anchors are either plain or barbed. All the anchors are fixed transversely to the length

Fig. 144. Skeleton of Synapta.

of the animal, lying with great regularity in the interspaces of the longitudinal muscular bands. Sometimes a thousand anchors are crowded into a square inch, each elegant in form, perfectly finished, and articulated to an anchor-plate, whose pattern as well as that of the anchor itself is characteristic of the species to which it belongs. In the Synapta digitata, which has four fingers and a small thumb on each of its twelve oval tentacles, the anchors are but just visible to the naked eye;[9] in all the other species they are microscopic. Besides the anchors, the skin of the genus Synapta contains innumerable smaller particles, 'miliary plates,' which are crowded over the muscular bands. The muscular system of the Synapta digitata is so irritable that, on being touched, it divides itself into a number of

---

[9] Messrs. Woodward and Barrett on the Synapta. Trans. of Zoological Society, London.

independent fragments, each of which keeps moving for a time, and ultimately becomes a perfect animal like its parent. Specimens of this Synapta have been found on the southern coasts of England and in the West of Scotland, but the genus is rare, although containing several species in the British seas; it is more common in the Adriatic; but they cannot be compared, as to size, with the great Synapta of Celebes, which is some-times a yard in length, and is known among the natives as the Sea Serpent.

The calcareous particles imbedded in the skin of the allied genus Chirodota are wheel-shaped when viewed

Fig. 145.   Wheel-like Plates of Chirodota violacea.

with a microscope (fig. 145). One species is British, but they are mostly inhabitants of warm seas. In Chirodota violacea, a Mediterranean species, the skin is full of groups of broad thin hya-line wheels lying upon one another and connected by a fine thread. The wheels have five or six flat radiating spokes.[1] The wheels are exceedingly small in the Chirodota lævis, and are ar-ranged in groups; in the C. myriotrochus they are im-bedded in myriads, as the name implies.

Echinodermata Sipunculidæ.

The Sipunculidæ, which form the last order of the Echinoderms, consist of several genera of marine worm-shaped animals which burrow in the sand, and form a link between the Holothuridæ and the true sea-worms. They have no calcareous particles in their flexible skins, nor have they any tubular feet, or special respiratory organs, but a vascular liquid is kept in motion in the

[1] 'The Microscope,' by Dr. Carpenter.

internal cavity by the cilia with which it is lined. The mouth of the Sipunculus is a kind of proboscis with a circular fringed lip and two contractile vessels, supposed to serve for raising the fringes. An alimentary canal extends to the end of the animal, turns back again, and the intestine ends in a vent near the mouth, so that the creature need not leave its burrow and expose itself to enemies in order to eject the refuse of its food. The locomotive larval zooids from the rose-coloured eggs undergo two metamorphoses; at last the young Sipunculus unites with the zooid, and no part is thrown off.

SECTION VII.

THE CRUSTACEA.

THE Crustacea are free, locomotive, articulated animals, covered with a crust or external skeleton, and distinguished by having jointed limbs, and gills that fit them for aquatic respiration. They are male and female, and, though extremely diversified, they have a similarity in their general structure. Many are microscopic.

The Crustacea constitute ten orders, many genera, and innumerable species. The Decapods, or the ten-footed order, are by far the most complicated in organization. They have prominent eyes, movable on jointed stalks, antennæ, gills in a cavity on each side of the throat, a mouth opening into a digesting apparatus, a heart, liver, circulation of the blood, and a nervous system, and are therefore animals of a higher grade than any that have come under consideration.

The Decapods are divided into three tribes :—the Macrura, or long-tailed Crustacea, of which the Lobster and Astacus fluviatilis, or fresh-water Crawfish, are types; the Anomura, or tailless tribe, of which the Hermit crab is the type; and the Brachyura, or short-tailed crustaceans, which are represented by the common Crab. The greater number of these animals are marine; some inhabit fresh water; and some are amphibious, living in holes in the ground; others climb reeds and bushes with their long claw-feet; the last two kinds come to water to spawn.

Macrura.

The body of the Macrura, or long-tailed crustaceans, consists of a number of segments or rings joined end to end, having jointed members on each side. Every individual joint is covered with a hard crust to afford support to the muscles. A certain number of the rings, which form the tail, are always distinct, similar, and movable on one another, whilst the remainder, which form the carapace or shell, are confluent so as entirely to obliterate the divisions. But generally the arrangement of these twenty-one rings is such that seven of them are confluent and form the head, seven confluent rings form the thorax or throat, and the seven non-confluent rings form the tail. In the Decapods the three last head rings greatly expanded are cemented to those of the thorax, so as to form the carapace or shell, which covers all the body of the animal except the tail. This structure may be traced on the under-surface of the crab.

A ring consists of an upper and an under arch, with a space between them, so as to let the feet and other appendages pass through. In the long-tailed tribe the tail is bent and unbent by muscles attached to the under and upper surfaces of each ring, which give the tail a powerful motive force, for, by bending it suddenly under the body, and then as suddenly stretching it out, the animal darts backwards through the water.

The Decapods have five pairs of walking feet; the front pair are claws employed to seize their prey, and occasionally for walking; the other four pairs are cylindrical, and end in sharp hooked points.

Brachyura.

The Brachyura surpass all the other Decapods in compactness and concentration, and are without exception the highest of the Crustacea. Though apparently without a tail, they really · have one, as their name implies; but it is short, rudimentary, and folded under the posterior end of the carapace. The genera and species are exceedingly numerous, many swim and inhabit the deep oceans, others live on the coasts · but never leave the water; a numerous tribe live as much in the air as in the water, hiding themselves under stones and sea-weeds on the rocky coasts, while some dig holes for themselves in the sand, and the land crabs only come to the sea or to fresh-water lakes to spawn. The Brachyura have two claws, and are divided into the two chief families of walking and swimming crabs, according as their posterior pairs of legs end in a sharp horny nail, or a ciliated lamellar joint.

The great shell or carapace which covers the body varies in form with the genera; it may be square, oval, or circular, longer than it is broad, or broader than it is long; it may be straight or beaked between the eyes; but its lateral edges always extend over the haunches of the feet. In the Cancri, or walking crabs, of which there are eighteen genera and many species, the carapace is generally much broader than it is long, and broader before than behind.

The carapace, or shell, of the common crab is too well known to require a particular description. · The deep lines which indent it correspond with the limits of the internal organs; the parts between the lines often bulge very much above the parts occupied by the stomach, heart, gill chamber, &c., but in the flat crabs these divisions are not so evident.

The compound eyes, which in all the crabs have hexagonal facettes, are on short jointed stems placed in deep and nearly circular orbits like cups, so that the stems are scarcely visible. These orbits, whose edges are sometimes smooth and sometimes notched, are so constructed that the crab can bend the eye-stems horizontally to the right and left, and the front of the carapace either conceals the orbit, or forms the eyebrow.

In all crabs the antennæ appear in front between the eyes. The first or interior pair are short, jointed, and capable of being bent into cavities, which contain their basal joints; these cavities are near the eye orbits, with which they are connected in certain species. Well-developed ears are placed in their basal joints. Fig. 146 represents a magnified ear seen from behind, and Mr. Gosse mentions that the large eatable crab, whether at rest or feeding, carries these antennæ erect and elevated, always on the

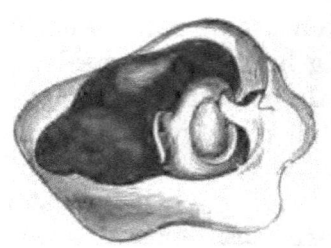

Fig. 146. Ear of Crab.

watch, and either vibrating them, or incessantly striking the water with them in a peculiar jerking manner.

The exterior or lower pair of antennæ are always longer than the interior pair; sometimes they are simple and similar to them, as in the flat crabs; and sometimes they have jointed filaments at their extremities. In all the species they are attached to the under-side of the crab, and the organs of smell are openings at the point of junction between their second and third joints. These openings, which lead into the mouth, are covered by a membrane, and closed by a calcareous lid. Each lid is fastened by a little hinge to the side of its cavity, and is opened and shut by muscles fixed at the extremity of a long tendon. Thus the lower antennæ are the organs of smell, while the upper pair are the organs of hearing, and both are probably the organs of touch.

The mouth of the crab is on the under part of the head, its lips are horny plates, and it has a pair of mandibles to cut the food; their action is from side to side. On each side of the mouth there are two pairs of

jaws, followed by three pairs of foot-jaws; so called because they are legs modified to serve as jaws, but in some crustaceans they are also instruments of loco-motion or prehension, and sometimes of both. The two last pairs have palpi, or feelers, at their base. All the jaws and foot-jaws, when not in use, are folded over the mouth; the joints of the two last are so broad that they completely conceal this complicated apparatus.

Posterior to the mouth and its organs there is a flat broad plate, which forms the ventral side of the body, with a groove in its surface, into which the rudimentary tail is folded back, as in the Carcinus mœnas (D, fig. 148), and the feet are fixed by movable joints on each side of this sternal plate. The first pair, which are a little in advance of the others, and bend forwards in a curve towards each other, may be called hand-feet, as they occasionally serve for both. They have very thick short arms and swollen hands, having a curved finger and a thumb with a movable hinge, armed throughout their internal edge with a row of blunt teeth, and ter-minated by sharp points. The other four pairs, which are the real walking feet, spread out on each side of the animal, and often bend a little backwards; they are rather thin, compressed, and end either in a horny nail, or flattened blade for swimming.

The gills, which are the breathing organs of the crabs and other Decapods, are spindle-shaped bundles of long, slender, four-sided pyramids, fixed by their points on each side of the mid line of the throat, so that they ex-tend in opposite directions, and their spreading bases fit and rest upon the vaulted sides of the carapace, or rather gill chambers, to the right and left. Each of the pyramids is formed of a multitude of parallel membra-nous cylinders fixed to the axis of the pyramid, and an infinity of capillary bloodvessels form a network in their surfaces.

The crab has nine of these bundles of gills in each

gill chamber; a few of them are shown in fig. 147. Each gill chamber has two openings; the water is admitted by a slit in the base of the claw feet, and ejected by another into the mouth. But the act of breathing is regulated by a plate on the second pair of jaws, so connected with the exterior pair of foot-jaws that, when the crab applies the latter to its mouth, the plate shuts the slit, the water in the gill chamber is ejected by the mouth, and in order to admit a fresh supply, the crab must open the foot-jaws

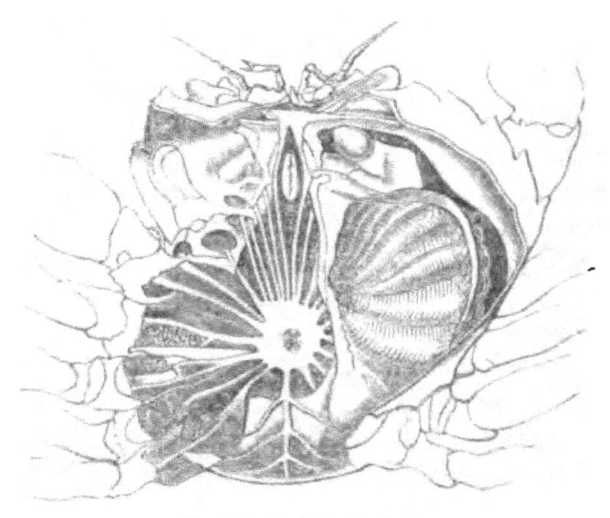

Fig. 147. Section of a Crab.

again, so that they are in constant motion. There are plates called whips on all the appendages of the crab, from the last pair of foot-jaws to the fourth pair of walking feet inclusive, which ascend and descend vertically between the bunches of gills to sweep particles of sand or other foreign matter out of them.

The heart of the crab, as in all the Decapods, is placed under the skin of the back next to the throat; and the blood, which is white or bluish, flows from the heart through a complicated system of vessels, and, having nourished the different organs, it is collected in reservoirs at the base of the gills, is aërated while passing through them, and returns to the heart again.

The mouth opens through a short gullet into a large globular stomach, from the walls of which calcareous toothed organs meet in the centre. One serves as an anvil, while the others bruise the food on it. Some of the long-tailed crustaceans can evert this apparatus and push it out of their mouth. The bruised food is liquefied by solvent juices from the liver and stomach, and the nutritious part enters the bloodvessels by imbibition.

The nervous system is condensed to suit the form of the crab. An oval nervous mass with a hole in its centre surrounds the gullet, from each side of which a nerve extends to a nerve-centre in the head. The organs of sense are as usual supplied with nerves from the latter, and, from the circumference of the massy ring, nerves radiate to every part of the animal, voluntary or reflex, as may be required.

Dr. Carpenter has proved, by microscopic observations, that the shell of the Decapod, in its most complete form, consists of three strata : the first is a horny structureless layer covering the exterior; the second, a cellular stratum ; and the third is a laminated tubular substance. In the large, thick-walled crabs, as the Cancer pagurus, the three strata are most distinctly marked. The tubuli of the lowest layer rise up through the pigment stratum in little papillary elevations, which give the coloured parts of the shell a minutely speckled appearance. There are various deviations from this general plan. In many of the small crabs belonging to the genus Portunus, the whole substance of the shell below the structureless horny investment is made up of hexagonal, thick-walled cells; and in the prawns there are large stellate coloured cells.

The eggs of the Brachyura are attached by gluten to the false ciliated feet of the tail of the female, which being bent up under the body forms a temporary protection till they are hatched. On leaving the egg the young have not the smallest resemblance to the parent; it is only after the fourth moult that they even acquire the crab form. When the young of our common shore crab, the Carcinus mœnas, leaves the egg, it is scarcely half a line in length. The body is ovoid, the dorsal shield large and swelled (fig. 148, A). On the middle of its upper edge there is a long, hollow spine bending backwards, in

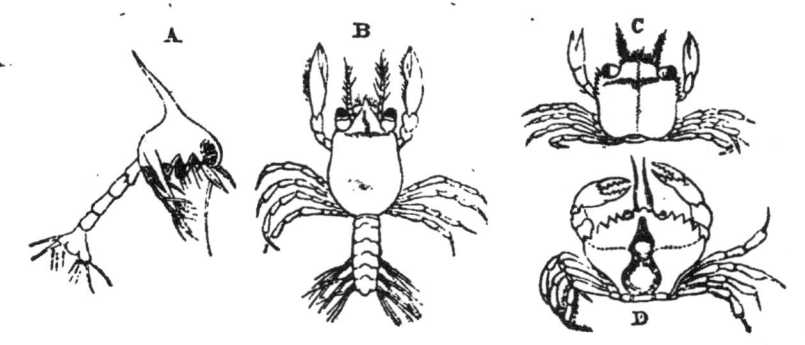

Fig. 148. Young of Carcinus mœnas in different stages of development:—A, first stage; B, second stage; C, third stage; D, perfect form.

which the white blood may be seen to circulate with a sufficient microscopic power. In front there is a pair of large sessile eyes, and the circumference of the pupils is marked by radiating lines : behind, there is a long, six-jointed tail, the last segment of which is forked and spined. On each side of the shield there is a pair of swimming feet attached to its waved margin. Fixed also to the margin, but in advance of these, there are three pairs of jointed feet ending in slender hairs. Immediately in front, between the eyes, there is a very long compressed appendage, which is bent backwards between the claws when the animal moves. Under each eye there is another appendage, shorter and rather more compressed. There are three pairs of claws, each composed of three joints, and ending in four long slender hairs : the claws stand at right angles to the body. The young, when it escapes from the egg, is quite soft, but it rapidly hardens by the deposition of calcareous matter on its surface. The progress of the consolidation is shown by the circulation of the white blood in the hollow dorsal spine. When the creature is yet soft, the blood globules may be seen ascending to its apex; but, as the consolidation advances, the circulation becomes more and more limited till at length it is confined to the base. This creature, whose shield is sap green and the rest transparent, swims with great activity, beating the water with his claws and tail. Such is the first stage in the life of the common shore crab. At this period the young of the Decapods bear a strong resemblance to one another, whether they are afterwards to become long or short tailed crustaceans.

After a time this creature loses its activity, moults, and is no longer to be recognised as the same, so great is the change (fig. 148, B). The dorsal spine has vanished, the shield has become flatter, its anterior part pointed, the eyes raised on stalks, and certain rudimentary organs that were below the eyes now form long antennæ. The first pair of feet have got hands, the others are jointed and simple, except the last pair, which are still natatory : with these and with the tail, which is now much smaller, these creatures swim and congregate round sea-weeds and floating objects. After the third moult they have the form of a crab, though neither that of the genus nor species of the parent (fig. 148, c). The tail is folded under a square carapace, the four pairs of walking feet spread widely and laterally, while the great hand-feet attached to the anterior sides of the carapace stretch straightforwards, the antennæ are short, and the eye-stalks bent to the right and left. It requires several moults to bring this creature to its final size and form.[2]

Crabs sometimes die while moulting, and occasionally are unable to extricate a limb from its shell, and consequently lose it. But if a limb be fractured they can cast it off at the second joint, and soon after a diminutive limb is formed, which attains its full size at the next moult; but if the crab has not strength enough to cast it off, it bleeds to death.

Anomura.

The Anomura is a family of Decapods intermediate between the long and short-tailed Crustacea. There are nine or ten genera and many species, chiefly distinguished by the development of the head and thorax, and the softness of a non-locomotive tail: of these the Pagurus, or Hermit crab, is assumed as the type or representative.

The carapace is long and convex, scarcely extending over the basal joints of the feet. The claw feet are short, with a very broad hand and sharp pincers; but the Hermit crab and some of its congeners are irregularly formed; for the last pair of walking feet, instead of being attached to the thorax, like the others, are fixed to the first part of the tail, are generally folded over the back, and are employed to sweep foreign matter out of the gills. The mouth and its masticating organs are similar to those in the crab, except the exterior pair of foot-jaws, which are longer and move like feet. But that which distinguishes the Pagurus and its fellows from every other Decapod is the softness of its unsymmetrical tail, all the appendages of which are abortive, and the extremity, instead of ending in a

[2] Mr. C. Spence Bate.

swimming fin, terminates in a pair of grasping organs. In order to protect this soft-skinned tail, the Hermit crab folds it up and thrusts it into some old empty shell, clasps the column of the shell with its grasping organs, draws in the rest of its body, and covers it with the broad hands folded in such a manner as to close the mouth of the shell, and to defend itself if attacked. It holds so fast that it cannot be drawn out; but, when in search of food, it stretches out its mailed head and legs, and walks off with its house on its back. However, it sometimes comes out of its shell to feed, and, like some other crustaceans, it holds its prey with one claw, and tears it to pieces with the other. They are very pugnacious, and come out of their shells to die. The larvæ of the Paguridæ undergo transformation, and they moult when full grown.

Stomapoda.

The Stomapods are all swimmers; they have long bodies with a carapace; but it is so varied in form and size, that no general description of it can be given. They have external, instead of internal, organs of respiration; gills in the form of tufts are in some cases attached to a few of the foot-jaws, but they are much more frequently fixed to the basal joints of their swimming feet, so that the blood in their capillary veins is aërated through their thin skin as they float in the water. In the Squilla mantis, or S. Desmarestii, members of a genus of this family, the gills, which are fixed to the basal joint of their last pair of feet, consist of a long conical tube, on each side of which there are numerous parallel tubes, like the pipes of an organ, and each of these has a row of many long cylindrical filaments that drag in the water. The mouth and its appendages are similar to those of the common Decapods, with the exception of the anterior jaw-feet, which are of a singular and formidable structure. They are bent outwards, and their basal joint is exceedingly large, broad, and compressed; the next joint is less, with a groove in its side; the third joint is a blade like a scythe, whose cutting edge is furnished with long pointed teeth. The Squillæ are carnivorous, and, if any unfortunate animal comes within their grasp, they bend back the toothed edge of the first joint into the groove of the second joint like a clasp-knife, and cut it in two. These prehensile foot-jaws, or ' pattes ravisseurs,' are like the fore-feet of the praying Mantis, and like them weapons of defence.

The genus Mysis, or Opossum Shrimps, have a long straight carapace, which covers most of the thorax, and folds down on each side so as to conceal the base of the feet: in front it is narrow, and ends in a flattened beak; at the posterior end it is deeply scooped out. The two last rings of the thorax are more or less exposed; the tail is long, almost cylindrical, tapering to the end, and terminating in a swimming fin composed of five plates spread like a fan. Both pairs of antennæ have jointed stems ending, the outer in one, the inner in two very long many-jointed filaments. On the top of the basal joint of the outer pair there is a very long lamellar appendage, ciliated on the side next the joint. Between the second and third joints of the exterior antennæ, Mr. Spence Bate found the organ of taste: the aperture is simply covered by a membrane, as in the lobster. The ears are in the last appendage of the tail.

The Mysis has two pairs of jaw-feet differing little from feet; five pairs of thoracic feet, all thin and divided into two branches, which increase in length as they are nearer the tail, and are all provided with a ciliated appendage to adapt them for swimming. In the female, broad horny plates, attached to the two last pairs of legs, are bent under the body so as to form a kind of pouch, destined to lodge the eggs and the young during the first period of their lives, whence their name, 'Opossum Shrimps': the young are crowded in this pouch, and acquire their adult form before they come into the water. The circulation of the white blood of the Mysis was discovered by Mr. Thompson : the pulsations of the heart are so rapid that they resemble vibrations. There are many species of these small shrimps.

The genus Lucifer is one of the most singular of the crustaceans from its almost linear form (fig. 149), the excessive length of the anterior part of the head, the extreme shortness of the thorax, the smallness of the

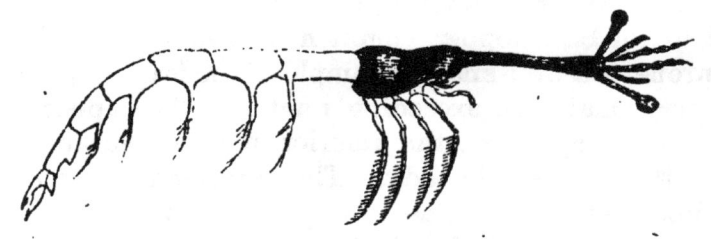

Fig. 149. Lucifer, a stomapod crustacean.

carapace or shell, and the great development of the tail, which is more than three times as long as the thorax. The thin eye-stalks, which are of exaggerated length, extend at right angles from the top of the long cylindrical part of the head, and terminate in large, staring, dark-coloured eyeballs covered with a multitude of facettes. The two pairs of antennæ are placed between and below the eye-stalks. The undermost pair, which are the shortest, have a little lamellar appendage at their base : in some Lucifers, when viewed in front, it looks like a cross. The salient mouth is placed at the base of the long organ that carries the eye-stems. It has strong toothed mandibles, two pairs of jaws with plates attached to each jaw, and three pairs of foot-jaws. The tail is very narrow, consisting as usual of seven rings movable on one another; but they are quite abnormal, for each of the rings is at least as long as the thorax ; the last has five plates spreading like a fan. All the bristly feet, which seem to hang loosely down from the animal, are fitted for swimming; those of the tail have long ciliated plates in their basal joints. These creatures are small, and inhabitants of warm seas.

Amphipoda.

The Amphipods are very numerous, and abound in the British seas. They have long, slender, and many-jointed bodies which have no carapace : the tail in some genera is more fitted for swimming, in others for leaping. The Talitrus, or Sandhopper, common on every sandy shore in Europe, is a well-known example of the leaping genus. It is very small and exceedingly active. The upper antennæ are very short, the inferior pair are large, and longer than the whole body. The anterior feet are thin and not prehensile. The first pair end in an immovable claw; the second pair have a kind of hand, and are folded beneath the body; the following feet end in a crooked nail. The appendages of the last three rings of the tail are thick and spiny, and the tail serves as a leaping organ.

The sandhoppers hide themselves between tidemarks in large communities under masses of wet sea-weeds, on which they feed. When disturbed they leap away with great agility, and bury themselves in the sand by digging with their fore-feet, and kicking the sand away with their tail-feet. They have a strong sense of smell, for if a dead fish be buried in the sand, it is devoured by these little voracious animals in a few days.

In the fin-tailed genera the gills are suspended between the bases of the thoracic legs: they swim lying on their side, and their feet are very varied in form, but always more or less furnished with spines and hairs.

There are several genera of Amphipods that are nest-building animals; all have hooks at the end of their tails,

The Amphithoæ enclose themselves in a cylindrical tube open at both ends. The animal is very active, running along the branches of the sea-weeds by means of its antennæ instead of its feet, which remain within the tube. In general only the first pair of antennæ are put out to catch prey. If the animal be prevented from advancing, it immediately turns its body within the tube, and protrudes its head from the other extremity.

Isopoda.

The order of Isopoda are so called because of the sharp and equal claws of their walking feet, which are often prehensile. Their body is short and flattened, and their small head is almost always distinct from the throat. They are very numerous, and are divided into walking, swimming, and sedentary animals; the females have horny plates on some of their feet, which fold under the throat and form a pouch, in which the eggs are hatched.

The Oniscus, common Wood-louse, or Slater, is a terrestrial Isopod. It is an oval jointed creature, which rolls itself into a ball when touched. The second of its six pairs of posterior limbs perform the part of lungs: they contain hollow organs in their interior, into which the atmospheric air penetrates directly through openings in their exterior covering: so the Oniscus and its congeners, which live on land, are drowned when put into water.

In the swimming Isopods, the five first pairs of tail-limbs are false feet, and are suspended under the tail. The gills, consisting of two great oval leaves, are fixed to them by a stalk; and are dragged through the water. This group is very numerous; many live among the sea-weeds on the coasts, others perforate submerged wood in all directions, and live in the winding galleries they have formed. The Limnoria lignorum is particularly destructive in the harbours on the British coasts, and in the locks of the canals. The tortuous holes it bores are from the fifteenth to the twentieth of an inch in diameter, and about two inches deep. The female Isopod is not more than a line or two in length, the male is a third less, and of a grey or greenish brown. These minute creatures bore their holes with their mandibles, which are so sharp and strong that they can penetrate the hardest wood, and appear to feed on it, from the quantity found in their stomachs. Their bodies are covered with pinnated hairs, their antennæ are short, and their posterior end or tail is rounded.

Most of the genus Cymothea are parasitical; they can bend the sharp nail of the three first pairs of feet upon the preceding joint, so as to form hooks with which they fix themselves to the fishes on whose juices they feed.

The Isopods bear a strong resemblance, an almost identity of structure, with the Trilobites, a jointed race of Crustaceans long extinct. Some of the Isopods roll themselves into a ball, as these most ancient inhabitants of the ocean were wont to do; whose large compound eyes are exactly like those of the Isopods; whence it was inferred by Dr. Buckland, that neither the constitution of the sea nor the light of the sun had changed for innumerable ages. The discovery of the Eozoön has proved that Nature has not varied during a period immeasurably prior even to that.

Entomostraca.

The Entomostraca form an immense group of the lower Crustacea, consisting of five orders. A vast number are just visible to the naked eye, and many are microscopic; they teem in every climate along the coasts, and in the deep blue oceans. The horny coat, enclosing the minute bodies of these animals, is often so transparent that their internal structure, and occasionally the process of the assimilation of the food, is distinctly seen by the aid of a microscope. Small as they are, their beauty is often very great; when transparent they sometimes radiate all the prismatic colours; when opaque, they are frequently of the most brilliant and varied hues, others shine with vivid phosphorescent light. The segments of their bodies are often very numerous, and similar to one another; but their appendages are very different. They form two distinct natural groups of the bristly-footed and gill-footed Crustacea.

Copepoda.

The first order, Copepoda, or oar-footed tribe, have a distinctly articulated body formed of movable rings, bristly swimming limbs; and the females carry their eggs in huge pouches suspended on each side of the posterior part of their bodies.

The Sapphirina fulgens is a beautiful example of the two-eyed tribe; its body is nearly oval, divided into nine distinct joints, and so flat that it is almost foliacious. The head has two brilliantly coloured eyes, with large cornea so connected with the shell that they look like spectacles. The two pairs of antennæ are silky, and the last pair of foot-jaws that cover the mouth are garnished with silky plumes. It has five pairs of swimming feet, and the tail ends in two little plates.

The Sapphirina is about a line and a half long, of a rich sapphire blue, and floats on the surface of the Mediterranean and tropical oceans. It shines with the most brilliant phosphorescent colours, passing from deep blue to a golden green, or splendid purple. The brilliant colouring is seated in the layer of cells that secrete the firm substance of the body. With a microscope the cells are seen to pass alternately from one colour to another. There is a little three-lobed body between the eyes connected with the central nervous system by a small nerve; it contains several corpuscules, which Professor Gegenbaur regards as the remains of the single eye of the larva which undergoes many transformations before it arrives at its adult form.

According to Professor Gegenbaur, the Sapphirina fulgens is a true Copepod and the Mediterranean Phyllosoma is a Decapod, although it has a lacunar blood system.

Some genera of the order Copepoda inhabit salt water, others fresh, as the Cyclops quadricornis (fig. 150), which abounds in the water with which London is supplied.

The genus Cyclops is a type of the bristly-footed group, distinguished by a single compound eye placed in the middle of the forehead. The head and thorax are almost ' entirely covered with an oval jointed buckler, which has an opening below to let the bristly limbs pass through (fig. 150); and the tail, which is five-jointed, ends in two plates furnished with

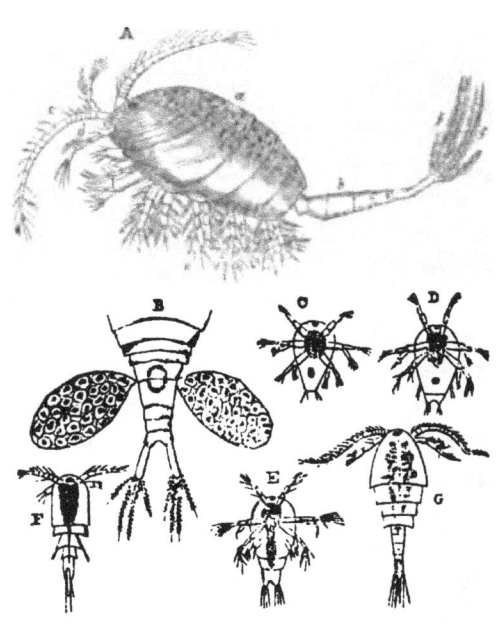

Fig. 150. Female Cyclops:—*a*, body; *b*, tail; *c*, antenna; *d*, antennule; *e*, feet; *f*, plumose setæ of tail; B, tail, with external egg-sacs; C, D, E, F, G, successive stages of development of young.

bristly plumes. It is traversed by the intestine, which ends near its extremity. The brilliant little eye in front consists of a number of simple eyes placed under one glassy cornea. It rests upon the base of a cone of muscular fibres, which give it a movement of rotation upon its centre. Its upper pair of antennæ, situated below the eye, spread to the right and left. In the female they have numerous joints with a bristle at each joint; the lower pair of antennæ are short-jointed and bristled. The mouth of the Cyclops has a pair of jaws, and two pairs of foot-jaws covered with bristles. The five pairs of branching legs, which are fitted for swimming, are thickly beset with plumose tufts. In the female the egg-sacs are hung on each side of the tail (B, fig. 150) by a slender tube, through which the eggs pass from the ovary within the mother into the sacs where they are deposited in rows, and there they remain till hatched. When the larvæ come into the water the sacs drop off, and the young undergo various changes before coming to maturity, as shown in fig. 150. The Cyclops swims with great activity, striking the water with its antennæ, feet, and tail; and the rapid movement of its foot-jaws makes a whirlpool in the water which brings minute animalcules to its mouth, and even its own larvæ, to be devoured.

Some species of the Calanus, a marine genus of the one-eyed group, are eminently social. Professor Dana found that the colour of those vast areas of what the sailors call bloody water, met with off the coast of Chili, was owing to shoals of the Calanus pontilla; and another immense area of bloody water he met with in the North Pacific was owing to a vast multitude of the Calanus sanguineus. Although this genus abounds more in individuals in the temperate seas, the species are more varied in the tropical. Those figured and described in Captain Maury's works were mostly microscopic and very beautiful; one fished up was grey with a bunch of yellow feathers at the end of its tail. The egg-bags were purple, another was green marked with scarlet tufted antennæ longer than itself spread out at right angles from its head. This creature shone with a bright phosphorescent light, visible even when a candle was burning. These and many more were taken in tropical seas. They were remarkable for the length of their antennæ; and it was observed that no eyes were perceptible in such Crustacea as had these exaggerated antennæ; these organs of intelligence and warning were probably sufficient for their wants. When animals live without eyes on the surface of a tropical sea, it is quite conceivable that similar instruments of touch may suffice for those who live in the dark abyss below.

The Ostrapods, which form the second order of the bristly-footed Crustacea, are defended by a bivalve carapace; they have swimming limbs and a confluent eye; that is, a number of simple eyes placed under a glassy cornea.

The genus Cypris belongs to this group. Several species may be seen swimming in our streams and fresh-water pools. The body of the common Cypris (fig. 151) is enclosed between two flat oval shells, united by a hinge on the back. The little animal can open and shut the valves by means of two slender muscles, extending from its back to the shells, which

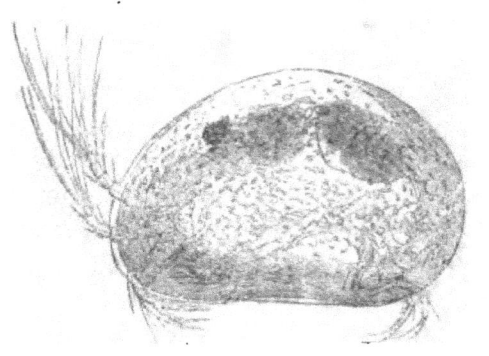

Fig. 151. Cypris.

are much curved above and rather flat below. There are two pairs of antennæ beneath the eye, they are perfectly transparent, many-jointed, and end in tufts of filaments. One pair projects forward and then bends gracefully backwards; the other pair are bent downwards. The mouth has no foot-jaws, and there are only two pairs of feet. Only one pair is seen in the female, for the other pair is bent upwards to support the egg sacs. The Cypris attaches her eggs to the leaves of aquatic plants by a greenish fibre. Not more than twenty or thirty eggs are deposited by one individual, while the heaps contain several hundreds; so many females contribute to form one heap. The young are hatched in the form of their parent in about four days and a half. As the pools dry up, the Cyprides bury themselves in the sand or mud at the bottom; if that

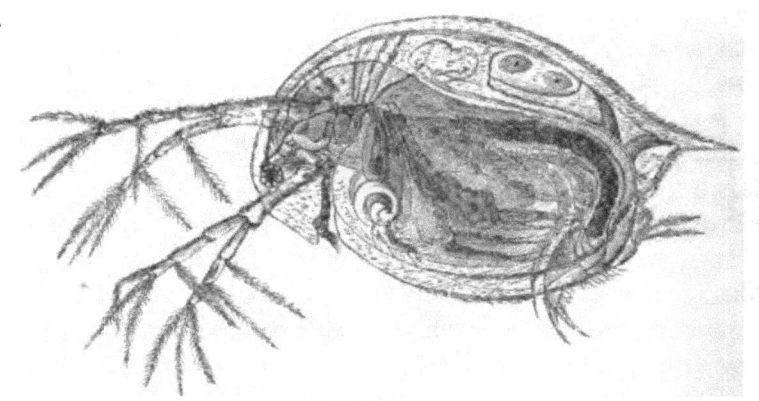

Fig. 152.   Section of Daphnia pulex.

remain moist they survive, if it becomes dry they perish; but the eggs remain dormant till the return of rain, when they are hatched, and the surface of the water is soon crowded with a swarm of young Cyprides.

The Cladocera is the first order of the gill-footed Crustacea: their body is defended by a bivalve carapace; they have from four to six gill-footed limbs, one compound eye, and two pairs of antennæ, one pair of which is large and adapted for swimming. The Daphnia pulex, or Arborescent Water-flea, of which fig. 152 is a section, is a common form of this tribe. It is very abundant in pools and ditches, coming in groups to the surface in the mornings and evenings in cloudy weather. The bivalve shell is transparent, flexible, and open below; it ends behind in sharp toothed peaks. The eye placed in front is moved by four muscles, and on each side of it are the great antennæ, which are jointed, branched, and garnished with feathery filaments, and are the chief organs of locomotion. This animal has no foot-jaws, but it has a nervous system and a heart, whose pulsations are repeated two or three hundred times in a minute, and the blood is aërated by gills at the extremities of six pairs of bristly feet situated behind the mouth, and only used for respiration and prehension.

The eggs, when laid, are deposited in a receptacle between the back and the shell of the female Daphnia, and after the young come into the water they undergo no transformations. Between each brood the Daphnia moults, and the egg receptacle is thrown off with the exuvia. After several changes of skin the young Daphniæ come to maturity and lay eggs, which produce successive generations of females throughout the spring and summer; but in the autumn males appear, and then the eggs are retained in the receptacle of the female and are not hatched till spring. If the female should moult after this, the case with the eggs in it is cast off with her outer skin, which then becomes a protection to the eggs during the winter, and they are hatched in spring, producing females.

Phyllopoda.

The second order of gill-footed Crustacea are called Phyllopoda, because they have gills like the leaves of a book attached to their lamelliform swimming feet. Their bodies are divided into many segments, and they form two groups, one of which has a carapace, the other has not. The Apus cancriformis is an example of the first. It is about two inches and a half long, and is a large animal compared with the others of its class. Its head and thorax are covered by an oval carapace, and its cylindrical body is composed of thirty articulations. It has a compound movable eye in the middle of its forehead, and a sessile eye on each side of it. All the members that follow the apparatus of the mouth have a foliaceous form, and are in constant motion even when the animal is at rest. The Apus has sixty pairs of jointed legs; the number of joints in these and in the other appendages is estimated to be not less than two millions. However, the instruments chiefly used for locomotion are the first pair of feet, which are very long and serve for oars; with these the animal can swim freely in any position, but when they are at rest it floats on the surface of the stagnant water in which it lives, and the fin feet maintain a constant whirlpool in the water, which brings the small animals on which it feeds to its mouth.

The Branchipes stagnalis, which may be taken as a type of the second order, has a perfectly transparent segmented body nearly an inch long, eleven pairs of pale red gill-feet, antennæ of bluish green, and a long tail ending in red bristles. The head has two large eyes on movable stems, and a sessile black oculus between them. Filiform antennæ spring from the upper part of the head; the other pair, like two large horns, are turned downwards. The last ring of the swimming tail has two plates with ciliated appendages.

The Artemia salina differs very little from the Branchipes. It abounds so much in the brine pans at Lymington and other salt works, as to give a red tinge to the nearly concentrated brine, the temperature of which is so high that no other animal could live for a moment in it.

Pycnogonoïdea or Spider Crabs.

Some of the Spider crabs hook themselves to fishes, while others live under stones, or sprawl with their long hairy legs over sea-weeds, and feed on the gelatinous matter these weeds afford. The throat with its members, and the head soldered to its first ring, forms nearly the whole animal. It has a pair of antennæ and four rudimentary eyes, set on a tubercule. A proboscis-like projection extends from the front; the mouth is furnished with cilia and one pair of foot-jaws. Four pairs of long hairy legs proceed from the throat, spread widely on each side, and end in a hooked claw. The stomach, which occupies the centre of the animal, sends off five pairs of long closed tubes like rays; one pair enters the foot-jaws, the others penetrate the legs. This digesting system is in a state of perpetual vermicular motion, which, as well as the movements of the animal itself, aërate its transparent blood through the skin, by keeping it in circulation. So this insignificant-looking creature has a very curious and complicated mechanism.[3]

Fossil Crustacea.

Analogues to the Anomura are found in the Chalk formation, but the Macrura are the prevailing forms. Extinct species of lobster, crawfish, and shrimps are met with in the secondary strata, from the Chalk to the Coal measures. In the Coal formation all these higher forms disappear, but then the gigantic King Crab, or Limulus, is found accompanied by the minute Entomostracan forms in infinite variety of species.

[3] 'Histoire naturelle des Crustacés,' par M. Milne-Edwards.

Epizoa, or Suctorial Crustacea.

The Epizoa infest the skin, eyes, and gills of fishes. Many of them in their adult state bear a strong resemblance to the lowest of the Crustacea; but, in general, the resemblance between these two classes of animals can only be traced during the extraordinary changes which the Epizoa undergo in their early life, and they differ so much in their perfect state that it is wonderful any connection should ever have been discovered between them. The Epizoa are extremely varied in their perfect forms, and the class generally is supposed to be more numerous than the whole race of fishes. In the lower orders of the Epizoa the mouth is suctorial; the higher orders adhere to their victim by jointed mandibles ending in hooks. The Epizoa are male and female: the male is small and free, the female is fixed, and generally has a pair of long egg-sacs hanging from her body.

SECTION VIII.

CIRRIPEDIA.

THE metamorphoses of the Cirripeds, and their resemblance to the lower Crustacea at each moult, are still more remarkable than those of the Epizoa. They form two primary groups, the Balanidæ, or Acorn shells, and the Barnacles or Lepadidæ, which have peduncles or stalks. Both are parasites, but they do not draw their sustenance from the substances they adhere to.

The Balanidæ (fig. 153) are grouped in innumerable multitudes, crowded together on the rocks of the southern and western coasts of England, like brown acorns. They have an obscurely articulated body, enclosed in a membrane, and defended by a multivalve conical shell. The base of the shell is a broad disk fixed to a foreign substance by a cement secreted by the animal. The walls consist of twelve triangular compartments. Six rise upright from the edge of the disk, and end in a point at the open margin of the shell; the other six are

Fig. 153. Balanus culcatus.

inverted and wedged into the interstices. The whole cone thus constructed is divided into from four to eight pieces by expansive seams. The mouth of the cone is closed by a lid formed of four triangular valves, which meet in a point in the centre, and shut in the creature.

Six pairs of long, slender, curly feet rise from the throat of the animal, and bend over the prominent mouth, which

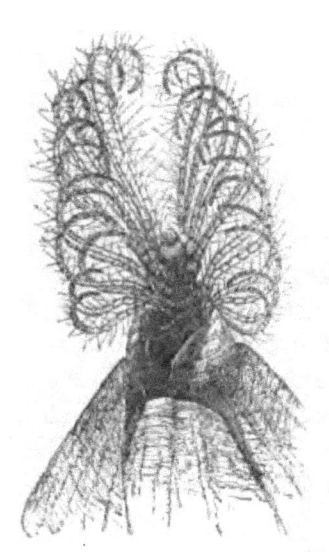

is placed at the bottom of a kind of funnel, formed by the divergence of these six pairs of thoracic feet. It is furnished with a broad upper lip, two palpi, and three pairs of jaws, of which the outermost are horny and toothed, the innermost soft and fleshy. Each foot is divided into two similar many-jointed branches: the shortest pair is nearest to the mouth, the others increase gradually in length and number of joints to the most distant (fig. 154). Mr. Gosse estimated that, in a specimen he possessed, the whole apparatus included nearly five hundred distinct articulations. Since each

Fig. 154. Tentacles or feet of the Balanus.

joint is moved by its own system of muscles, the perfection of the mechanism may be conceived. But it is as sensitive as flexible, for every separate joint is furnished with a system of spinous hairs, which are no doubt organs of touch, since the whole of the branches are supplied with nerves. These hairs, which extend at somewhat wide angles from the axis of the curling filaments, are barbed, for they have numerous projections, or shoulders, surrounded by whorls of microscopic hairs.[4]

This beautiful and complicated structure is the fishing apparatus of the animal, which it is continually pushing out and drawing in through the valved lid of the shell. When the whole is thrown out it is widely spread, and

4 'Evenings at the Microscope,' by Mr. Gosse.

the filaments uncurled; then, as they close again, the innumerable hairs meet and form a sieve through which the water escapes, but whatever minute particles it may contain are inextricably entangled, and when the small animals fit for food have been selected, the filaments curl inwards, and carry them to the mouth; there they are seized by the jaws and sent through a short gullet to be digested.

The feet and cirri are moved by very strong muscles, the valves of the lid are opened and shut by muscles attached to the mouth of the shell; and when the animal wishes to protrude its cirrhated feet, the longitudinal muscles attached to the lid come into action, and it draws itself in again by short muscles attached to the base. All the organs of the animal are supplied with nerves by a double nerve-centre in the head, and a circle of nerve-centres round the gullet. The ears are situated at the base of the first pair of cirrhated feet, and consist of a cavity enclosing a vesicle closed by a nerve, and containing a liquid, but no otolites.

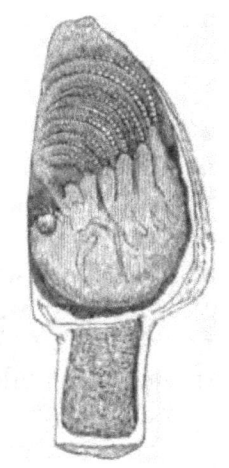

The common Lepas anatifera, of which fig. 155 is a section, as well as its allies, have a thick stem and a conical shell closed on the back, but gaping in front. Their internal structure does not differ essentially from that of the Balanidæ, and it has been proved by Mr. J. V. Thompson and others, that there is no material difference between their transformations during the early stages of their lives.

Fig. 155. Section of Lepas anatifera.

Each individual cirriped is both male and female, and the eggs are hatched before they come into the water. Mr. Gosse mentions that he had seen the Balanus porcatus throw out a dense column of atoms from the mouth of its shell for several successive days; each column was composed of thousands of active microscopic creatures, bearing a strong similarity to the young of the Cyclops Crustacea. A, fig. 156, represents one of these creatures. Its body is enclosed in a carapace with a pair of flexible organs like horns, six swimming feet, and a very black eye deeply set in front. The creature swims and sometimes rests, but never alights on anything. After some changes this

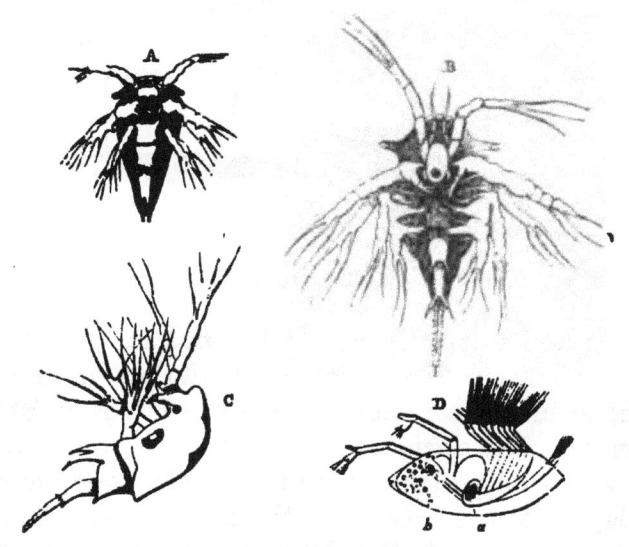

Fig. 156. Development of Balanus balanoïdes :—A, earliest form ; B, larva after second moult ; C, side view of the same ; D, stage preceding the loss of activity ; a, stomach ; b, nucleus of future attachment.

creature takes a form whose front is represented at B, and its side by C, fig. 156. It is larger, more developed, and swims with its back downwards.

A new series of transformations changes this embryo into the form represented by D, fig. 156, which is closely allied to the Daphnia pulex, or Water Flea. The body is enclosed between two flat oval shells, united by a hinge on the back, and is capable of being opened in front for the protrusion of a pair of prehensile limbs; and six pairs of swimming feet cause the animal to swim by a succession of bounds. Instead of the single eye, it has now two raised on pedestals, attached to the anterior part of the body.

This animal having selected a piece of floating wood for its permanent abode, attaches itself to it by the head, which is immovably fixed by a tenacious glue exuded from glands at the base of the antennæ. The bivalve shell is subsequently thrown off, a portion of the head becomes excessively elongated to form the peduncle of the Barnacle or Lepas, and in that state it is exactly

Fig. 157. Lepas.

like the Lucifer Stomapod. In the Balanus, on the contrary, the head expands into a broad disk of adhesion, and the animal resembles the Mysis or Opossum Shrimp.

From the first segment of the throat a prolongation is sent backwards which covers the whole body, and the outer layer is converted into the multivalve shell; and the three pairs of cirrhated feet, which were formed in the larval state, now bend backwards from the other three rings of the throat.

Though the Cirripeds lose their eyes in their mature state, they are sensitive to light. They draw in their cirrhated feet, and the Balanus even closes the lid of its shell under the shadow of a passing cloud.

SECTION IX.

BRYOZOA, OR POLYZOA.

A BRYOZOON is a microscopic polype, inclosed in an open horny or calcareous sheath, out of which it can protrude and draw in the anterior part of its body. It is seldom or never seen alone, on account of its tendency to propagate by budding. When the buds spring from the sides of the sheath or cell, it is known as the Sea Mat, or Flustra. The Flustra, which is common on our coasts, spreads its hexagonal cells like a delicate network over sea-weeds, shells and other marine substances. Sometimes the polypes are so closely arranged on both sides of a leaf that a square inch may contain 1,800. In the calcareous genera, Eschara and Cellipora, the cells have a lid movable by two muscles, so that the polypes can close the orifice, and shut themselves in.

In the greater number of the Polyzoa the polype has a cylindrical form, a mouth at its anterior extremity surrounded by an annular disk, which forms the roof of the internal cavity containing the stomach and the other digestive organs. The disk is furnished with eight, ten or a greater number of tubular tentacles, which surround the mouth, their tubes being continuations of the internal cavity below. The mouth leads into a funnel-shaped space, separated by a valve from the gullet; and the gullet ends in a capacious stomach. Short vibratile cilia are arranged like a fringe on the opposite sides of each tentacle, which form two currents in the surrounding water—an ascending stream on the outside, and a descending one on the inside. When any particles of food that may be carried down the inner surface of the tentacles arrive at the mouth, a selection is made, the rejected particles being carried off by the stream, while those that are chosen are received by the funnel-shaped mouth, and pass through a valve in the gullet into the stomach, where they are kept in continual motion by cilia, and the refuse is ejected by an orifice near the mouth.

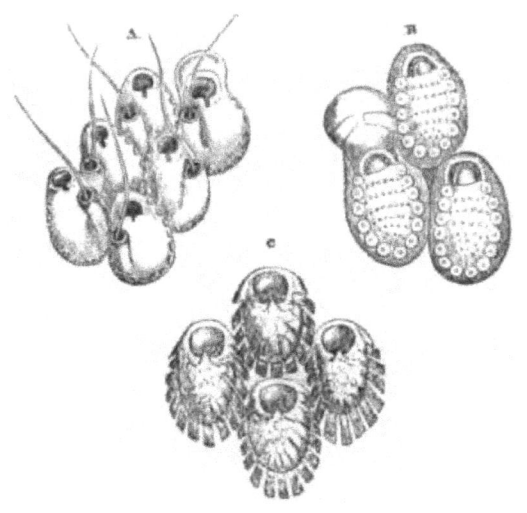

Fig. 158. Cells of Lepraliæ.—A, L. Hyndmanni; B, L. figularis; C, L. verrucosa.

Fig. 158 represents the cells of different species of the genus Lepralia, which form crusts upon marine objects. Other genera grow as independent plant-like structures, and some take an arborescent form, and creep over rocks and stones. The Cellularia ciliata, of which fig. 159 is a magnified portion, rises in upright branching groups like little shrubs; and as many are commonly assembled together, they form miniature groves, fringing the sides of dark rocky sea pools on our coasts. Most of the

Polyzoa have pedicellariæ attached to their stems, either sessile or stalked. Their forms are various: a jointed spine, a pair of pincers, &c. But on the Cellularia they are like a bird's head with a crooked beak, opening very wide, and attached by a stem. B, fig. 159, represents a highly magnified pedicellaria in the act of seizing another. These bird's head appendages are numerous

Fig. 159. A, Cellularia ciliata; B, 'bird's head' process of Bugula avicularia, highly magnified, seizing another.

on the Cellularia ciliata, and in constant motion; the jaws are perpetually snapping little worms, or anything that comes in their way, while the whole head nods rhythmically on its stalk. Two sets of muscles move the jaws; when open, a pencil of bristles projects beyond them, which is drawn in again when they are closed; they are supposed to be organs of feeling. The Polyzoa have organs also called vibracula, which are bristle-shaped, as on A, fig. 158; these sweep over the surface of the Polyzoon to remove anything that might injure the polypes.

It is believed that the polypes of the Polyzoa are male and female, and that the ciliated locomotive larvæ which appear in spring are developed from eggs. The fresh-water Polyzoa are as worthy of microscopic examination as the marine.

SECTION X.

TUNICATA, OR ASCIDIANS.

THE form of the Tunicata is irregular. They have two orifices—one at the top, for the entrance of a current of water, and another at one side for its egress. They have two tunics only adhering to one another at the edges of these orifices, which are furnished with a circle of cilia. The irregular or scattered condition of the nerve-centres, as well as the alternation in the circulation, are eminently characteristic of the whole class. They consist of three distinct groups: the compound or social gelatinous Ascidians; the solitary Tunicata, with leathery coats; and the Salpæ, which are gelatinous. The two first, though mobile when young, become fixed when they arrive at maturity; the third floats free on the surface of the ocean.

The fixed gelatinous Ascidians resemble the Polyzoa in structure and tendency to gemmation; nevertheless, they differ in their circulating and respiratory systems. The Perophora Listeri is an example which is found on the south coast of England and Ireland (fig. 160.)

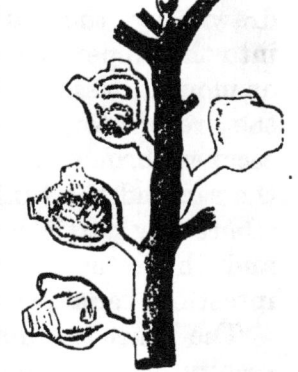

Fig. 160. Magnified group of Perophora.

It consists of minute globes of clear jelly, not larger than a pin's head, spotted with orange and brown, and attached by a foot-stalk to a silvery stem like a thread which stretches over the surface of stones, or twines round the stalks of sea-weeds; and as the stem increases in length, buds spring from it, which in time come to maturity, so that the silvery thread connects a large community; but, though thus connected, every member has its own individuality. Fig. 161 represents one of these transparent individuals very highly magnified.

The respiratory sac occupies the upper part of the body. It is perforated by four rows of narrow slits, edged with cilia, whose vibrations are distinctly seen through the transparent tunic of the little animal. A portion of the water which is drawn by the cilia into the upper orifice or mouth, passes into the respiratory sac,

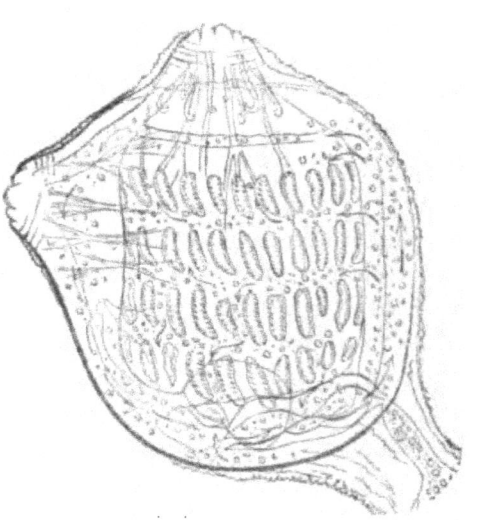

Fig. 161. Highly magnified Perophora.

escapes through the narrow slits into the space between the sac and the tunic, and from thence into the stomach, where any particles of food it may bring are digested, and the refuse is carried by the current through the intestinal canal, and ejected at the lateral orifice.

The heart is a long multiform muscle, attached to the respiratory sac, from whence capillary vessels spread over that sac and throughout the body. The pulsations of the heart drive the blood through the general system, and bring it back to the heart again. After a time the pulses of the heart become faint, and the blood ceases to flow. A short pause takes place, the heart gives an opposite impulse, and the blood makes its circuit in a direction exactly contrary to what it did before. The circulation in all these little globes is brought into connection by a simultaneous circulation through two tubes in the silvery thread to which they are attached.

The average duration of the ebb and flow of the blood is probably the same, but the period between the changes varies from thirty seconds to two minutes. As the blood is colourless and transparent, it probably would have been impossible to determine its motion had it not been for solid particles floating in it.

The larva of the compound sessile Ascidians is like the tadpole of a frog, which swims about for a time ; it then fixes itself by the head to some object, the tail falls off, and in a few days it becomes a solitary Ascidian, with its two orifices and currents of water. This solitary animal gives origin by budding to a connected group, which in its turn lays fertilized eggs, so that there is an alternation of generations.

The Botryllidæ or Star-like Ascidians, appear as masses of highly coloured gelatinous matter, spread over stones or fuci in which from ten to twenty minute oblong Ascidians are arranged in a circle round a common open centre which is the discharging orifice of the whole group, for the mouth of each individual is at the opposite extremity. The only indication of life given by this compound creature is the expansion and contraction of an elastic band surrounding the discharging orifice. The organization of each of these individuals is similar to that of the Perophora.

Although many Tunicata form composite societies, the most numerous and largest in size are always solitary, as the Ascidia virginea (fig. 162). Its outer tunic contains cellulose, it is pale and semitransparent, the inner tunic is orange-coloured or crimson. These creatures vary in length from one to six inches : therefore they are not microscopic, yet their internal structure, which is similar to that described, cannot be determined without the aid of that instrument. The organ of hearing is a capsule containing an otolite and coloured spots placed between the orifices; the uppermost orifice or mouth is surrounded by eight eye-specks, and six of a deep orange colour surround the

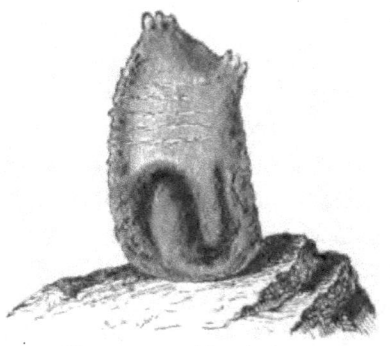

Fig. 162. Ascidia virginea.

lateral one, a nerve-centre between the two supplies the animal with nerves. These Tunicata live on diatoms and morsels of sea-weeds, and, like all the fixed Ascidians, they show no external sign of vitality except that of opening and shutting the two orifices. More than fifty species of these solitary Ascidians inhabit the British coasts from low-water mark to a depth of more than one hundred fathoms.

Pyrosomidæ.

The Pyrosomidæ are floating compound Ascidians, composed of innumerable individual animals united side by side, and grouped in whorls so as to form a hollow tube or cylinder open at one end only, and from two to fourteen inches long, with a circumference varying from half an inch to three inches. The inhalent orifices of the component animals are all on the exterior of the cylinder, while the exhalent orifices are all on its inside, and the result of so many little currents of water discharged into the cavity is to produce one general outflow which impels the cylinder to float with its closed end foremost. The side of each animal in which the nerve-centre is placed is turned towards the open end of the cylinder, the whole of which is cartilaginous and non-contractile. Each of the Ascidians forming this compound creature has its outer and inner tunic united and lined with a vascular blood system, a respiratory cavity of large size completely enclosed by a quadrangular network, and digesting organs. The sexes are combined, and they are propagated by buds and single eggs. The Pyrosomidæ are gregarious and highly luminous; vast shoals of them extend for miles in the warm latitudes of the Atlantic and Pacific Oceans, and as soon as the shade of night comes on they illuminate ships with bright electric flashes as they cleave the gelatinous mass; half a dozen of these animals give sufficient light to render the adjacent objects visible. The intensity depends upon muscular excitement, for Professor Fritz Müller observed that the greenish blue light of the Pyrosoma Atlantica is given out in a spark by each of the separate individuals; it first appears at the point touched, and then spreads over the whole compound animal. This species appears in such aggregations in the Mediterranean as to clog the nets of the fishermen.

Salpidæ.

The Salpidæ are another family of free-swimming Ascidians. The tunic is perfectly hyaline, the body is somewhat cylindrical, but compressed and open at both ends (fig. 163). The mouth is a slit, the discharging orifice is tubular and can be opened and shut. The breathing apparatus is in the form of a ribbon extending obliquely across the cavity of the tunic, the ear with four otolites is in the ventral fold, and the flux of the pale blood is alternate as in other Tunicata.

The Salpidæ are produced by alternate generation.

A solitary floating Salpa is always found to contain a chain of embryos joined end to end winding spirally

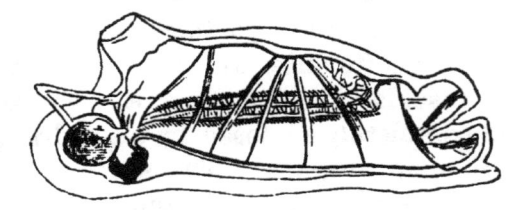

Fig. 163. Salpa maxima.

within her. They are all of one size, and portions are liberated in succession through an aperture in the tunic. In a little time these connected larvæ are developed into a chain of adult Salpæ. The individuals are from half an inch to several inches long, according to the

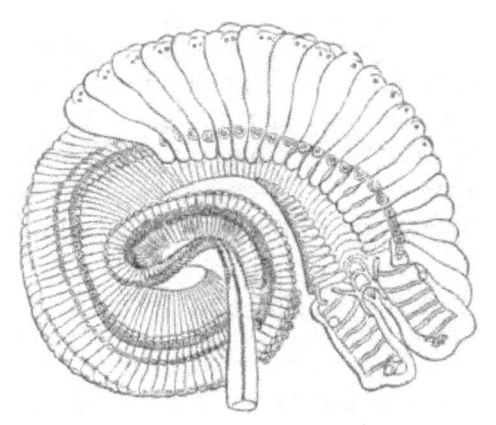

Fig. 164. Young of Salpa zonaria.

species, and when joined end to end the chain may extend many feet, but the attachment is so slight that they often break up into shorter portions. The chains swim with an undulating serpentine motion either end foremost by the simultaneous expulsion of water from the muscular tunic of each individual. A single egg is formed by each of these creatures, which remains within the parent till a solitary Salpa is hatched, and then it comes into the water, and after a time produces a chain of larvæ.

The aggregate young of the Salpa zonaria, instead of being united end to end, are applied side to side, and as the individuals are broad at one extremity and narrow at the other, they constitute groups continually diminishing in size, which take a spiral form.

The reproduction of the whole genus of Salpidæ is rapid and enormous. Dr. Wallich mentions that while sailing between the Cape of Good Hope and St. Helena, the ship passed for many miles through water so crowded with the Salpa mucronata that it had the appearance of jelly to apparently a great depth. The Salpæ, which were from one to two inches long, had yellow digestive cavities, about the size of a millet seed, which contained diatoms, Foraminifera, Polycystinæ, small shrimps, and other microscopic creatures.

SECTION XI.

MOLLUSCA.

ALTHOUGH the Mollusca do not come within the limits of this work they nevertheless afford objects worthy of microscopic investigation. The gills of a bivalve mollusk are like crescent-shaped leaves fixed by their stalks to the transverse extremities of the mantle, so that the greater part floats freely in the water.

To the naked eye the gills appear to be formed of radiating fibres of admirable structure; but the microscope shows that each leaf consists of a vast number of straight transparent and tubular filaments, arranged side by side so close that 1,500 of them might be contained in the length of an inch. These filaments, however, apparently so numerous, in fact consist of only one exceedingly long filament in each gill, bent upon itself again and again throughout its whole length, both at the fixed and free ends of the leaf. These long filaments are fringed on both sides by lines of cilia continually vibrating in contrary directions. By this action a current of water is perpetually made to flow up one side of the filaments and down the other, so that the blood which circulates in their interior is exposed throughout their long winding course to the action of oxygen in the water. The duration of these vibrations in the mollusca is marvellous. The cilia on a fragment of a gill put into water by Mr. Gosse fifteen hours after the death of the mollusk caused a wave to flow uniformly up one side of the filaments and down the other. Even twenty-hours after the death of the animal the ciliary motion was continued on such parts as were not corrupted, a remarkable instance of the inherent contractility of the animal tissues.

The refined mechanism of the gills of the common Mussel enables it to live when attached to rocks above high-water mark, so as only to be immersed at spring tides. By the movements of cilia, water is retained in the gill-chamber, which derives oxygen from the atmosphere, and animalcula supply the Mussel with food.

The mollusks that burrow in sand or mud have two tubes fringed with cilia, which they protrude into the water above them. The water which is drawn into one of these tubes by the action of the cilia passes in

Fig. 165. Cardium or Cockle.

a strong current over the gills, aërates the blood, brings infusorial food for the animal, and is expelled in a jet from the other tube. The foot at the other extremity of the shell is the organ with which the mollusk makes its burrow in sand, clay, chalk, stone or wood.[5]

The common Cockle digs into the sand, and uses its foot both for digging and leaping; it is cylindrical, and when the Cockle is going to leap, it puts out its foot and

[5] Jeffrey's 'British Conchology.'

bends it into an elbow; then having fixed the hooked point firmly in the sand, by a sudden contraction of the muscles it springs to a considerable height and distance, and leaps actively along the surface of the sand. The lowest part of fig. 166 is a magnified section of the foot, showing the muscular system which gives the animal that power. It consists of many rows of longitudinal muscles, interlaced at regular distances by transverse fibres. When the foot is extended, the Cockle has the power of distending it by filling a network of capillary tubes with water till it is almost transparent. The water is also distributed through the body and into the gill-chamber, which opens and shuts every ten minutes or oftener, in order to maintain the supply; and it has egress through the pores in the mantle and foot, for some burrowing mollusks squirt it out through the foot when disturbed. This water-system is unconnected with the circulation of the blood.

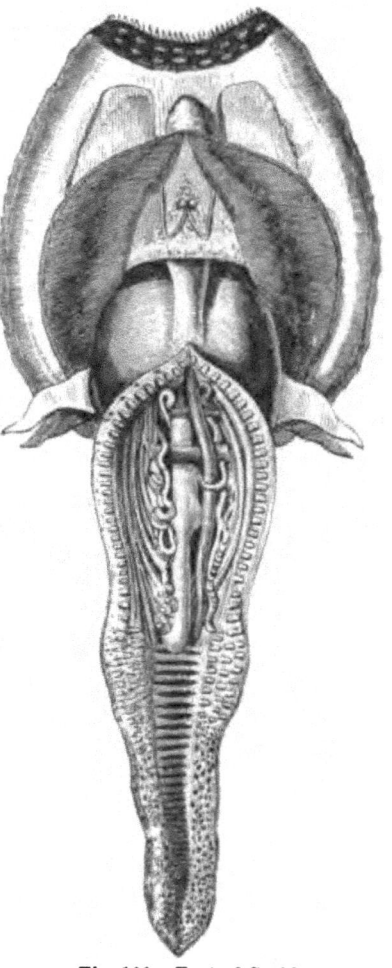

Fig. 166. Foot of Cockle.

Each bivalve mollusk is both male and female; and the fertilized eggs pass into the gills of the parent, where they undergo a kind of incubation. At a certain time the yellow yolk of the egg is divided into a granular mass, which separates from the liquid albumen and produces cilia. The cilia cause the albumen to revolve round the interior of the egg; at last the granular mass revolves with it, while at the same time it rotates about its axis in a contrary direction at the rate of six or eight times in a minute. When still in the egg, all the organs of the little embryos are formed in succession, even the little valves of the shells are seen to open and shut, but the embryos are hatched before they leave the parent, and swim about in the cavity of the external gill.

Shells of the Mollusca.

When these mollusks come into the water, they soon find their transparent white shell too small, and begin to increase its size by means of the mantle, which is an exquisitely sensible fleshy envelope applied to the back of the animal, extending round its sides like a cloak, only meeting in front, and it is for the most part in close contact with the whole interior of the shell. Its edges are fringed with rows of slender tentacles, and studded with glands, which secrete the colours afterwards seen in the shell; the glands in the rest of the mantle secrete only colourless matter.

When the animal begins to enlarge its shell, it attaches the borders of the mantle to the margin of the valves, secretes a film of animal matter, and lines it with a layer of mucus containing carbonate of lime and colour in a soft state, which soon becomes hard, and is then coated internally by the other glands of the mantle with colourless carbonate of lime.

The two strata thus formed, one richly coloured, the other white, often nacreous and brilliantly iridescent, are highly organized substances. Examined with the microscope, they present remarkable varieties in some of the natural groups of bivalve Mollusca; the structure of the Monomyarian Oyster is characteristic of the division which has but one muscle; the Dimyaria, having two muscles, are represented by the Cockle.

The exterior laminæ at the edge of the fragile valves of a Pinna are often so thin and transparent that the organization of the shells may be seen with a low magnifying power. A fragment has the appearance of a honeycomb on both

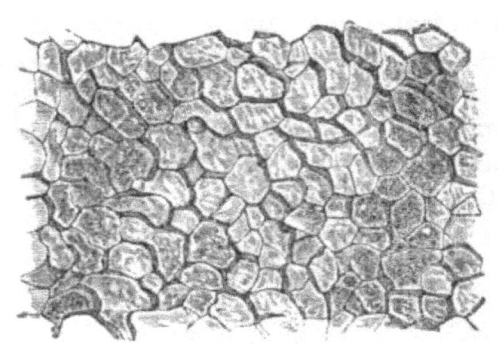

Fig. 167. Section of shell of Pinna transversely to the direction of its prisms.

surfaces (fig. 167), whereas its broken edge resembles an assemblage of basaltic columns. The exterior layer of the shell is thus composed of a vast number of nearly uniform prisms, usually approaching to the hexagonal structure, whose lengths form the thickness of the lamina, their extremities its surfaces. When the calcareous part of the lamina is dissolved by dilute acid, a firm membrane is left, which exhibits a

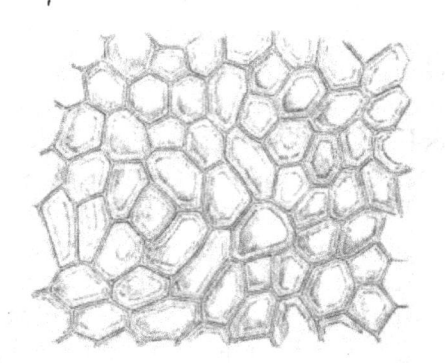

Fig. 168. Membranous basis of the shell of Pinna.

hexagonal structure (fig. 168), as in the original shell; but it is only in the shells of a few families of bivalves nearly allied to the Pinna that this combination of the organic and mineral elements is seen in this distinct form; it is beautifully displayed in the nacreous shells.

In many shells the internal layer has a nacreous or iridescent lustre, shown by Sir David Brewster to depend upon the striation of its surface, by a series of nearly parallel grooved lines. When Dr. Carpenter had dissolved the calcareous matter from a thin piece of nacreous substance, taken from the shell of the Haliotis

Fig. 169. Section of nacreous lining of the shell of Avicula margaritacea
(pearl oyster).

splendens, or Ear Shell, there remained an iridescent membrane, which presented to the microscope a series of folds or plaits somewhat regular, and splendidly iridescent, but when the plaits were unfolded and the membrane stretched, the iridescence vanished. So the varied hues of mother-of-pearl are owing to the folds of an organic membrane.

The shells of the Gastropoda, or crawling mollusks, have a structure peculiar to themselves, but by no means so much varied as that of the bivalve class. The Strombus gigas, or Queen Conch, the Cassis, or Helmet

Shell, and the beautiful porcellanous Cyprææ or Cowries, are much valued by the artists who cut cameos, on account of the structure of their shells, which consists of three strata, the same in composition, but differing in arrangement, and sometimes in colour. Each stratum of the shell is formed of many thin laminæ, placed side by side, perpendicular to the plane of the stratum, and each lamina consists of a series of prismatic spicules with their long sides in close approximation; the laminæ of the inner and outer strata have their spicules parallel to one another, while the spicules of the intermediate lamina are perpendicular to those on each side. According to Dr. Bowerbank, who discovered this complicated structure, the spicules are microscopic tubes filled with carbonate of lime.

The Spondylus gædaropus has sixty ocelli constructed for accurate vision. One can form no idea of the effect of so many eyes, unless they combine to form one image as our eyes do. The common Pecten, or Scallop, pretty both in form and colour, has a number of minute brilliant eyes arranged along the inner edge of the mantle, like two rows of diamond sparks. Some families of mollusks are destitute of eyes, even of the simplest kind; and it has been observed that those mollusks most liberally provided with eyes are also endowed with the most active and vigorous motions. The bivalves do not appear to have either taste or organs of hearing, but they are exceedingly sensitive to touch. It is singular that animals which have neither head nor brain should have any senses at all. A nerve-collar round the gullet with a trilobed nerve-centre on each side supplies the place of a brain; nerves extend from these; besides there are nerve-centres in various parts of the unsymmetrical bodies of the acephalous mollusks.

The Gastropoda, or crawling mollusks, have a head, and are consequently animals of a higher organization than the Conchifera or bivalve class. Their mantle forms a vaulted chamber over the head and neck, and envelopes the foot or crawling-disk; all these the animal can protrude or draw in at pleasure. The head is of a globular form, with two or four exceedingly sensitive tentacles, arranged in pairs on each side of it, as in the garden snail, which has four, two long and two short. These tentacles, which the snail can push out and draw in at pleasure, are hollow tubes, the walls of which are composed of circular bands of muscle. The tentacles are pushed out by the alternate contractions of these circular bands, but they are drawn in again like the inverted finger of a glove by muscular cords proceeding to the internal extremity of the tentacle from the muscle that withdraws the foot. The structure of the tentacles is the same in all the crawling mollusks; they are most sensitive in the Helix or Snail family, but they are believed to be delicate organs of touch in all.

The Gastropod mollusks never have more than two eyes, either placed on the tips, or at the base of one pair of tentacles; in the snail they may be seen as black points on the tips of the longest pair. In some of the higher Gastropods they are of great beauty, and appear to be perfectly adapted for distinct vision. Organs of hearing were discovered by Dr. Siebold at the base of one of the pairs of tentacles, consisting of vesicles containing a liquid and calcareous otolites, which perform remarkable oscillations due to the action of vibratile cilia. In the Snail and Slug group the number of otolites varies from eighty to one hundred.

The mouth of a Gastropod is a proboscis, with fleshy lips, generally armed with horny plates or spines on the jaws. The Snail has a crescent-shaped cutting plate on its jaw, and a soft bifid lip below, but the tongue is the most remarkable microscopic object in this group of Mollusca. In the terrestrial Gastropods, it is short and entirely contained within the nearly globular head. It is tubular behind, but in front it is spread into a nearly flat narrow plate, traversed by numerous rows of minute recurved teeth, or spines set upon flattened plates; in the Garden Snail or Slug each principal tooth has its own plate. Fig. 170 represents a magnified portion of a Snail's tongue by Dr. Carpenter; the rows at the edge are separated to show the structure.

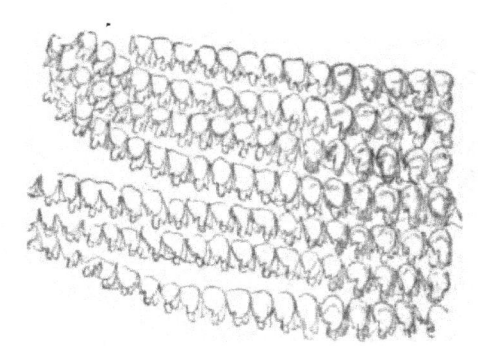

Fig. 170. The tongue of Helix aspersa.

The teeth are set close one to another, and are often very numerous. In the Helix pomatia, a snail found in the middle and southern counties of England, they amount to 21,000, and in the great slug (Arion ater), there are 26,800. This kind of tongue only serves for rasping vegetable food. All the Trochidæ, which are marine mollusks that are supposed by some naturalists to live on fuci, are remarkable for the length and beauty of their narrow spiny tongues. Fig. 171 is a small portion of the tongue or palate of the Trochus zizyphinus, highly magnified; the large teeth of the lateral

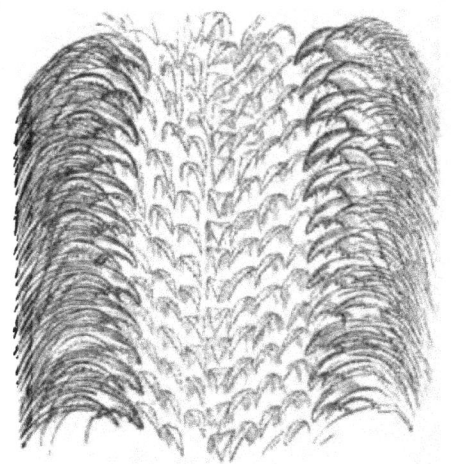

Fig. 171. Palate of Trochus zizyphinus.

bands, as well as the small teeth in the centre, have minutely serrated edges. Fig. 172 shows the Trochus granulatus in the act of crawling.

The Limpet lives on sea-weeds. The animal is large in proportion to the size of its conical shell; it has a long

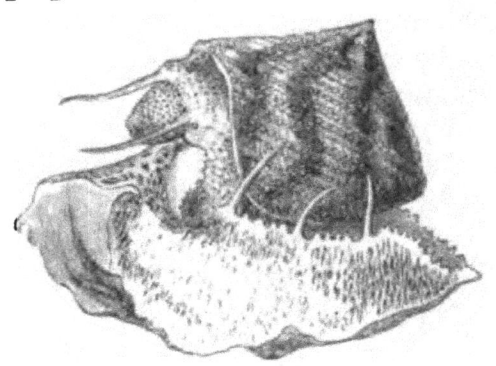

leaf-shaped gill under the edge of the mantle. The head has a short proboscis and pointed tentacles, with eyes at their base. The mouth has a horny jaw and a very long tongue, moved by muscles rising from firm objects on each side of

Fig. 172. Granulated Trochus.

it. Fig. 173 represents the tongue beset with recurved hooks, and A shows a portion highly magnified. These recurved teeth are transparent, amber-coloured, and in the Limpet, as in most of the other Gastropods, they are chitinous. The teeth towards the point of the tongue are sufficiently hard to rasp the food; and it is said that when they are worn down, the part of the tongue support-

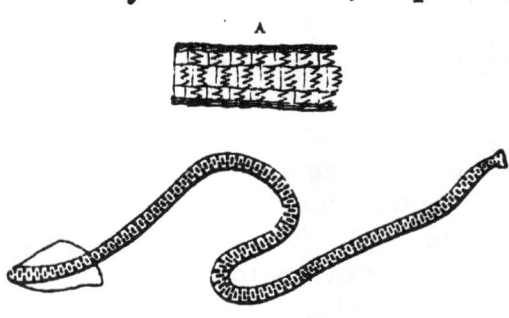

ing them falls off, and that the waste is supplied by a progressive growth of the tongue from behind, and a hardening of the teeth in front. The soft reserved portion is coiled in a spiral when not in use.

Fig. 173. Tongue of Limpet:—A, portion of surface magnified.

All the species of Patellidæ, or Limpets, have the power of making cavities with their foot in the surface of the rocks to which they adhere. The cavity exactly corresponds in shape and size with the mouth of the shell, which is sunk and very strongly glued into it, yet the Limpet dissolves the glue with a liquid secretion, roams in quest of food, and returns again to its home: both fluids are secreted by a multitude of glands in the foot, which is the instrument of adhesion.

The tongue of the carnivorous Gastropods is a very formidable weapon, used for boring holes in the hardest shells. The round holes in dead shells frequently met with on our coasts show that their inhabitants had fallen a prey to some of these zoophagous Mollusks. The tongue of these predatory Gastropods is a narrow mechanical file, sometimes twice or even three times the length of the whole animal, and when not in use it is curled up near the foot. It is spined in various microscopic patterns according to the genus, and is supported by two firm parts from whence the muscles spring that work the rasp.

The Periwinkles have a ribbon-shaped tongue, rough with hooked teeth; the Scalariæ have also predatory tongues, but of all the Gastropod mollusks, the Whelk and its numerous allies are the most predacious. The Purpura or Dog Whelk especially is the most ravenous of mollusks. Its long tongue is armed with hooked and spined teeth, placed three in a row; with this weapon and a proboscis capable of boring, they have been known to exterminate a whole bank of Mussels.

The Common Whelk is represented in fig. 174. When in the act of crawling, its head, with two tentacles, is at one extremity, its foot at the other, sometimes used as an organ of prehension; and it has a siphon for carrying water to the gills at the end of the shell.

All the families of the naked mollusks or Sea Slugs, furnish beautiful objects for the microscope. The two sexes are united in the same individual, and in their embryonic state they have a shell, which is cast off long before they come to maturity. The gills placed on the naked body are capable of being withdrawn into a cavity in the medial line of the back, and are either plumose, or

Fig. 174. Whelk.

like the leaf of a plant pinnated again and again, but they vary in form and position in the different genera.

Fig. 175. The Crowned Eolis.

In the group of the Eolidæ, the gills are like leafless trees in most genera, but in the principal genus Eolis, they are long, spindle-shaped, sharp-pointed papillæ, arranged in transverse rows or clusters along the sides of the back, leaving a space between them, as in fig. 175. They are covered with long cilia, whose vibrations send a perpetual current of sea-water along each of them, the respiration is aided by vibrating cilia, scattered almost over the whole body, and the circulation of the blood is very simple.

The Eolis has a head prolonged into a pair of tentacles which are active and as sensitive as antennæ. Another pair on the back have ten or twelve narrow plates twisted in a spiral round them; the eyes are at the base of these horns. The mouth contains horny jaws and a spiny tongue like a mere strap covered by numerous transverse plates armed with recurved spines not more than a sixth part the thickness of a human hair. Fig. 176 repre-

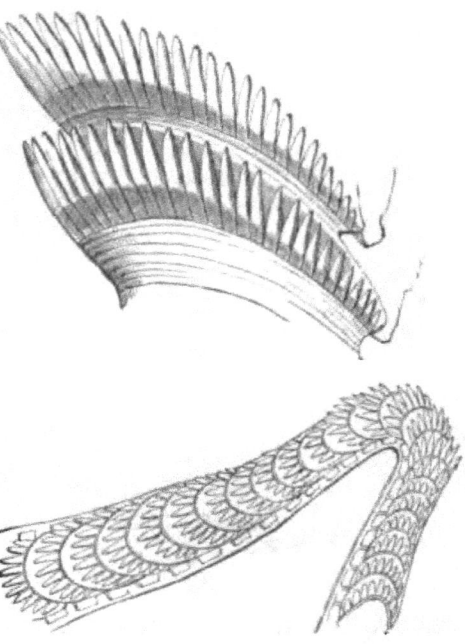

sents the tongue and some of the spines greatly magnified. The mouth leads into a short and large membranous stomach, from each side of which branches are sent off, from whence long canals traverse the papillæ longitudinally, and perform the part of a liver. In many species these tubes are brilliantly coloured, but none are more beautiful than those in the Eolis

Fig. 176. Tongue-teeth of Eolis coronata.

coronata, which is found under stones, like a mass of jelly, not larger than a pea, at low spring tides, on our own coasts. When put into sea-water it expands till it is about an inch long (fig. 175). It is then pellucid, tinged with pink, and the central tubes in its numerous papillæ are of a rich crimson hue, their surface reflects a metallic blue, and their tips are opaque white; as the animal keeps its papillæ in constant motion the effect is very pretty.

The Eolis coronata, like all its congeners, has a stinging apparatus, consisting of an oblong bag, full of thread cells, placed at the extremity of each papilla, from whence darts can be ejected through an aperture in the tip. The whole of the Eolididæ are carnivorous, fierce, and voracious, setting up their papillæ like the quills of a porcupine when they seize their prey; they tear off the papillæ of their weaker brethren, and even devour their own spawn, though their chief food consists of zoophytes.

The Pteropoda, or wing-footed mollusca, are very small; they are incapable of crawling or fixing themselves to solid objects, but they are furnished with two fins like the wings of a butterfly, with which they float or row themselves about in the ocean, far from land in vast multitudes. The shell of the typical species Hyalæa (A, fig. 177), which resembles the thinnest transparent glass, consists of two valves, one, which is placed on the front of the animal, is long, flat, and ends in three points; the other valve, which is applied to the back, is short and convex, and in the lateral fissure between the two, the mantle is protruded. The head and fins project from an opening at the top of the shell. The fins, which are formed of muscular fibre, are fixed on a short thick neck, with the mouth lying between them, containing a tongue crossed by rows of long reversed teeth. The head has no tentacles, and the animal appears to be blind, but it has an auditory vesicle lined with cilia, which keeps a few otolites in motion. This little animal is highly organized; it has a gullet, a kind of crop and gizzard, a liver, a respiratory tube, a heart, a circulating and nervous system, which enables it to swim with a flapping motion of its fins.

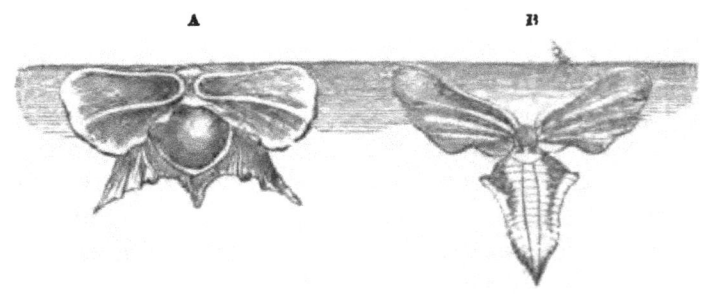

Fig. 177. A, Hyalæa; B, Clio.

The Clio pyramidata (B, fig. 177) is an elegant animal belonging to the same class. Its fragile transparent shell has the form of a triangular pyramid; and from its base proceeds a slender spine, and a similar spine extends from each side of the middle of the shell. The posterior part of the body is globular and pellucid, and in the dark it is vividly luminous, shining through the glassy shell. The fins of the Hyalæa and Clio or Cleodora are of a bright yellow, with a deep purple spot near the base. Both are inhabitants of the ocean.

The Clione borealis (fig. 178), which exists in millions in the Arctic Seas, is the most remarkable instance of the Naked Pteropods. It has neither shell nor mantle; its membranous body is not more than half an inch long, its head is formed of two round lobes, on each side of the neck there is a large muscular wing or fin; in swimming the animal brings the tips of the fins almost in contact, first on one side of the neck and

Fig. 178. Clione borealis.

then on the other. In calm weather, they come to the surface in myriads, and quickly descend again. There is a pair of slender tentacles close to the head, which are organs of feeling, a pair of eyes are placed on the back of the neck, and acoustic vesicles lined with cilia keep otolites in motion. Besides these organs of sense, the Clione has respiratory, digestive, and nervous systems. The latter consists of a nerve-collar round the gullet, with two nerve masses in its upper part, so the Clione is well supplied with nerves.

Upon each of the two round lobes of the head, there are three tentacles, totally different from those of feeling. They are, in fact, organs of prehension, which can be protruded or withdrawn at pleasure into a fold of the skin. When protruded, these six tentacles form a radiating crown round the mouth, which is terminal, and furnished with fleshy lips. Each of these tentacles is perforated by numerous cavities, appearing like red spots to the naked eye; however, Professor Eschricht discovered that each spot consists of a transparent sheath, enclosing a central body composed of a stem terminated by a tuft of about twenty microscopic suckers, capable of being thrust out to seize prey. The whole number of these prehensile suckers in the head of one Clione was estimated by Eschricht to amount to 330,000. Notwithstanding the vast prehensile power and multitude of these animals, they find abundance of food in the Arctic Ocean, for although the water is generally of the purest ultramarine blue, one fourth of the Greenland Sea, extending over 10° of latitude and some hundred feet deep, is green and turbid, with a profusion of minute animal life. The indefinite increase of the Clione borealis is checked by the whales, who feed upon them, and other minute inhabitants of the Arctic Seas. The Pteropods first appear in a fossil state in the Lower Silurian strata.

Naked Cephalopods.

The Naked Cephalopods have an internal skeleton instead of a shell, in the shape of a transparent horny pen in the Calamary, or the well-known internal shell of the Cuttle Fish; they are divided into Octopods and Decapods, according to the number of their tentacles: the Poulpe, or Octopus vulgaris, is a type of the first, the Sepia or Cuttle Fish, fig. 179, and the Loligo vulgare or Squid, are types of the last. These creatures may be seen on rocky coasts, or in the ocean hundreds of miles distant from land. They are nocturnal, gregarious, carnivorous, and fierce,—their structure enables them to be tyrants of the ocean. They are strange-looking, repulsive creatures, with staring bright-coloured eyes, while crawling awkwardly on their fleshy arms head downmost; yet they are the most highly organized of all mollusks.

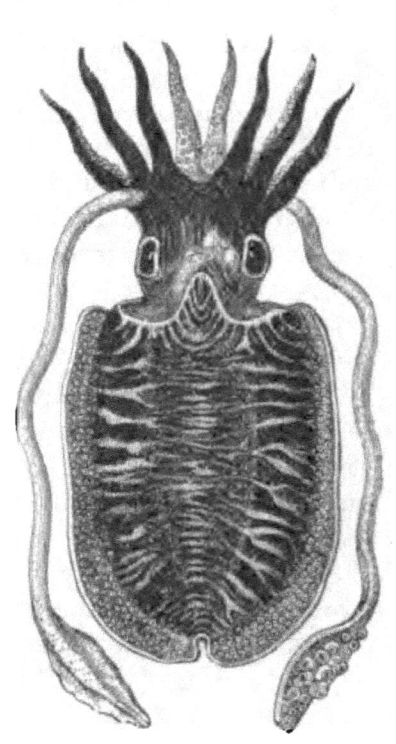

Fig. 179. Cuttle Fish.

They have a distinct brain, enclosed in a cartilaginous skull, and all their muscles are attached to cartilages. The lower part of their body is surrounded by a mantle, which extends in front to form a gill chamber, in which there is a pair of plume-like gills; a funnel or siphon projects from the gill chamber immediately below the tentacles. All the naked Cephalopods propel themselves back foremost in the sea, by the forcible expulsion of water from the gill chamber through this siphon.

The head protrudes from the top of the mantle; it has a pair of large eyes on sockets, and some species of these animals have eyelids. The ears are cavities under the cartilage of the skull, containing a small sac and an otolite. The mouth, which is terminal, and surrounded by the tentacles, has powerful jaws like a parrot's beak reversed, acting vertically. The tongue is large, the posterior part is covered with recurved spines, and the organ of smell is a cavity near the eyes. The Naked Cephalopods are remarkable for having three hearts, or propelling vessels—one for the circulation of arterial blood through the body, the others for projecting venous blood through the gills, at whose base they are situated.

The arms or tentacles of all the Naked Cephalopoda are formidable organs of defence and prehension, but are most powerful in the Loligo vulgaris, the Poulpe, and the Cuttle, on account of one pair of the tentacles being long slender arms, dilated at their extremities into flat clubs. On the inner surface of each of the tentacles, and upon the lower surface of the dilated extremities of the long ones, there are multitudes of sucking disks, which, once fixed to an object, adhere so firmly that it is easier to tear off a portion of the animal's tentacle than to make it release its hold. These sucking disks, which are placed in parallel rows, are represented magnified in fig. 180. Each sucker consists of a firm cartilaginous or fleshy ring (e), across which a disk of muscular membrane (f) is stretched, having a circular opening (g) in its centre. A cone-shaped mass of flesh fills the opening like a piston, capable of being drawn backwards; the membranous disk can also be drawn in. When one of these sucking-disks touches a fish, the fleshy piston is instantaneously retracted, a vacuum is formed, and the edges of the disk are pressed against the victim with a force equal to the pressure of the superincumbent water and that of the atmosphere. The fish is powerless when embraced by the eight tentacles and their hundreds of suckers; but, if large enough still to struggle, the force is increased by drawing in the membranous disk. The Poulpe, the most powerful of the group which swims far from land, and has to contend with large slippery fishes, has a hooked claw in the centre of each sucking-disk, which is clasped into the fish the instant

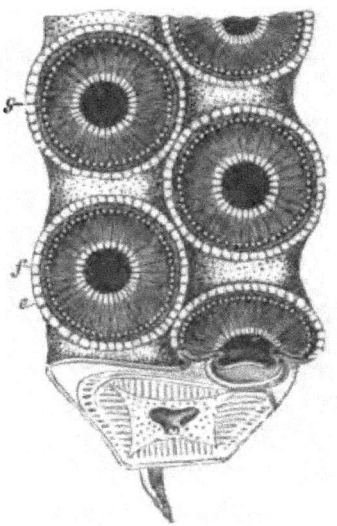

Fig. 180. Arm of Octopus.

the vacuum is formed. The expansions at the extremities of their two long arms, which are thickly and irregularly beset with hooked sucking-disks, not only drag the fish into the embrace of the eight short tentacles, but they clasp round it and interlock, so that the fish can be torn to pieces by the parrot-like jaws, and eaten at leisure. The tentacles, long and short, have strong nerves, and a little nerve-mass occupies the centre of each sucking-disk, which gives the tentacles great power.

The sepia, or inky liquid, which all the Naked Cephalopods possess as a means of defence, is secreted in a pyriform bag, which has an outlet near the respiratory siphon. If the animal be alarmed when devouring its prey, it instantly lets go its hold, discharges the inky liquid into the water, and escapes unseen.

The skin of this class of animals is thin and semi-transparent; the surface immediately below it consists of numerous cells, of a flattened oval or circular form, containing coloured particles suspended in a liquid. The colour is seldom the same in all these cells; the most constant kind corresponds with the tint of the inky secretion. In the Sepia there is a second series of cells, containing a deep yellow or brownish colour; in the common Calamary, or Squid, there are three kinds of coloured cells—yellow, rose-coloured, and brown; and in the Poulpe there are red, yellow, blue, and black cells. The cells possess the power of rapid contraction and expansion, by which the coloured liquid is drawn into deeper parts of the surface, and is again brought into contact with the semi-transparent skin—thus constantly varying. In consequence of the high development of the nervous system, the skin of the Naked Cephalopods is of extreme sensibility; a mere touch brings a blush on that of the Poulpe, and they all assume the colour of the surface on which they rest as readily as the chameleon. Many of these nocturnal animals are luminous, and are easily attracted by bright metallic objects.

RECAPITULATION.

NUMEROUS instances of microscopic structure may be found in the vertebrate series of marine animals, but the field is too extensive for the Author to venture upon.

In the first section of this book, an attempt has been made to give some idea of the present state of molecular science—far short, indeed, of so extensive a subject; yet it may be sufficient, perhaps, to show the views now entertained with regard to the powers of nature, the atoms of matter, and the general laws resulting from the phenomena of their reciprocal action. By spectrum analysis it has been shown that not only many terrestrial substances, in a highly attenuated state, are constituents of the luminous atmospheres of the sun and stars, but that the nebulæ in the more distant regions of space contain some of the elementary gases of the air we breathe.

In the succeeding sections it has been proved that the atmosphere teems with the microscopic germs of animal and vegetable beings, waiting till suitable conditions enable them to spring into life, and perform their part in the economy of the world. The life history of the lower classes of both kingdoms has been a triumph of microscopic science.

The molecular structure of vegetables and animals has been investigated by men of science in their minutest details; the fragment of a tooth, bone, or shell, recent or fossil, is sufficient to determine the nature of the animal to which it belonged ; and, if fossil, to assign the geological period at which it had lived, whether on the earth, in the waters, or the air. By the microscopic examination of a minute Foraminifer or shell-like organism, it has been proved beyond a doubt that the Eozoön, an animal which existed at a geological period whose remoteness in time carries us far beyond the reach of imagination, only differs in size from a kind living in the present seas. Simplicity of structure has preserved the race through all the geological changes which, during millions of centuries, have swept from existence myriads of more highly organized beings. The Eozoön is the most ancient form of life known, and was probably an inhabitant of the primeval ocean. Patches of carbonaceous matter imbedded in the same strata show that vegetation had already begun; so at that most remote period of the earth's existence, the vivifying influence of the sun, the constitution and motions of the atmosphere and ocean, and the vicissitudes of day and night, of life and death, were the same as at the present time.

INDEX.

INDEX.

—•—

A

Acetylene, chemical composition of, i. 128

Achlya prolifera, structure and reproduction of, i. 220

Acids, their affinity for alkalies, i. 96

Acineta, structure and mode of reproduction of, ii. 77, 78
food of, and mode of seizing it, ii. 78

Acorn-shell, structure of the, ii. 213

Acrocarpi, characters of the group, i. 328

Acrocladia mammillata, spines of the, ii. 180, 181

Acrosticheæ, characters of the, i. 359, 360

Actinia sulcata, structure of, ii. 132

Actinian polype, structure and mode of reproduction of, ii. 130, 131

Actinian zoophytes, characters of, ii. 130, 131
thread-cells, ii. 132
structure of, ii. 134–136

Actinism of star-light, i. 55
of moon-light, i, 55
of sun-light, i. 56

Actinocyclus undulatus, structure of, i. 199, 200

Actinomma drymodes, structure of, ii. 21

Actinophrys sol, structure and reproduction of, ii. 16–18
certain degree of instinct exhibited by, ii. 18
its enemy, the Amœba, ii. 18

Adder's tongue fern, i. 365

Adiantieæ, characters of the groups, i. 358

Adiantum Capillus-Veneris, or maiden's-hair fern, structure and habitat of, i. 359

Adriatic sea, Foraminifera in the ooze of the bed of the, ii. 51

Adularia, or moonstone, fluorescent property of, i. 66

Æcidium, characters of, i. 280

Ægean sea, zones of Algæ in the, i. 259

Æthalium septicum, structure and habitat of, i. 270–272
Amœba-like motions of, i. 270
mode of reproduction of, i. 271

Affinity, chemical, of kind and of degree, i. 95
relation between chemical affinity and mechanical force, i. 98

Agaricini, the order, i. 261

Agaricus, the genus, i. 261, 263
structure of the, i. 263

Agaricus arvensis, spawn of, i. 262

Agaricus campestris, or common mushroom, i. 261
structure and mode of reproduction of, i. 261

Agaricus gardneri, luminosity of, i. 264

Atoms : effect of catalysis, i. 91
 of matter, i. 2
 cohesion of, i. 25
 unit of mechanical force, i. 26
 the atomic theory, i. 93
 the law of definite proportions, in combination and resolution of the component parts of substances, i. 94
 affinity of kind and of degree, i. 95
 force of chemical combination, i. 97, 98
 relative atomic weights, i. 99
  table of atomic weights compared with that of hydrogen, i. 100
  relation between the atomic weights and the specific gravities of substances, i. 100
  capacities of atoms for heat and electricity, i. 100, 101
 law of equivalency in weight and volume, i. 102, 103
  substitution the basis of this law, i. 104
  sequence of atomic numbers, i. 105
 groups of substances whose atomic weights are in regular arithmetical series, i. 106
 groups of combined atoms called compound radicles, i. 106
 the polyatomic theory, i. 107
 the force of molecular attraction more powerful than gravitation, i. 109
 internal movement of molecules of matter in a gaseous state, i. 113
Aulocantha scolymantha, structure of, ii. 21
Avicula margaritacea, or pearl oyster, nacreous lining of shell of, ii. 234
Azores, the black mildew of the, i. 297
Azote in vegetable organisms, i. 423
Azuline dye, production of, i. 123

. B

Babylon, the asphaltic mortar used in building, i. 126 ·
Bacillaria cursoria, motion of, i. 203
Bacillaria paradoxa, motion of, i. 203
Back, Sir George, his arctic journey, i. 308
Bacteria, their structure, size and habitat, ii. 64
Bæomyces, structure of, i. 306
Balanidæ, structure of, ii. 213
Balanus balanoïdes, development of, ii. 216

E

H

I

M

N

Nitric acid, combination forming, i. 95
Nitrogen gas, i. 12
    combination of nitrogen with chlorine, i. 20
    absorptive power of, i. 39, 41
    fulminates compounds of, i. 92
    number of combinations of, with oxygen, i. 95
    atomic weight of, compared with that of hydrogen, i. 106
    one of the illuminants in coal gas, i. 113
    spectrum analysis of, i. 140, 145
        in high temperature, i. 144
    binoxide of, combination forming, i. 95
    chloride of, catalysis of, i. 91
    iodide of, catalysis of, i. 91
    protoxide of, or laughing gas, combination forming, i. 95
Nitrous oxide, absorption of, radiant heat by, i. 41, 43
    combination forming, i. 95
Noctiluca miliaris, structure and mode of propagation of, ii. 73, 74
Noctiluci, their food, i. 205
Nodosaria, characters of the genus, ii. 39
Nodosaria rugosa, shell of, ii. 28
    structure of, ii. 39
Nodosaria spinicosta, form of, ii. 28
    structure of, ii. 39
Nostoc commune, wide distribution of, i. 212
Nostochineæ, structure and habitat of, 211
    reproduction of, i. 212
    wide distribution of, i. 212
Nullipores, structure and habitat of, i. 142
Nummulites, structure of the, ii. 44–46
    circumstances favouring their existence in the Tertiary period, ii. 53

O

Ocean, force exerted in the creation of the, ii. 31
Octoblepharum albidum, leaves of, i. 330
Octopoda, structure of, ii. 245
Octopus vulgaris, or poulpe, structure of, ii. 245–247
Odonthalia, structure of, 242
Œdogonian capillare, reproduction of, i. 216
Oïdium, structure and habitat of, i. 290
Oïdium Tuckeri, or vine mildew, fungus producing, i. 295

P

S

Sea-serpent of Celebes, ii. 186
Sea-slugs, structure of, ii. 239, 240
Sea-weeds, former and present uses of, i. 128
Seeds of two lobes, i. 177
    of one lobe, i. 177
    of plants, i. 381, 382, 383, 404
Selaginella, structure and habitat of, i. 374
Selenium, atomic weight of, i. 105
    its properties analogous with those of sulphur and tellurium, i. 105
Sepedonium mycophilum, spores of, i. 286
Sepia, or cuttle fish, structure of, ii. 245, 246, 247
Serpentine marble of Tyree and of Connemara, composition of, ii. 56
Serpula, structure of, ii. 155
Sertularia cupressina, structure of, ii. 87
Sertulariidæ, characters of the family of, ii. 90, 91
    modes of propagation of, ii. 91
Shells of mollusks, ii. 234
Shrimps, opossum, ii. 199, 200
Sigillaria, structure of the fossil, i. 375
Silex, quantity of, in the Equisetaceæ, i. 369
    in the grasses, i. 386
Silica, abundance of, i. 17
    in the stalks and leaves of the grasses, i. 386
    effect of electricity on, i. 32
Silicon, i. 17
    combined with oxygen gas forms rock-crystal, i. 17
    three different states in which it exists, i. 18
    analogy between silicon and carbon, i. 18
    Professor Graham's limpid solution of, i. 18
Silk, dyes for, i. 125
    mode of preparing it if it is to be moiré, i. 125
    advantages of the climate of Lyons in the manufacture of, i. 126
Silk-worm, a fungus parasite of the, i. 274
Silver, affinity of, for oxygen, i. 5
    conduction of heat and radiation, i. 5
    iodine found in combination with, i. 19
    crystals of, formed artificially by electricity, i. 74
    transmissive power of, of electricity, i. 90
Sipunculidæ, structure and mode of reproduction of, ii. 186, 187
Sky, probable cause of the blue colour of the, i. 58
Slate, polishing, of Bilin, of what it consists, i. 206
Smoke, i. 14

T

U

CPSIA information can be obtained
at www.ICGtesting.com
Printed in the USA
BVHW082045200622
640215BV00001B/189

9 783375 047948